HUNGRY BUG

CARLTON MELLICK III

ERASERHEAD PRESS
PORTLAND, OREGON

ERASERHEAD PRESS
205 NE BRYANT
PORTLAND, OR 97211

WWW.ERASERHEADPRESS.COM

ISBN: 1-62105-137-4

Printed in the USA.

Praise for
Carlton Mellick III

"Easily the craziest, weirdest, strangest, funniest, most obscene writer in America."
—*GOTHIC MAGAZINE*

"Carlton Mellick III has the craziest book titles... and the kinkiest fans!"
—CHRISTOPHER MOORE, author of *The Stupidest Angel*

"If you haven't read Mellick you're not nearly perverse enough for the twenty first century."
—JACK KETCHUM, author of *The Girl Next Door*

"Carlton Mellick III is one of bizarro fiction's most talented practitioners, a virtuoso of the surreal, science fictional tale."
—CORY DOCTOROW, author of *Little Brother*

"Bizarre, twisted, and emotionally raw—Carlton Mellick's fiction is the literary equivalent of putting your brain in a blender."
—BRIAN KEENE, author of *The Rising*

"Carlton Mellick III exemplifies the intelligence and wit that lurks between its lurid covers. In a genre where crude titles are an art in themselves, Mellick is a true artist."
—*THE GUARDIAN*

"Just as Pop had Andy Warhol and Dada Tristan Tzara, the bizarro movement has its very own P. T. Barnum-type practitioner. He's the mutton-chopped author of such books as *Electric Jesus Corpse* and *The Menstruating Mall*, the illustrator, editor, and instructor of all things bizarro, and his name is Carlton Mellick III."
—*DETAILS MAGAZINE*

Also by **Carlton Mellick III**

Satan Burger
Electric Jesus Corpse
Sunset With a Beard (stories)
Razor Wire Pubic Hair
Teeth and Tongue Landscape
The Steel Breakfast Era
The Baby Jesus Butt Plug
Fishy-fleshed
The Menstruating Mall
Ocean of Lard (with Kevin L. Donihe)
Punk Land
Sex and Death in Television Town
Sea of the Patchwork Cats
The Haunted Vagina
Cancer-cute (Avant Punk Army Exclusive)
War Slut
Sausagey Santa
Ugly Heaven
Adolf in Wonderland
Ultra Fuckers
Cybernetrix
The Egg Man
Apeshit
The Faggiest Vampire
The Cannibals of Candyland
Warrior Wolf Women of the Wasteland
The Kobold Wizard's Dildo of Enlightenment +2
Zombies and Shit
Crab Town
The Morbidly Obese Ninja
Barbarian Beast Bitches of the Badlands
Fantastic Orgy (stories)
I Knocked Up Satan's Daughter
Armadillo Fists
The Handsome Squirm
Tumor Fruit
Kill Ball
Cuddly Holocaust
Hammer Wives (stories)
Village of the Mermaids
Quicksand House
Clusterfuck

AUTHOR'S NOTE

About three days after I finished my last book, Clusterfuck, I went to a beach house on the Oregon Coast with bizarro authors Jeff Burk and Cameron Pierce. We were on a writing retreat, something we'd planned to do for months. Yet by that time, I was completely burned out on writing—having just come off of a six week marathon at an airport hotel. So, instead of writing, I decided to read some comics. I read a few volumes of the brilliant manga *Dorohedoro* by Q Hayashida, *Stray Bullets* by David Lapham, and some of the *Sandman* series by Neil Gaiman (all of which ended up influencing the hell out of this book whether I wanted them to or not). I had a blast reading comics and hanging out with my author friends, roasting fresh shellfish on the barbeque and drinking local beers on the beach. On the last night, I was inspired to get back into writing again and wrote the first chapter of this book. I really didn't know where I was going with this at the time, but I really enjoyed getting into the world and its characters. It reminded me why I got into writing in the first place.

This book is about addiction. It's the first time I've written a theme-driven book since the sex allegory novella, *Razor Wire Pubic Hair*, twelve years ago. Addiction is something everyone is very familiar with. Perhaps not everyone has gone through something as serious as heroin addiction, but we've all gone through small addictions such as internet addiction, video game addiction, food addiction, caffeine addiction, or breakdance addiction (my main crutch), all of which are so common that we hardly see them as addictions until we watch a news story about some South Korean kid dying of malnutrition from being unable to pry himself away from World of Warcraft. When I decided I wanted to write a fantasy book in a modern urban setting, I thought about what sort of problems would arise from living in a world of magic. The number one problem I kept coming back to was addiction. People would become obsessed with using magic and would cast their spells no matter the consequences. That was my main focus in writing Hungry Bug and I'm happy with the results.

I also decided to approach this book using an unusual structure. A lot of authors write short story collections that read like novels (for example, Chuck Palahniuk's *Haunted* or Ray Bradbury's *The Martian Chronicles*). Well, Hungry Bug is a novel that reads like a story collection. It's definitely a novel, but it's told through a series of stories from different characters' points of view. The stories are not just connected by the setting and theme; they also build on each other. One character's story will continue in the background of another's, with all plot arcs resolving by the end of the book. It was a fun approach to writing a story and I might have to repeat it another time. I'll let you decide whether the structure was successful or not.

So, here it is: my 43rd book. I hope you enjoy it.

—Carlton Mellick III 12/19/2013 6:10am

CONTENTS

THE
ENDLESS
CHILDHOOD

It was the fifth time Elmore Wormwood turned twelve years old.

He sat at the dining room table, a violet rose pinned to his charcoal-black suit, looking down at the red velvet birthday cake with faded blue frosting. Only candlelight illuminated his pale slender face.

"Blow out your candles, my darling," the mother said, standing behind him in her dinner dress burnt with age.

Elmore looked up at her, a party hat made of old newspaper leaning off the side of his forehead. He didn't care to blow out his candles. He had blown out so many candles in his eighty-nine years that he never wanted to blow out another for the rest of his life. The number of candles didn't mean anything to him anymore. The whole idea of birthdays seemed pointless.

"Why should I?" Elmore said.

"It's your birthday, sweetheart," said the mother, rubbing his shoulders with her thin bony hands. "My little baby's growing up."

"How exactly am I growing up?"

His mother's twisted smile dropped from her lips. Her eyes pierced into the boy. She didn't like when he pointed out his never-ending cycle of childhood.

"What did you say?" asked the mother, removing her hands from his shoulders and placing them against her tiny waist, revealing a prominent hourglass figure beneath the dress.

"Nothing," Elmore said. "I'm sorry."

Elmore didn't want to be turned into a baby again. His mother knew the spell of Age Reversal and was always turning him back into a baby whenever she felt like it, whenever she wanted to hold her adorable baby boy in her arms once again. He had been forced to restart his life at least seventeen times.

The endless cycle of growing and shrinking and starting life all over again was completely maddening to him.

The mother threw her arms around the boy and kissed him on the cheek. "What did you wish for?"

He wished he could become an adult. He wished his mother would finally let him grow up past the age of sixteen. He wished something horrible would happen to his mother and he'd never have to see her ever again. He wished he could just die.

"I can't tell you," Elmore said. "Wishes won't come true if I tell you."

The mother laughed and kissed his tiny hand.

"It's okay, I already know what you wished for," she said, as she cut into the cake with an iron spatula. "You wished that you'll get to stay mommy's little angel forever and ever."

Then she put a glob of blue frosting on the tip of his nose and giggled at how cute and sweet he looked.

Elmore pretended to be excited as he played with the toy robots he'd gotten for his birthday. He didn't want to let on that he hated playing with toys. The worst thing he could do was show his mom that he was too old for childish things.

The mother sat on the couch behind him, drinking half a jug of wine as she admired her beautiful child. She'd never seen a prettier boy in her life. He was so delicate, so soft and sugary like warm caramel. He was the complete opposite of his father—a weathered, lumpy man who died a coward in the First World War.

"My beautiful little boy," she said to him, her voice languid from alcohol. "You love Mommy more than anything in the world."

Elmore didn't like to be around his mother during the evenings, which was when she drank. It was always the most dangerous time for him to be near her, because she so often yearned to have her baby back when she was intoxicated. Every single time she drank it was always the same conversation, over and over again. She rambled on about how perfect her life was after he was born.

"You're so cute when you're a baby, when I pick you up and snuggle you in my arms." The mother pretended to be cuddling an infant version of Elmore in her lap. "You're always so happy when Momma holds you, smiling with your chubby cheeks and giggling when I kiss your tiny little feet."

There was nothing Elmore hated more than being an infant. It was frustrating enough that he was unable to speak or move his body properly, but even worse was the way he was treated. His mother didn't see him as human anymore. She treated him like a pet, a play-thing who was completely at her mercy. She ignored the fact that he'd ever grown up at all, imagining herself back in the time of her life when she was at her happiest. She didn't seem to notice how miserable it made him.

"Do you remember how cute you were?" his mother asked, pouring another glass of Carlo Rossi chardonnay. "Do you remember how much you loved snuggling with me as a baby?"

It was getting late and his mother was getting too drunk. Elmore knew it was time to gather up his toys and go to bed.

"It's my bed time," he told her, holding his toys in his arms. "I'm going to go to sleep."

His mother shook her head. "It's your birthday. You get to stay up until whenever you want."

"I'm tired. I'd prefer to go to bed."

"You're not tired." His mother held out her arms. "Stay up. Come snuggle with Mommy."

"I'm really tired, though."

"Just stay awake. I'm not ready for your birthday to be over. Come here."

"I'd prefer to go to sleep."

"Come *here*." She yelled so loud the wine bottle shook against the glass coffee table. Her face instantly changed from the drunken smiling mother to a furious demonic monster.

"Okay," Elmore said, sitting next to her on the couch.

He knew not to make his mother too angry. She would

always win every argument with him by threatening to shrink him down to a baby if he didn't do exactly as he was told. One time she even said that she would keep him as a baby forever and never let him grow old enough to walk if he didn't do what she wanted.

"Cuddle with me, my cute boy," said the mother, wrapping her arms around her son.

She squeezed him tight against her bosom, rubbing his hair from his eyes and planting kisses on his forehead, her bony arm practically strangling him.

"You love being held by your Mommy," she said. "You love Mommy so much. You love her more than anything, don't you cupcake?"

"Yes."

"Twelve years old," she said with a sigh. "You're growing up too fast again."

Elmore didn't like the smile that was growing on his mother's face. He'd seen that smile many times before.

"I want my little baby back," she said, giving him another quick squeeze. "Don't you want to be my baby again?"

"No," Elmore said.

"What?" His mother was surprised. "Don't lie, of course you do."

"I don't want to be a baby again. It's humiliating."

"But it will make me so happy. Don't you want Mommy to be happy?"

"It won't make you happy," Elmore said, resting his head gently on her shoulder, trying not to be too aggressive. "You always think it will make you happy, but after the first week you get exhausted and stressed out over the responsibility of taking care of an infant again. Always having to change diapers, feeding and burping, not getting enough sleep—you hate it."

Elmore made sure to be especially difficult when he was an infant, in order to get back at his mother. He would cry all night, throw food on the kitchen floor, and try to crawl away whenever she left the front door open. He always thought that if he made it exhausting enough she'd someday lose interest in raising him as a baby and allow him to grow up, but his plan never worked. When she was drunk, she only remembered the good times.

"No, it makes me so happy," his mother said. She grabbed his foot and rubbed his toes through his sock. "Your cute little footsies. Your tiny little nose." She rubbed her nose against his. "I would just snuggle you all day."

Elmore pried himself from his mother's grasp.

"Where are you going?"

"To sleep. You're too drunk."

"I am *not* drunk." His mother's words were slurred and angry. "I've only had a few glasses."

"Goodnight," Elmore said.

"No, come back," his mother said. She stood up and unbuttoned her dress. "I want you to be a baby again. I want you to be cute and little, lying in my arms all night long."

The mother dropped her dress on the ground, standing nude before her son. Elmore hated seeing his mother without her clothes. It reminded him of how inhuman she had become.

"Come to me," the mother said, wrapping her fingers around her tiny fragile waist.

His mother's torso was an hourglass. There were no organs in her body, no muscle, no blood. From her collar down to her pelvis, she was made of glass. Red sand slowly trickled from the region of her upper chest down to the region of her lower belly, each grain a second of her life.

"You can't do this," Elmore said. "It's my birthday."

"But your birthday is the perfect time to be reborn," his mother said, gripping her hourglass body.

Elmore ran to his bedroom and locked the door.

"What are you doing?" said the mother. "Come out of there and be my baby again."

She pounded on his door.

"You're too drunk," Elmore said. "Wait until morning."

"I want my baby boy *now*. Open the door."

"I'm going to sleep."

He knew she wouldn't be this way in the morning. All he

had to do was hold her off until then. She couldn't use the magic unless she held his hand.

"I hate when you're this age," said his mother. "I'm never going to let you be this age ever again."

Elmore turned off the lights and crawled into his dinosaur-shaped bed. He watched his mother's shadow linger through the crack under the door. The woman just waited for him to come out, assuming he would eventually obey her wishes and succumb to giving up his current life for her. But he wasn't going to give it up without a fight.

Elmore's mother was in the kitchen looking at herself in the mirror when he woke up the next morning. She was still naked, cleaning wine stains from her glass breasts. It looked as if she drank all night until she passed out on the couch again. Everything smelled of egg farts and menthol cigarette smoke.

"You're finally awake," she said, not looking at him.

His breakfast was on the table. Cold eggs and cereal that'd gone soggy. Elmore wasn't hungry anyway.

He could tell she didn't remember much from the previous night. "You tried to turn me into a baby again."

She ignored him, pulling her dress over the glass sections of her body.

"Do you know how much I hate being a baby?"

She turned to him, making eye contact for only a second. "Eat your breakfast."

"You think I don't remember anything when I'm that small, but I do," said Elmore. "Just because my body restarts doesn't mean my memories do as well."

"Are you going to eat or not?"

Whenever Elmore spoke to her about her resetting his childhood, she either responded with anger or just ignored him completely. That day she chose to ignore him.

"I'm not hungry," Elmore said. "Yesterday was my birthday. Do you know how old I turned?"

"Well, I'm dumping it then," said the mother. "You can just starve."

She took his dishes and scraped them off into the garbage disposal.

"Do you know how old I am now?" Elmore repeated. "My *real* age?"

"You're twelve," said his mother.

"I turned eighty-nine," Elmore said. "I'm an eighty-nine-year-old man trapped in a twelve-year-old's body."

"Don't be ridiculous."

"I should be at the end of my life by now," Elmore said. "I shouldn't still be forever trapped at the beginning."

His mother turned on the garbage disposal to drown out the sound of his voice. It was a childish move, but his mother was always childish—scary, powerful, and childish.

"You need to let me grow up," Elmore said, the second she turned off the garbage disposal.

She glared at him. Her eyes said to him, *How dare you speak to me like this, after all I've done for you? You never used to be this way. It's because you're growing up. You wouldn't be this way if you'd never grow up...*

But when she finally opened her mouth to respond, she said, "Fine." She tossed the dish towel on the kitchen counter and walked away. "Grow up and leave me. See if I care."

Elmore watched his mother as she left the kitchen.

"I'm tired of taking care of you anyway," she said. Then she went to her room and slammed the door behind her as loudly as she could, pouting like an upset teenager.

Elmore went to the front door and turned the knob. It wouldn't open. There were seven locks lining the doorframe and he didn't have a key to a single one of them. He went to the side door, then the back door, then he checked the strength of the bars on all the windows. Everything was locked tight, as always. This was his routine whenever his mother wasn't watching him.

He hoped that someday she would forget to lock a door and he would be able to escape.

"One day…" Elmore said.

Two restarts ago—back when he was able to leave the house, attend school, play with friends, and do all the things a normal kid should be allowed to do—he ran away from home, trying to escape his mother for good. He made it to the age of sixteen before she tracked him down. She shrunk him in his sleep, while he lay naked in his girlfriend's arms. He was already too small to fight back by the time he opened his eyes and saw his mother hovering over him, his girlfriend's gargantuan form pressed against his chubby little body. She might as well have murdered him in his sleep that night.

From that moment on, Elmore was his mother's prisoner. She kept him locked away, hidden from the rest of the world. He wasn't allowed to leave for anything, not even school—not that there was anything left for him to learn in school anyway. The only purpose he had in life was to be his mommy's little boy, forever.

But Elmore didn't waste his purgatory. He used it to learn as much as he could about the world. In his father's library, Elmore opened a book on German history. Collecting knowledge was the only pleasure left in his life. He didn't care what knowledge he absorbed. He wanted to know everything there was to know about everything. He mostly read science and history books, language textbooks, and technical manuals. He also read a lot of fiction so that he could learn about the world he was missing out on.

The only problem was that he was running out of books to read. His mother refused to buy him anything but children's books. When he had the freedom to leave the house, he used to shoplift every book he could find, maybe a dozen books a day every day after school. He had enough books to last anyone else a lifetime, but it just wasn't enough for Elmore. He had too many lifetimes to fill.

"Your move," Elmore said.

It was family game night, as it was every Friday. Elmore sat at the dining room table, across from his mother who was already down half a bottle of wine, still dressed in the elegant clothes she wore out that day.

"This is such a cute game," said the mother, shaking the red and blue dice in her hand. "Isn't it such a cute game?"

They were playing Monkey Trap, a board game for little kids that wouldn't have appealed to Elmore the first time he turned twelve years old. He couldn't have been more bored.

"How was your customer today?" Elmore asked her, gesturing toward the briefcase filled with money by the front door. "How much did you get?"

Elmore's mother made a fortune selling her Age Reversal spell to the old and wealthy. Her spell was very rare. Not many people knew it even existed.

"He was a cheapskate," she said. "He only wanted eight years removed, so people wouldn't be too suspicious."

"That's still eight hundred thousand dollars," Elmore said.

"Pocket change," said the mother. "It was hardly worth the three hour drive."

"You should charge more," Elmore said. "You have no idea how much money some people make these days. You could easily charge a million per year you remove."

His mother moved her piece quietly across the board, then pulled a tiny plastic monkey up a rope. "I don't need to discuss my business with a child. You know nothing of the adult world."

Elmore smiled and rolled the dice. He knew far more about the world than his mother did. Although she was probably a century older than he was, she drank most of her years away. She did nothing to better herself or better the world. Every day was the same, year after year, decade after decade.

"I miss you being small and innocent," she said, pouring more wine into her glass. "You don't act like a kid when you're this age."

"I'm eighty-nine years old," Elmore said. "No matter what age I look, I will never be a child again."

"You'll be a child again if I say so."

"No. I won't."

His mother took a long drink.

"You wouldn't have a choice," she said.

Elmore moved his plastic monkey across the board.

"You said you'd let me grow up this time," Elmore said.

"I said nothing of the kind."

"What if I killed myself?" Elmore said.

"What?" His mother nearly spilled her wine glass.

"I'd rather be dead than restart my life again," he said. "If you use your magic on me one more time I will kill myself."

"No, you wouldn't," his mother said, shaking her head and laughing as she poured more wine.

"I'm serious. I loathe being a child. If I can't grow up then I'd rather just die."

"You'd just be a baby. Babies can't commit suicide. They wouldn't even know how."

"I can choke on pretty much any small object in the house. I can take a tumble down the basement stairs. I can eat all sorts of pills or toxic chemicals."

"You'd really do it?" His mother's face was turning red. "You'd really kill yourself?"

"Yes. If you don't let me grow—"

His mother interrupted him. "How could you do that to me? How could you be so selfish?"

Tears ran her makeup down her cheeks.

"You've kept me a prisoner in this house, in this tiny body, for decades. How can you—"

"Don't you know how much I love you? I would do anything for you. Anything."

She was sobbing so much he could hardly understand her words.

"Then let me grow up."

"Fine…" she said, staggering out of her chair. She walked as if somebody had punched her in the stomach. "Grow up then, you spoiled brat."

She took the bottle with her when she left the dining room, turning off the overhead light, leaving her son to play the game by himself in the dark.

Elmore woke up in the middle of the night. The sound of his drunken mother tripping over toys echoed through his bedroom, startling him awake. He flipped on his lamp.

"Mom?" he asked. "What are you doing?"

She was naked and too drunk to stand.

"My sweet little baby," she said, her voice distant. "I just wanted to snuggle with you."

She stood up and tried to balance. With every step toward him, she crushed another toy robot he'd gotten for his birthday.

"Get out of here," Elmore said. "You're drunk."

"I want my little baby back," she said, slurring her words. "You'll like being my baby. You'll see. You love it."

Elmore jumped out of his bed and held out his pillow like a shield.

"I told you I'll kill myself if you do this to me again," he said.

She languidly shook her head. "No, no… you won't. You'll love being my baby."

"I promise," he said. "I'll do it."

"You won't remember…" she said, stepping toward him. "You'll just be a baby."

"I always remember everything."

"Not if I cast the whole spell," she said, reaching out with her bony silver-painted fingers.

When her hand came near him, Elmore shoved it out of the way with his pillow. As long as she didn't touch him, she wouldn't be able to cast her magic.

"You think you remember everything," she said. "You think you've been alive for eighty-nine years. But that's not true."

Elmore had no idea what she was talking about.

"You're really two-hundred-and-thirty-seven years old," said the mother.

Elmore froze. He stared at his mother. Her face was blank, emotionless. She was serious.

"No, I'm not…"

"You just don't remember the first one hundred forty-eight years of your life," she said.

"How is that even possible?"

She grabbed at him again, trying to maintain her balance. Elmore protected himself with his pillow.

"If I cast the full spell, you'll revert back to before you were born, before your brain was developed enough for intelligent thought." His mother rubbed her stomach. "You'll return to the womb and one day be reborn anew, with no memories of ever having lived before."

"You've been doing this to me for 237 years?"

"I would have cast the full spell every time, but childbirth has become such a pain over the centuries." She looked down at her glass body. Elmore had no idea how she'd even be able to carry a child in her freakish form. "I guess I don't have any other choice this time."

Elmore shook his head.

"That's murder," he said. "You'll murder me."

"It's not like that," said his mother. "You'll be reborn. It'll be beautiful."

"But everything I am will be dead," Elmore said.

"Don't be so selfish," she said. "I need a baby. You wouldn't know how pointless and lonely eternity can be without having a purpose, without having a child to look after."

"Then have other children," Elmore said. "Stop recycling the one you have."

"I can't have any other babies," she said. "There's only you."

She tore Elmore's pillow away and grabbed him by the wrist.

"No!" Elmore cried.

He tugged and thrashed, trying to make her let go.

"It'll be over in just a minute, my darling. Then you'll be at peace."

His mother clutched her giant hourglass torso and chanted her spell, whispering the ancient words, her eyes glowing purple, her fingers glowing red. Then she flipped the hourglass over. Her torso moved as if it were just hovering in thin air—her other body parts floating next to it. Then the magic poured through her arm and into her son.

"Stop!" Elmore cried.

As the sand flowed through the hourglass, moving hundreds of times faster than normal, Elmore could feel himself becoming younger. Year after year was peeled from him like the skin on an onion. His pajamas loosened against his body.

"Please!" he yelled. "You're killing me…"

But his mother wouldn't look at him, wouldn't hear him. Her eyes were off in the distance. A smile brightened across her face, imagining the thought of having her baby in her arms once again.

"No…" Elmore sobbed. Tears flowing down his cheeks.

When he'd lost five years, his body that of a seven-year-old, he reached down to the floor and grabbed one of the broken toy robots he'd received for his birthday. With all the strength a seven-year-old could muster, he tossed it at his mother's head.

She let go of his arm and tumbled backward.

"Elmore…" she cried, as she fell.

She landed against the back of the door. There was a loud cracking noise. It took both of them a moment before they realized the doorknob had pierced her glass torso, cracking the lower half of the hourglass. Glittering shards crumbled down the back of her thighs as she tried to move. She was stuck.

"My baby… help me," she asked her son.

Elmore went for her. But instead of helping her, he ducked under her arms, squeezed past the cracked door and ran.

"Elmore!" his mother called. "Help me!"

Red sand flowed out of the crack in her torso, piling onto the bedroom floor.

Elmore tightened the straps on his pajama bottoms so they wouldn't fall down his legs. Then he searched the house for his mother's purse.

"All the sand is falling out!" she yelled, her voice echoing through the hallways.

Elmore found the keys in a side compartment. He ran to the hall closet, took out a pair of sneakers and an old coat that was small enough to fit him.

"Please!" she yelled. "You're killing me..."

He ran to the front door. Each key went to a different lock, but he'd studied his mother locking them over the years. He knew exactly which key went with which lock.

"Elmore... My baby..."

The cold night air hit him when the door flew open. He raised his arms and felt the cool wind. It had been a very long time since he had stepped outside.

"Elmore..."

He turned to see his mother stagger out of his bedroom, a trail of red sand forming on the carpet behind her. As she lost sand, she looked as if she were getting younger and older at the same time. Her features were becoming cuter and more childlike, while her skin withered and wrinkled.

"You can't go..."

Elmore glanced at the briefcase beside the door, the one filled with $800,000. He grabbed it, ran outside, and closed the door. As his mother ran toward him, he locked her inside. Just as she had locked him in there for so many years, it was her turn to feel trapped. He knew from experience, there was no way out.

"I'm sorry, Mommy..." Elmore said in his seven-year-old voice. "But I have to finally start living my life."

"Elmore..." she said.

He could hear her dying in there. The sand was her lifeblood. She couldn't survive after losing that much.

"I will always love you..." he said. "I despise you, too. But I will always love you."

"You can't leave, Elmore..." His mother's voice was weak and fading.

"But I have to leave. I want to finally grow up."

"You don't understand," she said, wheezing between words. "They're looking for you. They don't recognize you as a child, but once you become an adult... they'll find you. You can't let them find you..."

"Who?" Elmore said. "What are you talking about?"

But his mother didn't say another word. She just gasped and moaned. Then she was silent. Elmore brought his key to the lock, wondering if he should check on her to see what happened, but then he stopped. He tossed the keys as far as he could into the neighbor's yard. Knowing his mother, she was just lying to get him to open the door. He knew better than to fall for her tricks. He was finally free and he hoped to never see his mother ever again.

THE BEE
WOMAN'S
OBSESSION

Bee's apartment was infested with porcelain dolls. They crawled out from behind the refrigerator at night, slithered up from the floorboards, squeezed out of the bathtub drain. As she tried to sleep, Bee could hear them scurrying between the walls, nibbling on scraps of food and building nests in the back of her cupboards. There was nothing more irritating than the sound of those tiny porcelain feet tip-tapping across the concrete floor.

"Will you please shut up," Bee moaned, holding her feather pillow against her yellow ears. All night she'd been tossing and turning.

It was mating season, so the dolls were even more active than usual that night. They whispered to each other with their squeaky voices, searching for mates, making love in the laundry baskets and leaving tiny pieces of white poop all over the bathroom floor. On nights like these, Bee fantasized about all the horrible things she would do if she ever tracked down the sorcerer who created this grotesque race of vermin.

"You're all dead," Bee announced to the dolls.

She flipped on the light switch and sat up in bed. The tiny porcelain creatures stared up at her with their smooth, white, expressionless faces. Then they scurried out of sight, ducking beneath the furniture.

"I guess I'll call it an early morning," she said to her tiny hiding guests.

As she stretched her arms in a yawn, her insect wings fluttered and the antennae on her head wiggled awake. Her black and yellow striped flesh glistened with morning sweat. She went to the kitchen section of her grimy studio apartment and made herself a cup of coffee with honey. A loud snapping sound echoed from the closet.

"Haha! Got you!" Bee said, raising a black fist in triumph.

When she opened the closet door, she saw the body of a porcelain doll twitching inside of a rat trap. Its neck was broken and its porcelain face was cracked apart, exposing the bloody pink insides. The dolls didn't have bones. Their porcelain exoskeleton was enough to keep them together. Inside them there was just a mass of goopy meat crawling with veins, nerves, and tendons.

"Gross…" Bee said, carefully picking up the trap and dumping the corpse into the closest trash bin.

There was a knock at the door.

"Hey Bee," said the deep voice on the other side.

It was Hoggins. Her boss.

"Wake up," he said, pounding on the door again. "We've got another one."

Bee stuck out her tongue in disgust as she shook droplets of doll blood off her glossy black fingernails.

"Are you awake in there?" Hoggins continued pounding on the door.

"Just like the others," Hoggins said, staring down at the body. "His eyes were removed, tongue split down the middle, all the blood drained out."

They were in an alley on the other side of Bee's neighborhood. It was considered the shitty side of the neighborhood, but it wasn't really any shittier than the rest of Hell's Bottom.

"Some local kids found him," Hoggins continued. "They snuck back here to cast fire spells. Nearly set the poor sap ablaze when they saw him."

Bee noticed movement under the dead man's coat. She lifted it up to discover three porcelain dolls hiding in there, eating his rotten flesh. Their tiny mouths filled with razor-sharp teeth, chewing the meat from his belly.

"Get out of there," Hoggins yelled at the dolls.

30

He stomped his foot at them and they scurried off, squeaking and whispering.

"The dolls already got to him?" Bee asked.

Hoggins nodded. "Dolls, rats, flies. You name it. He's been here at least twenty-four hours. My guess is he died yesterday morning, sometime before dawn."

Bee was hot. Even though it was supposed to be the coldest time of the day, she was sweating. Steam billowed out of the sewers like it was coming from the saunas of hell. She was thankful that she didn't need to wear clothes anymore. Because of her yellow and black striped skin, nobody could tell if she were naked or clothed. Nobody except for Hoggins, who regularly stole glimpses of her yellow breasts.

"So that makes three bodies in one week," Bee said.

"Definitely a serial killer, just like I said." Hoggins lit up a cigarette and offered one to Bee.

"I still don't think so." She took his cigarette and put it behind her ear. "I think there's a predator in Hell's Bottom, someone who feeds on human blood."

Hoggins laughed. "Are you saying we've got vampires now?"

"No, but we've got a non-fictional race of bloodsuckers living amongst us."

Hoggins turned away. "Don't say it…"

"I think it's the work of the Arachne."

Hoggins leapt at her and wrapped his chubby pink fingers around her mouth. "I said not to say it!" He looked around. "You don't know who's listening, Bee. Come on. You don't talk about them. Ever. Especially not around me."

"Who else could it be?" Bee asked.

"Dumping bodies in alleys isn't their style," Hoggins said. "When they target a man as prey, he just disappears, never to be heard from again. No, this is the work of one of our own. Somebody local."

Bee knelt down and shrugged. "Too bad we don't know anything about forensics…"

"Well, see what you can figure out. I need to get over to the restaurant. I'm late enough as it is."

Bee and Hoggins weren't actually the police, but they were the closest thing to it in Hell's Bottom. There wasn't any government or authorities of any kind in this neighborhood. It was just the strong versus the weak. Hoggins helped keep order in this place. He owned the biggest restaurant in the neighborhood. He had money, connections, and a large staff. He was in a position to help protect the weak from those who might take advantage of them and that's exactly what he tried to do.

Hoggins wiped mucus from his snout and turned to the three men holding the blockade at the end of the alley.

"Give Bee all the assistance she needs," he told them. "I want this body out of here within the hour."

As her boss left the scene, Bee exhaled a sigh. Just because she once worked dispatch didn't mean she knew the first thing about being a cop. Hoggins thought she was the right person for the job, though. She did what she could.

"At least it's steady work," Bee said, lighting up her cigarette.

A group of porcelain dolls stared at her from behind the garbage cans, waiting for the right moment to sneak across the alley and continue to feast on the rotting corpse.

"This is where he lived?" Bee asked, staring up at the apartment.

"Fifth floor," said Angry Eddie, pointing at the window with black moth-chewed curtains. "His name was Richard Cayman."

Eddie, Bee, and Big Strange were checking out the victim's residence, while Torko transported the body across town. Big Strange and Angry Eddie were Hoggins' two most intimidating thugs in his employ, who triple-timed as bouncers, chefs, and police backup.

"Well, get climbing," Bee told them, pointing at the fire escape.

"You first," Eddie said.

"I'll meet you up there." Bee pointed at the wings on her back.

The two men groaned as they climbed the fire escape up to the fifth floor apartment. Because overpopulation was such a problem in Hell's Bottom, a lot of apartments were divided up into two or three different units. It wasn't uncommon for an apartment's only entrance and exit to be a single window accessible only by fire escape.

Bee cast the spell of Flight and flapped her wings, buzzing like an insect up to the fifth floor ledge. As she waited for the two thugs to catch up to her, Bee looked through the window into the apartment. It was incredibly neat for Hell's Bottom, but just as small as Bee's. She had no idea why anyone would bother to take such good care of such a shitty place.

"Let's go, slackers," Bee said, as the two men reached her.

"Fuck you, bug bitch," said Angry Eddie. "We don't have flying magic."

Big Strange was huffing and puffing, his three pairs of arms grasping the railing tightly. He was mostly muscle, covered in tattoos and hardly spoke. His head was that of a rhino beetle.

Bee opened the window to the apartment and squeezed inside. Angry Eddie followed her. But when Big Strange tried to enter, he smashed through not only the window, but also the frame and curtain rod. Shards of glass rained onto the carpet.

"Way to go, garbage truck," Bee said.

Big Strange picked up the tiny pieces of glass and tried to put them back together, but they just crumbled into smaller pieces.

"At least the guy who lived here's not ever coming back," said Eddie.

"Bloopa-bloo…" said Big Strange.

Every time Big Strange spoke, it always sounded like he was saying bloopa-bloo, but that's just how people heard it. Only Angry Eddie could understand what he was really saying.

"Don't bother," Eddie said to Big Strange. "The landlord will take care of it."

"Bloopa-bloo…" said Strange, making a sad face.

"Just don't break anything else."

Bee ignored the two thugs and scoured the apartment. It was mostly one room, but there was a walk-in closet that was big enough to be used as a bedroom—at least, that was what Bee assumed when she saw an old urine-stained mattress on the closet floor. There was also a kitchenette and a shared bathroom. No couches, no television. Just a desk in the center of the main room.

"This guy was researching new spells," said Angry Eddie.

"How do you know?" Bee asked.

Bee went to the work desk. There were stacks of pages from old spellbooks. Eddie showed her a notebook filled with diagrams, formulas and recipes, proving he was some kind of arcane scientist.

"The other victims did not appear to be arcanists," Bee said. "It might just be a coincidence. I think the murder was just a random attack."

"I don't know..." Eddie said. "If I had my hands on a new spell I'd have reason enough to murder somebody."

"But why would you drain his blood and gouge out his eyes?" Bee said.

Bee really had no idea what she was doing investigating a murder, but at least she was trying to use her brain. She looked over the notes, scanned the formulas, but it didn't seem like the man was very close to making a breakthrough on anything. As far as she knew, it had been years since a new spell had been discovered. It was unlikely this guy was killed because he had the key to new magic.

"Bloopa-bloo!" Big Strange cried, pointing at the window.

"What's that?" Eddie asked.

Three pairs of black spiked boots lowered down onto the fire escape outside the apartment window.

"It can't be..." Bee said.

The three figures out on the fire escape were kneeling down to the entrance, preparing to enter.

"Hide," Bee whispered to the others.

They ducked into the closet/bedroom. Dust billowed up from the mattress as Big Strange belly-flopped onto it.

Only Bee peeked out. She saw two men and one woman enter the apartment. They looked like ghosts, not a part of their world—white skin, translucent clothes, steam rising from their mouths and nostrils. Their hair was black with white stripes, long bangs covering half of their six red spider-like eyes.

"They're Arachne," Bee told the others, keeping her voice quiet.

"What?" Eddie cried, not keeping his voice quiet.

She hushed him.

The ghostly figures entered the room. They looked like shiny morticians with their elegant top hats and dress gloves. Even the boys wore makeup—shiny black and silver highlights.

"The boss said there's no way the Arachne are responsible for these murders," Eddie said.

"I'm telling you," Bee whispered. "They're fucking spider people. They have to be Arachne."

"What are we going to do?" Eddie said. His pointy eyebrows reached to the top of his head. "If they find us we're fucked."

Bee looked into the main room. The three spider people were spitting web from their tongues, creating a wall across the windows.

"They're trapping us," Bee said. "They must know we're in here."

"What are we going to do?" Eddie said.

The thug was practically crying with panic.

"We're going to fight our way out," Bee said.

Eddie nearly had a heart attack. "What!"

"What spells do you know?" Bee asked.

Eddie shook his head. "We can't use magic to get out of this."

"Answer the question," Bee said.

Eddie hit himself in the knees three times.

"I'm a goddamn pastry chef," he said. "I only know one spell."

"What's that?" Bee asked.

"What do you think? The only spell I can cast is Pie Conjuring. What good is that going to do?"

"Pie Conjuring? Are you serious?"

"I told you, I'm a fucking pastry chef."

"What about Big Strange?" Bee asked.

"Bloopa-bloo!" Strange said.

"What's that mean?" Bee asked.

"He knows Ground Upheaval and Waste Disposal," Eddie said.

"What the hell are Ground Upheaval and Waste Disposal?"

35

Bee said. "I've never even heard of those spells."

Eddie tried to be as quiet as he could. "Basically, he can dig holes and teleport small pieces of garbage into trash cans."

"What good is that!" Bee whisper-screamed.

She looked back into the main room. The three spider people were digging through the desk, pulling apart the notebook. One of them was guarding the only exit.

"Well, what spells do you know?" Eddie asked Bee.

"Sting… Flight…" Bee said. "I've got enough to take out one of them if I get lucky, but definitely not three."

"Only two spells?" Eddie asked. "I thought you were a higher level sorcerer than that."

Bee knew more than two spells, but those were the only ones she wanted people to know about.

"We've got to work with what we have," Bee said.

Angry Eddie smacked his hands into the chef hat-shaped head.

"Bloopa-bloo!" Big Strange said, trying to talk them out of it.

The spider people were cold and without much emotion. They packed up what they wanted and set the rest on fire.

"Who's the buggy-bug spying on us, Little Sister?" said one of the Arachne, as he spread the fire from the desk to the walls.

"A tasty little pest, Big Brother," said the female Arachne. "Should we make her our lunch?"

They had seen Bee poking her head in and out of the closet as they were searching the apartment.

"She's trapped in our web, Big Sister," said the smallest of the three. "We might as well feed."

Bee stood up and stepped out of the closet.

"You're the ones who killed Richard Cayman?" Bee asked the spider people. "Why?

The Arachne just laughed at her.

"Who is Richard Cayman, Big Brother?" said the smaller Arachne.

"I think he's the man who lives here, Little Brother," said the older Arachne. "The one whose research we've stolen."

"So you didn't kill him?" Bee asked.

The Arachne laughed.

"We've never even met him, have we, Little Sister?" said the older Arachne.

The fire grew larger around them.

"The bug doesn't even know we've come for her, Big Brother," said the female Arachne.

The spiders snickered.

"You've come for me?" Bee asked, stepping away from the rising flames.

"She's been a naughty little bug, Big Sister," said the younger Arachne.

"A gluttonous selfish little bug, Little Brother," said the older Arachne. "Always tampering with the order of things…"

"I think it's time we taught her a lesson, Big Brother," said the female Arachne.

"Go on then," Bee said. "Teach me a lesson."

The Arachne came closer, then Bee's backup crew leapt from the closet.

"Pie attack!" Eddie yelled, pointing at the Arachne and conjuring pies. Eddie didn't have powerful spells, but he was masterful at casting pie magic. He could conjure any pie he wanted in any location he wanted.

When the pies splatted into their faces, the three spider people tumbled backward, blinded. They dropped to their knees, thrashing and shrieking in pain.

"Ummm…" Bee was confused.

She looked at Eddie. He shrugged.

The plan was just to blind them with the pies. Eddie forgot that the pies he conjured were always piping fresh-from-the-oven hot. The apple syrup scalded their spider faces like boiling oil, cooking their red eyes inside their tiny sockets, searing their flesh.

"It burns, Big Sister!" cried the younger Arachne.

"My face is melting off, Big Brother!" said the female Arachne.

The oldest of the three Arachne tossed the pie from his face, raising his fists to cast a powerful magic spell.

"Bloopa-bloo!" Big Strange cried, as he leapt at the Arachne.

The muscular rhino beetle dug right through the spider man in an instant, using his digging magic spell. The Arachne screamed through apple syrup as his chest was ripped open.

"They killed him, Little Brother!" the female Arachne cried, wiping the pie from her face. "The vermin killed him!"

Bee jumped on the female Arachne, wrapping her arms and legs around her torso. Then Bee stabbed her stinger into the woman's stomach. The red-glowing blade emerged from Bee's anus, inserting poison into the spider woman. Her prey fell to the ground as the Paralysis spell took effect.

"Bloopa-bloo! Bloopa-bloo!" Big Strange jumped up and down, pointing at the third Arachne as he made his escape.

"We can't let him go!" Bee cried.

Angry Eddie jumped for the spider boy's ankles, but he wasn't quick enough. The Arachne slipped out of the window, even with scalding pie in his eyes, and disappeared into the sky.

"Fuck!" Eddie cried.

"It's okay," Bee said. "We survived."

Eddie kicked over a table of papers.

"Are you kidding?" he said. "They know what we look like. The Arachne won't let something like this go."

Bee shook her head. "They weren't real Arachne. We wouldn't have been able to survive that if they were real Arachne."

"Then what the hell were they?"

"Trainees, probably," Bee said. "Errand boys. The weakest of the weak."

"They're still going to want revenge," Eddie said. "They could have even been children of Arachne Lords."

The spider woman moaned beneath Bee. Although she was paralyzed by Bee's poison, she was still alive.

"What do we do with her?" Eddie said.

"Kill her," Bee said. "If I sting her again it will probably do the trick."

Big Strange grabbed the yellow part of her arm.

"Bloopa-bloo…" Big Strange told her, shaking his grotesque head.

"He's right," Eddie said. "Let's take her to Hoggins. Killing her will only piss off the Arachne even more." He pointed at the corpse. "Let's take the body as well, just in case somebody has revival magic."

"Bloopa-bloo," said Big Strange.

"Exactly," said Angry Eddie.

"Are you fucking kidding me?" Hoggins yelled at his three underlings. The boss's pig-shaped face was especially frightening when he was angry. "You killed an Arachne? Do you know how fucked we are?"

The boss paced back and forth. They were in the alley behind *Le Petite Provence*, Hoggins' restaurant and center of operations. Big Strange held the bodies over each of his shoulders. Compared to his mammoth build, the two spider people seemed as light as towels.

"Not necessarily," said Angry Eddie. "If we knew somebody with revival magic—"

"Who the fuck knows revival magic these days?" Hoggins said. "You can't just go pick it up at the local spell shop."

"The Arachne could know," Eddie said. "If we return the body it might be enough."

Hoggins hit himself in his fat head. "Now you've involved me in this mess. I would've been better off if they killed you back there and left me out of it."

"Sorry we inconvenienced you," Bee said, rolling her eyes as she lit up a cigarette. "Next time we'll just let them kill us."

The boss opened the back door. "Just get the bodies out of sight before somebody sees us."

Just as he said that, there were two people standing at the edge of the alley. A man and a woman. They stared with their mouths and eyes wide open, drool slipping from their lips. A red mark centered each of their foreheads.

"It looks like we've already been spotted," said Eddie.

Hoggins squinted his eyes. "Nah, they're just hollow-heads. They couldn't even spot what planet they're on."

The two zombie-like people stared down the alley at Bee, yellow fluids leaking from their ears and nostrils, crackling sounds emanating from within their empty bodies.

The boss asked Bee to question the Arachne girl, but she wanted to do it in private. She didn't want anyone else to know what the spider had to say.

"There was another body found around the corner from here," Hoggins said. "If the Arachne are responsible I want to know immediately so we can just dispose of the bodies and be done with this case. I'm not going to try to stop them from doing whatever they want to do."

"Do you want me to check out the scene after I question her?" Bee asked.

"Eddie and Torko can take care of it."

Once Hoggins went back to work, Big Strange let her inside the meat locker.

"Stay out here and don't let anyone inside," Bee told the muscular bug man.

"Bloopa-bloo," Strange said.

"I'll call you if I need help."

"Bloo—" Strange didn't get to finish his sentence before Bee closed the door on him.

She turned to the spider girl.

The Arachne was hanging from a meat hook, tied up with her own webbing. The dead brother was on the hook next to her.

"Where are we, Big Brother?" the woman asked as she regained consciousness. "I'm so dizzy."

The spider's white face was covered in red splotches. The burn marks were already swelling into blisters.

"That's my poison working its way through your body," Bee said.

"The little bug's poison is weak, isn't it Big Brother?"

"If I sting you again you will most likely die," Bee said. "It's designed to paralyze, but too much and it will slow your heart until it stops. Does that sound weak to you?"

"We should show her what real poison feels like, Big Brother," said the spider girl. "Arachne poison rots flesh from the inside out."

"Your brother's dead," Bee told her, pointing to the corpse. "You can stop talking to him now."

The spider girl smiled up at Bee and blinked all six of her red eyes. "The little bug doesn't know what kind of trouble she's in, Big Brother. She thinks she's still safe."

"So it's true?" Bee asked. "You weren't after Richard Cayman? You were after me? Why were you after me?"

"She knows what she's been doing, Big Brother," said the Arachne. "We don't have to explain her sins to her."

"Why do you care about my sins? I haven't done anything that affects the Arachne."

"If it affects Hell's Bottom it affects the Arachne, doesn't it Big Brother? We are the caretakers of this realm."

"You are parasites who feed on the weak," Bee said. "You've done far worse things than I've ever done."

The spider snickers.

"She thinks her reasons are just, Big Brother. She has no idea the repercussions of her actions."

"You're mistaking me for somebody else," Bee said.

"She defeated us, Big Brother, but she'll never last against the Viceroy. He'll punish her for her sins."

"I'm telling you, you've got the wrong person," Bee yelled.

"The Viceroy will avenge us, Big Brother."

The spider girl laughed in Bee's face, opening her gray mouth and exposing two black fangs behind her human teeth.

Bee leapt into the air, her wings buzzing at full speed. Before the spider could finish laughing, Bee's stinger pierced through her black leather clothing into her chest. Poison flooded her lungs. The insect fell limp within her bondage.

Once her feet were back on the ground, Bee pressed her palm against the girl's ribcage. The heartbeat grew faint. She wasn't sure if she made the right call injecting her with more of her poison magic, but Bee couldn't let her say anything to anyone else. If the boss knew the Arachne were only after her, he would have quickly fed her to them to save his own ass. As much of a humanitarian the fat bastard was, he wasn't above selling out his friends in the name of self preservation.

"The Arachne didn't kill Cayman," Bee told Hoggins.

She sat in the bar section of the restaurant, sipping on a glass of red mushroom whiskey.

"Are you shitting me?" asked the pig man.

"They were at Cayman's place for a completely different reason," she said. "He was an amateur arcanist. They must have thought he was on to something and came to steal his work. They didn't even know he was dead."

"She said that?" Hoggins asked.

Bee took a sip of whiskey. She didn't like lying to the man. He wasn't the kind of boss who easily forgave liars.

"And you believed her?" he asked.

Bee shrugged. "I don't see why she'd lie. Besides, you said the murders weren't Arachne style."

Just hearing the word *Arachne* sent nerves crawling down Hoggins' spine. "We might still be able to fix this. It was just a misunderstanding, right? I know some guys who do business with the Arachne. They might be able to smooth things over for us. We only killed one of them in self-defense, right?"

"Well..." Bee paused and took a sip.

"What aren't you telling me, Bee?"

"The girl," Bee said. "I don't think she's going to pull through."

"What? How is that fucking possible? You only used a Paralysis spell."

"Some people's hearts can't take the poison," Bee said. "They go into cardiac arrest."

"Shit, why didn't you say so, Bee..." Hoggins left the bar, heading for the kitchen. "I know Counter Magic."

Bee forgot that Hoggins was able to undo the poison magic. Because he knew the spell of Counter Magic, he'd made a lot of friends around Hell's Bottom. It was why so many people owed him favors.

"It's probably too late, Boss," Bee said, following after him. "She was hardly breathing."

They raced through the kitchen, squeezing past the bustling chefs and waiters who used food magic to enhance the flavor of their dishes. A dessert chef cast Growth to create a pumpkin-sized strawberry which would be hollowed and filled with ice-cream and chocolate. A waiter cast Telekinesis so that he could carry twelve dishes at once, which hovered in midair, orbiting him like planets around a sun.

"Bloopa-bloo?" Big Strange asked, as Bee and Hoggins arrived at the meat locker.

"Open it up," Hoggins said.

When Big Strange opened the walk-in fridge, all they saw was a pile of webbing where the two Arachne had been. Hoggins ran inside and looked around. They were long gone, even the dead one.

"Where the hell are they?" Hoggins yelled.

"They vanished…" Bee said.

Hoggins went to the guard. "Did you let anyone through here? What the hell happened?"

"Bloopa-bloo, bloopa-bloo," said Big Strange.

"What the fuck does that mean?" Hoggins yelled.

"Bloopa-bloo…"

"Where the fuck is Eddie when you need him?" Hoggins said.

Bee scanned the area, looking for clues. She wondered if somebody had teleported in there and taken them out. Nobody she knew had any teleportation magic, but the Arachne knew more spells than most.

"Here," Bee said, pointing at a thin trail of blood leading up to a ventilation shaft. "Shrink magic."

Hoggins investigated the vent. "How can you be sure?"

"What else could this be?" She pointed at the tiny footprints going up the wall.

"Then they're still in the building," Hoggins said. "We have to find them."

"Bloopa-bloo!" said Big Strange.

"Don't bother…" Bee said.

Her boss looked at her.

She led them outside the refrigerator and showed them a tiny hole in the vent, then a tiny hole in the wall leading outside.

"They're already gone," Bee said.

Hoggins didn't care. He still ran outside, searching the alleyway for a sign of the Arachne, looking into the sky, scanning the fire escapes. The place was deserted. The only sound was the hot wind blowing through garbage bags.

"Shit…" the boss said, falling to his porky knees. "They're going to kill us all."

Back in the restaurant, Hoggins was eating like there was no tomorrow. The table was piled high with cheesecakes, double-decker pizzas, and bacon-wrapped meatball sandwiches. When times were dire, the fat bastard didn't drink his problems away like everybody else. He ate his problems away. And his next day food-hangovers were ten times worse than anything caused by alcohol.

"I'm going to take some time off," Bee told him.

"Like hell you are," Hoggins said, choking down a plate of pepperoni lasagna.

Bee sat backwards in the chair across from him, leaning in close. "Look, the Arachne are after me. I'm the one to blame for this. If I steer clear of you and this place then you'll be safe."

"Bullshit," Hoggins said, spitting pickle bits across the table. "I'm your boss. That means I'm responsible for everything you do. The Arachne will blame me for all of this."

Bee looked down at her shiny black fingernails, not sure how to respond to that.

"No, I need you here," Hoggins said. "If the Arachne retaliate for this I'm going to need every guy at my disposal."

"You're really going to fight them?" Bee asked.

Hoggins laughed, nearly coughing up an avocado eggroll. "You don't fight the Arachne. At best, we might be able to defend ourselves long enough to meet some kind of peace agreement. But we'll most likely…"

He paused to eat a slab of ham. It almost seemed like cannibalism as the pig man ate the pig flesh.

Bee finished his statement. "We'll most likely go out in a blaze of glory?"

Hoggins nodded. "More like a puff of smoke, but you get the idea."

"I guess it's something to look forward to," Bee said, stepping out of the chair and fluttering her insect wings.

"Check on Eddie and Torko," Hoggins said. "Get them back here as soon as possible. We're closing up early tonight."

"Got it," Bee said.

As she left the fat man to his banquet-for-one, Bee stepped out of the restaurant and took one look back.

"Sorry, big guy," she said to his figure in the window, "but you don't know the full story."

She watched her boss through the window as he ate his way through all of his favorite foods, believing it was mostly likely the last chance he'd have to taste them.

"The further away from you I get, the safer you'll be," Bee said. "I owe you at least that much."

The bee girl hopped up into the air and flew away, through the blanket of smog over Hell's Bottom, disappearing above the maze of crumbling architecture. If the Arachne were only after Bee, she wasn't going to make it easy for them to find her.

PARTY
GAME

"Is this the animal party?" Brian asked, holding up the fuzzy green flier.

The butler at the door fluffed his rabbit suit and bowed at the guest.

"Yes, you've come to the right place," the butler's voice was squeaky to impersonate a cartoon rodent.

Brian laughed at the bowing rabbit. He raised a half-empty can of Budweiser in a salute and took a swig.

"Dude, sorry I'm late," Brian said. "It took a while to find the place and shit."

The rabbit man stared at him through the eyeholes in his mask. He seemed displeased with Brian's attire—ripped jeans and a stretched out Iron Maiden t-shirt from three decades ago. But Brian was a serious metalhead. He didn't own any other clothes.

"It is understandable," said the butler. "This manor is deep in the country, miles from civilization. It's not easy to find."

Standing before the butler, Brian felt like a skunk who wandered up to a picnic. He rubbed moisture out of his grubby long hair and then laughed out loud for no particular reason. He had no idea why he was even there.

"Well, I'm here now, bro," Brian said, shrugging his chubby shoulders.

"Please, come in," the rabbit said.

Brian stepped over the butler's massive fluffy feet as he entered the mansion. The entry room was vast and white, and so clean it sparkled. His footsteps echoed across the tile floor. The place was dead quiet apart from the faint bouncing of electro-pop music issuing from a distant room.

"This is what I call a party house, bro," Brian said, nodding his head at the interior. "I feel like I'm in a museum."

They were the only two people in sight. Brian was obviously out of place and normally would have felt awkward in such a situation, but he was so stoned he decided to just go with it.

"So where is everyone?" Brian asked.

"They're in the lounge," said the butler in the rabbit suit.

"Are they all dressed like you?" Brian asked, pointing at the butler's costume.

"No, I am the only rabbit at this party. Everyone here is dressed as a different animal."

"Hmmm…" Brian nodded his head, scratching the scruffy black hair on his chin. "You know… when the flier said 'animal party,' I didn't think you really meant *animal* party."

"What else would we mean?"

"I thought it was going to be, you know, a crazy party. Where everyone listens to heavy metal and goes wild. You know. This sounds more like some kind of *furry* party."

"We don't use the term *furry* here," said the butler. "This is a party for those who wish they were animals. It's a role-playing event. For one night, our guests are transformed into wild beasts and are given the opportunity to experience what it's like to live as an animal."

Brian shrugged. "Well, take me to them. I could use another beer after that drive."

"You're not going anywhere looking like that." The butler pointed at the Iron Maiden shirt.

"What do you mean?"

"Only animals are allowed at the animal party. You must transform yourself into something more suitable."

"Like what?"

"Follow me."

The rabbit butler led Brian to the coat room. There were dozens of animal costumes hanging on a rack.

"Take off your clothes," the butler said. "And choose the animal you'd like to be."

Brian looked at the animal costumes, then at the butler.

Shaking his head, Brian told him, "You know, maybe this

party isn't for me…"

"Of course it's for you."

"I'm not into that furry shit."

The butler gave him an evil eye. He didn't want him using that term anymore.

"Just tell me what kind of animal you want to be."

Brian sighed and then removed his shirt. "Fine, make me a squirrel."

"A squirrel?" The butler squished his finger into Brian's belly fat. "Wouldn't you rather be a larger animal?"

"Why do I have to be a larger animal?"

"You're at least three-hundred pounds. You should be a moose."

"I'm not dressing up as no moose. And I'm only two-eighty, asshole."

"Then what would you like to be?"

"I'll be… a dragon."

"A what?"

"Yeah, make me a dragon. Like the one on that Dio album cover. That would be badass. "

"Choose a *real* animal."

"Fine, a T-rex then."

The butler pointed at the tattoo on Brian's chest. "Is this a tattoo of a bear paw?"

"More like a bear *claw*," Brian said. "My nickname was Big Bear on the rez." He paused for a moment and then shook his head. "It wasn't a gay thing."

"Very well, you will be the bear."

The butler handed Brian a brown bear costume.

"Lame… I'm always the bear…" Brian said.

Brian liked crashing parties. It was the best way to spend a Saturday night when he couldn't afford to go to the bar. His plan was usually to just pop in, drink all the beer he could chug down, then pop out—unless there were any hot chicks he thought he could score with. But now that his clothes, shoes, wallet, cell phone, and car keys were locked up in the coat closet, it wouldn't be so easy for him to sneak out of there whenever he wanted.

When Brian stepped into the lounge, he found himself surrounded by people in furry costumes. They were already drunk and stumbling over their big fluffy feet.

"Everyone," the butler announced to the group. "Allow me to introduce you to Brian, the mighty bear."

The animals clapped for him.

Brian raised his fist in the air and yelled, "Iron Maiden!"

Nobody knew why he shouted the name of his favorite band, but they applauded his words anyway.

"Enjoy yourself," the butler told the large man, before leaving him alone with the other guests.

Although the mansion was enormous, the lounge was small, as if the hosts were going for a more intimate setting. Less than twenty people were in the room. The small numbers made it even more uncomfortable for Brian. He went right for the bar and pulled a bottle of Corona from the sink full of ice.

"Hello, Mr. Bear," said an older obviously gay man in a white duck costume, the duckbill wide open so that his face was exposed. He waved at Brian with just his fingers.

Brian ignored the duck. He was too busy trying to figure out how to open the beer with his squishy bear paw gloves. It kept slipping against the fabric.

"Here, let me open that for you," the duck said.

The duck slipped the Corona from Brian's hands and popped the cap against the bill of his duck costume. The smirk on his face was meant to be seductive, but it was just downright creepy. Even if Brian was gay he would have been creeped out by this man. Then the duck wrapped his lips around the bottle and took a swig before handing it back.

"Keep it," Brian said.

He removed the bear-shaped gloves and tossed them aside. Then he grabbed himself a fresh beer, twisted off the top and drank it through the eyehole of his costume as quickly as he could.

The other guests felt right at home in their fuzzy costumes. A fox girl whipped her tail at a wolf boy. An elk woman tapped her horns against the tusks of a short pudgy man in a wild boar outfit. Two dog men made barking noises and butted their heads together, trying not to dip their long droopy ears into their shot glasses filled with tequila.

"This is fucked up," Brian said to no one in particular. He felt like a gamma wolf during mating season.

He chugged two beers before taking a third and stepping toward the back of the room. A guy in a big turkey costume was there, leaning against the wall, sipping a martini. His turkey mask was raised up so that he could drink, exposing a bristly lumberjack beard.

"You ever been to one of these parties before?" Brian asked the turkey.

"Not this one," the turkey said with a southern drawl. "But I never pass up the chance to dress up like a turkey. It's kind of my thing."

"Yeah?" Brian found himself cracking up.

"It's always been a dream of mine to be a big turkey."

"This isn't some kind of weird sex party is it?" Brian asked the turkey, then he chuckled until he coughed.

"I sure hope so," the turkey said. "I haven't gotten laid in over a year."

"This isn't my scene, man." Brian shook his head. "I'm not into furry shit."

"I'm not into furry shit either, my friend," the turkey man said. "That shit is de-sgust-ing."

"Tell me about it." Brian raised his beer to the turkey man. "I just came for free alcohol. I don't have no fucking furry fetish."

"Me, I'm a vore-fetish man," said the turkey. "My fantasy is to be roasted alive in an oven with a bunch of apple stuffing shoved up my ass. You know, *all* the way up there. Then, once I'm cooked, I'd be carved up and served for Thanksgiving dinner. Just like a turkey. That's what gets me off. Fuck this lame cosplay crap."

Brian nodded at him, trying to pretend that what he just

heard was the most normal thing in the world.

"That's fucked up, bro," Brian said, then chugged the last of his beer. "I'm out of here."

Moving as fast as he could away from the turkey guy, Brian grabbed as many more beers as he could carry and ran for the exit. But before he could escape the lounge, the rabbit butler appeared, blocking his path.

"Can I have your attention, please," the butler said to the crowd of furries.

Brian turned his back to him, hiding all the beers in his fluffy arms.

When the room quieted down, the butler continued, "The festivities are about to begin." The crowd cheered the bunny until he raised his paw, requesting their silence. "But first, your hosts wish to greet you now. Please make your way through the hallway toward the back door. The party will continue in the yard."

Brian couldn't squeeze past the butler in time. He found himself stuck in the middle of the crowd of party guests as they stumbled down the hallway toward the backyard.

The backyard was just a big green field surrounded by forest. The guests mingled, chatting in cartoon animal voices, finishing their cocktails, rubbing each other's fur. Excitement was in the air, fueled by their animalistic sexual energy. Half of them looked ready to go for a romp in the woods right then and there. Brian wondered how the hell he was going to get out of there without having to butt-fuck a chipmunk first.

"Quack, quack," the man in the duck suit whispered into Brian's ear.

When Brian turned around, the duck winked and then wiggled his butt feathers at him. Brian moaned so loud that it sounded almost like a bear growl. The manly sound sent visible shivers down the duck's spine.

"I need to get the hell out of this costume," Brian said to

himself, struggling to pull the mask from his face. He couldn't find the zipper that secured the mask to the rest of the costume. The butler was the one who put it on him. All Brian managed to accomplish was dropping his extra beers onto the ground, which exploded into geysers of foam.

Brian wanted to get the hell out of there, but just couldn't figure out a plan of action. He felt like a turtle stuck on his back, unable to roll over.

Before the group got too rowdy, the hosts of the party made their appearance. It was a young husband and wife, walking elegantly down the steps into the yard, holding each other's hands.

"Welcome to the party, my animal friends," said the female host in a cheery voice. She sounded like some kind of cross between a country girl and a rich sorority chick.

Although nobody else seemed to think it was odd, Brian noticed that the hosts of the party weren't dressed as animals. They were dressed as hunters, each of them resting shotguns on their shoulders. Their camo vests were filled with ammunition.

"My wife and I would like to welcome you all to the sixth annual animal hunt," said the male host.

The furry crowd cheered.

"We've invited you all here because you wished to experience what it was like to live as wild animals," said the female host. "Today your dream will become a reality."

The husband continued her statement, "Because today you will be hunted down and killed, just like wild animals."

The furries laughed and clapped.

"But it's not just for the sport of it," the wife said with a giddy smile. "We always eat everything we kill. By tomorrow night, you'll all be turned into steaks and sausages."

The guests cheered and shouted. Turkey man pumped his fists.

Although everyone else thought the hosts were just messing around, Brian could tell they were serious. These people were really planning to hunt the furries down like animals in some kind of sick game. If it wasn't for the fact that the guests already had their shoes, cell phones, and car keys taken away from them, Brian wouldn't have been so suspicious. It didn't help that they were all the way out in the woods, miles from the highway.

"And then your heads will be stuffed and mounted in the game room," said the husband with a smug smile on his face. "Just like real wild animals who were hunted down by a superior species."

This wasn't a joke at all. No matter how sarcastic the smiles on their faces appeared, these two hunters were for real.

The adrenalin coursing through his system sobered Brian up fast. He looked around. It was a long way into the woods. Because the hosts mentioned this was the sixth annual animal hunt, Brian assumed they had to be good at playing this twisted game without getting caught or letting anyone get away. Brian had been in enough bar fights to know what to do in a situation like this. When you're up against an opponent who's far more powerful than you are, your best chance is to strike first, before your opponent's ready. If you wait until they are in control of the situation, you're going to get fucked up.

"I need another beer," Brian announced.

He pretended to be a lot drunker than he was, stumbling toward the hosts as if he had no idea what was going on or what they were saying.

"We'll give you a thirty second head start," said the female hunter.

The furries still didn't know what was going on, but a few of them were wondering why the hunters continued their lame joke for so long. Brian knew the hunters were laughing their asses off inside their heads, excited for the moment when their guests finally realized what was about to happen. He hoped that excitement would keep them distracted long enough for him to make his move.

As Brian stumbled up to the hunters, the husband smiled at him and said, "Where do you think you're going, Mr. Bear? You're about to be hunted."

Things slowed down for Brian. He felt the spotlight on him, the adrenalin pumping. It reminded him of the time he ran on stage at an Iron Maiden show, getting ready to stage-dive into the crowd before security caught him.

"I forgot my gloves," Brian said in as slurred a voice as he could make. He held up his hands to the hunters to reveal the missing bear claws that should have come with the costume. "I'll go get them…"

The husband and wife just snickered at his drunken stumbling, not sure whether they should let him get the gloves or send him back to the others.

Before the male hunter could open his mouth, Brian fake stumbled and fell toward him. The hunter instinctively reached out his arms as if to catch him, giving Brian the opportunity he needed.

"What the fuck?" the hunter yelled as Brian pulled the shotgun out of his hands.

The furries laughed and cheered at Brian. The female hunter panicked. She pumped her shotgun and pointed it at Brian.

"Put it—"

Before the woman could say *down*, Brian fired. The blast took her face clean off, spraying the white porch with a coat of chunky red paint. Her body fell to the floor with a thud.

The guests went quiet. For a moment, everything was perfectly still. Everyone became very sober, yet not quite sure what just happened. Only the sound of the cold wind and the blood trickling down the steps could be heard.

At first, Brian wondered if he'd fucked up. He wondered if it really was just a joke and the two hunters decided to use real guns as props instead of fake guns. But then the male hunter burst into laughter. He clapped his hands and chuckled, the smug smile returning to his face.

"Somebody grab the other gun," Brian yelled, looking back at the other guests.

They were frozen in place, not sure what to do.

"This isn't a game," Brian said. "This dude was really planning to hunt you, dumbasses. Pick up the other gun."

A man in a bloodhound suit stepped toward the gun. As he leaned toward it, Brian pointed the gun at his head.

"Not you!" Brian yelled.

"What?" the bloodhound asked.

"Not the dog," Brian said. "Somebody else pick it up."

"Why not the dog?" asked the duck man.

"The bloodhounds are on their side," Brian said. "You don't hunt bloodhounds, they hunt you." He moved the gun, telling the dogs to move behind the hunter. "The rest of us are dressed as wild game for a reason."

When the two frat boys dressed as bloodhounds passed Brian, they flexed their muscles, growled at him and then said "Woof! Woof! Woof!"

Brian kept his gun pointed at them. He felt like a badger trying to threaten a whole pack of wolves.

"Thanksgiving," Brian said to the turkey man. "Grab the gun."

The turkey hesitated for moment. "But I kind of like the idea of being hunted down like an animal…"

"Just grab the fucking gun, pervert," Brian yelled.

The turkey took the shotgun away from the dead woman, then he wiped her blood from the handle with his orange wing.

The male hunter was still laughing at Brian. The smug look on his face made the bear want to shoot it off.

"What's so funny?" Brian asked. "I just killed your wife."

The man raised his hands as Brian pointed the barrel of the shotgun at his guts. "That woman wasn't actually my wife. She's Walter's daughter. Man, he's going to be so pissed when he sees what you did."

"Who's Walter?"

"You'll see. He'll be down in a minute. With his friends."

The two bloodhounds howled behind him.

"Come on, we can take him," said one the bloodhounds.

The hunter gave him an annoyed expression. "Shut up, Mike. Dogs don't talk."

"That's a double barrel shotgun," the dog said. "He's only got one shell left in there. He can't get all of us."

"I said shut up."

The bloodhound eyeballed Brian and said, "Woof! Woof! Woof!"

Brian fired the last shell, tearing through all three of the guys at once. The talking bloodhound fell to the ground with the top of his skull removed. The other bloodhound dropped to the ground screaming. The spray caught him down his chest and face. As for the hunter, he was still standing. The blast only grazed his shoulder, causing a minor flesh wound. He held in the blood with his left hand. The pain wasn't enough to wipe the annoying smile off his face.

"Keep pointing at them," Brian told the turkey, as he pulled extra shells from the dead woman's vest and reloaded his double barrel shotgun.

"Aren't you going to give me extra ammo?" the turkey asked.

"That's a pump-action shotgun," Brian told him. "You won't need to reload as much as I do."

While digging, Brian found a handgun on the woman. He pulled it out of its holster and gave it to the wild boar who held onto it with shaky hands.

"What are we going to do?" a fox woman asked.

"We need to call the police," said a raccoon.

Brian ignored them. He was more focused on the hunter.

"Turn around," Brian told him. "Keep your arms raised."

"I'll bleed to death if I don't apply pressure to this wound," the hunter said.

"Good."

The hunter let go of the wound on his shoulder and raised his arms. Then he turned around. Brian searched him and found a handgun in a holster on his back, just like the female. He gave this one to the fox girl.

"How many more of you are there?" Brian asked the hunter.

"I don't know," the hunter said. "Count them yourself."

A group of older men stepped out of the house with rifles in their arms. The leader of the pack was a fat middle-aged man with a gray beard and plaid sweater.

"Goddamnit, Steven, why the hell haven't you gotten things started yet?" asked the man with the gray beard. "The prey should be out in the woods by now."

"I'm sorry, Walter," Steven said. "There were some complications."

That's when the older hunters realized what was going on. Steven stood there with a double barrel shotgun in his back. There were two dead bodies on the ground and neither of them were prey.

"What the hell happened?" Walter cried.

"The bear is tough this year," Steven said.

"Where's Sarah?" Walter asked.

Steven pointed at the dead body next to him.

The fat man's beard dropped open when he saw her.

"Sarah…" He went toward her. "How…"

"The bear did it," Steven said.

Brian aimed his shotgun at the fat man's chest. The guy was in such a daze he didn't realize when the elk woman took away his hunting rifle and pointed it at his buddies.

Walter looked up, "You killed her…"

"What do you expect, asshole?" Brian said. "She wanted to hunt us."

"You filthy animals…"

"Dude, it's your fault, not ours."

"You monsters…"

Brian had enough of him.

"Hunters, drop your weapons," Brian said, pointing his shotgun at Walter's head. "Or the fat guy gets it."

"Just do it," Steven said to his hunting buddies.

The hunters put their guns down on the porch.

"Now what?" asked the wild boar.

"We should kill them all," said the elk woman.

"We should hunt *them* like animals," said the duck, almost excited by the idea.

The fox girl stopped them. "We haven't done anything wrong yet. This was just self-defense. We should call the police."

Brian nodded. "Go inside and get a cell phone. Call for help."
She nodded.

"We're all waiting here until the police arrive," Brian announced
to everyone. "Nobody else has to die."

Before Brian finished his statement, the fox girl fired her
gun, putting a bullet in the head of the unarmed rabbit butler
as he stepped out through the back door.

The police arrived twenty minutes later, a whole caravan of
them. Brian's buzz was beginning to fade and he wished he
would have had some beers during the wait. The blue and red
lights filling the country sky made him feel dizzy and not quite
a part of his own body. He felt like an eagle flying upside-down.

"Drop your weapons!" the police shouted, running toward
the furries with their guns drawn.

"It's okay," said the fox girl, holding up her phone. "I'm the
one who called."

"Put them down! Now!" The cops were ready to shoot down
the whole group of furries. But it made sense to Brian. The
furries were armed and wearing costumes, like bank robbers,
pointing guns at rich white people. Of course they would seem
like the bad guys.

"It's okay," Brian said to his furry comrades. "Put the weapons
down. Let the police take it from here."

Brian hated the cops, but he'd rather have to deal with them
than the rich psychopaths. He'd probably have to spend a few
nights in jail, but in the end the hunters would be proven the
guilty party.

"Thank God you arrived, Officer," Steven said to the ranking
policeman. "These animals have gone out of control."

"Oh, shut up," Brian told him.

The cops took all the guns away from the furries. Everyone
just stood there, keeping their hands in the air.

The ranking officer had a thick Nick Nolte head, his lips
were chapped, razor burn marks down his neck. "Now will

somebody please explain to me what's going on here?"

"Those people are trying to hunt us!" yelled the fox girl.

"It's true!" yelled the duck. "Look at their outfits!"

The elk woman said, "They made us dress up like these animals and planned to hunt us down and murder us for sport."

Then all the furries tried to speak at once. It was so much clatter that not a single one could be understood by the cops.

"Okay, okay, calm down," said the head cop.

None of them would calm down.

"Just shut up!"

When the cop raised his voice, everyone went quiet.

He turned to the rich people. "Is this true? You were really planning to hunt them down and kill them?"

"They also said they'd eat us afterward," said the turkey man. "I distinctly heard them say that."

Steven paused for a minute, lowered his head and then nodded.

"It's true," Steven told the cop. "We were most definitely planning to hunt them down. We are hunters. That's what we do."

"Are you fucking kidding me?" the cop said.

"It's okay, though. We have a hunting permit." Steven flashed his smug smile at Brian.

"What do you mean a hunting permit?"

Steven took some folded up papers from his pocket. The cop retrieved them, looking them over.

"All of these animals are in season right now," Steven said. "We have the license to hunt each and every one of them. Even bear."

The cop's fingers were shaking as he read through the pages. He looked up at Steven and Steven flashed him a smile. When he handed back the papers, he composed himself and cleared his throat. Brian wondered what was printed on those papers to make the cop so nervous.

"These look in order," said the cop. "Very well. It looks like no crime is being committed here."

"What!" cried the fox girl.

"You've got to be shitting me," yelled the elk woman.

The wild boar pointed at the dead people. "What about them? People have been killed. Of course a crime has been committed here."

The cop saw the dead woman below Walter who was still sobbing and red with rage.

"Oh yes, I guess there are bodies to deal with," said the cop. "How did this happen?"

Steven pointed at Brian. "The bear did it. The big guy went nuts and killed my wife and my dog."

"Well, if he attacked a human…" the cop pulled out his handgun and pointed it at Brian's head. "I guess we'll have to put him down."

Before the gun was fired, Steven yelled, "No, Officer!"

The cop looked back at him.

Steven continued, "I like the bear this year. He's fun."

The cop lowered his weapon.

"We can't blame him for what he did," Steven said. "It's only his nature to defend himself. It's part of what makes hunting them so interesting."

"Are you sure?" the cop asked.

Steven nodded.

"What the fuck is wrong with you, dude?" Brian told the cop. "Are you seriously letting them get away with this?"

The cop looked at him for a second and then lowered his eyes in shame. "I'm sorry, son. There's nothing I can do."

As the cops went back toward the front of the house, Steven yelled at them, "Aren't you forgetting something?"

When the policemen looked back at them, Steven pointed at the guns they carried. "Aren't you going to return our property?"

The cops nodded and gave them all their guns back. As they were leaving, the furries pleaded for their mercy.

"Where are you going?"

"Please don't go!"

"You have to help us!"

"This can't be real…"

"You fucking asshole pigs!"

Steven, now pointing his double barrel shotgun at Brian, just chuckled out loud. "What a lively bunch of animals this year…"

The guns were now pointed at the furries and there was nobody coming to help them. Brian wished he would have killed the hunters when he had the chance. But how could he have known the cops would side with the hunters?

"Well, shall we get started then?" Steven said, smiling at Brian.

"I'm going to rip your guts out and eat you alive," Brian said to the smug prick.

The hunters just laughed at him.

"You're dead, boy," Walter said to Brian, rage flowing through his eyes. "I'm going to put your head above my fireplace after I kill you."

"Not if I kill you first, old man," Brian said.

Walter raised his rifle and pointed it at the bear's face. "Maybe I should blow you away right now."

"Walter…" Steven lowered the barrel of the rifle. "Walter, please. That's not very sporting of you. We need to give them a thirty second head start."

"He killed my daughter, Steven. Fuck your head start."

"You know the rules. If you kill any of them before the countdown then you'll be disqualified."

Walter thought about it for a moment. Then he lowered his weapon and said, "Fuck… Fine, motherfucker." His voice was a grumble. "But nobody kill the bear. The bear's mine."

"That's not how it works, Walter. If you want the bear you'll have to beat me to him."

"Go ahead and try to go after him, you little shit, and I'll fill your ass full of buckshot."

Steven just chuckled.

Then he faced the furries and announced, "Without further ado, my wild creatures. You are free to go. Run deep into the woods and try to survive. We will give you a thirty second head start."

The animals cried out in protest.

"Please don't do this," cried the fox girl. "I'm a kindergarten teacher. I'm a good person."

"Walter, start the countdown," Steven said.

The old man nodded and then shouted, "Thirty."

"You can let us go," said the wild boar. "We won't tell anyone."

Walter raised his voice. "Twenty-nine."

"Are you really going to eat us if you kill us?" asked the turkey man. "Make sure to prepare me like a real turkey if you're going to eat us."

"Twenty-eight."

"I'm going to kill each and every one of you motherfuckers," Brian said.

"Twenty-seven."

Steven chuckled as he said, "Why are you all still here? You'll make it too easy for us to hunt you if you stay here."

"Twenty-six."

The furries looked at each other.

"Twenty-five."

Then the party guests in animal costumes took off running, drunkenly stumbling across the lawn with their floppy fuzzy feet, heading into the woods.

"Twenty-four."

Steven raised his voice so they could hear him from across the yard. "Make sure to spread out, dumbasses. You'll be too easy to hunt if you stay in a big group."

The furries spread out and ran in different directions.

"Twenty-three."

"What a bunch of idiots," Steven said.

"Twenty-two."

All of the animals were out of sight, heading deeper into the woods—all of them except for Brian, who stayed behind, staring the hunters deep in their eyes.

"Twenty-one."

"You're still here?" Steven asked.

Brian glared at him. "I'm not going anywhere, you fucking prick."

"Twenty."

"How disappointing. I was expecting so much from you on this hunt, Big Bear."

"You're all a bunch of cowards."

"We're hunters."

"Nineteen."

"You're not hunters. There's no sport in hunting people."

"Man is the most dangerous game, as they say," Steven said. "It is the biggest challenge for hunters of our ilk."

"Eighteen."

"Dude, hunting them's not a challenge. Did you see those idiots? They're fat suburbanites. They don't know how to survive out there. Most of them probably haven't even been out in the woods since they went camping as kids."

"Seventeen."

Brian continued, "Not only that, but they're drunk, unarmed, brightly colored, and don't even have shoes or proper clothing. By the end of the night, most of them will be so cold and busted up that they'll be begging to be found even if it kills them."

"Sixteen." Walter's eyes pierced deeper into Brian with every number he counted.

"Just start running, Big Bear," Steven whined. "I beg you. I was so looking forward to hunting you."

Brian just ignored him. "Have you ever hunted a predator before? Have you ever hunted a *real* bear? Now *that* is dangerous game."

"Fifteen."

"Bears can cut through a man like a machete through bamboo," Brian said.

"Fourteen."

"They run at speeds of forty-miles per hour. There's no way a hunter like you could get away from a bear once it starts charging you."

"Thirteen."

"Their hide is so thick that you can shoot them with a hundred rounds and they'll keep coming for you."

"Twelve."

Brian looked at the old man's rifle. "You wouldn't be able to kill a real bear with that peashooter you've got. It would just piss him off. Like a mere bee sting."

"Eleven."

"Imagine what it would be like if you were to hunt a real bear," Brian told the hunters.

"Bears are stupid," Steven said. "Compared to men, they are easy kills."

"Ten."

"What if you were faced with a bear that had the intelligence of a human?" Brian said. "The whole group of you would be fucked."

"Nine." Walter smiled at Brian. "Almost time, boy. Your ass is going to be mine."

"I don't think so."

"Eight."

"You see, I have a close relationship with animals," Brian said. "It's something that was passed down through the generations in my family."

"Seven."

"That's one reason I came to this party. I mostly came for the free beer, but I also kind of hoped there might be more people like me. More people who were able to bring out their inner animals."

"Six."

"It's a somewhat common type of magic," Brian said. "But still, I'm the only person I've known since my grandfather who was capable of casting the spell of Animal Spirit."

The hunters looked confused. They didn't know if the guy in the bear costume was just fucking with them or really believed what he was saying.

"Five."

"I'll show you what it's like to face a real bear," Brian said.

"Four."

Brian stumbled backward. At first, he was worried that he was too drunk to cast the spell, but he's done it so many times that it was second nature. In less than a second, the spell was cast.

"Three." Walter was drooling with excitement as the countdown was almost finished.

Brian's muscles swelled out five times their normal size, ripping open the back of the fuzzy bear suit.

"Two?" Walter said, his voice getting soft.

"You hunters are about to become the hunted," Brian roared. His voice was no longer human as his mouth changed shape—teeth stretching, tongue flopping out.

The hunters trembled in their boots. The voice coming from the bear suit was deep and monstrous. They couldn't believe what was happening in front of them.

Walter gulped. "One…"

A grizzly bear exploded from the bear costume and ripped Walter's throat out.

"What the fuck!" Steven cried, finally dropping that smug smile from his face.

Blood gushed out of the old man's neck as his spine cracked in the beasts jaws.

"Shoot him, goddamn it!" Steven's voice was now that of a high-pitched little girl. "Shoot the fucking thing!"

The hunters opened fire but their low-caliber rounds couldn't pierce the monster's hide. Brian hadn't just transformed into an ordinary grizzly bear. He was the biggest beast any of them had ever seen in their lives, something out of prehistoric times—like the mammoth short-faced cave bear which fed on Neanderthals a hundred thousand years ago.

"Don't run!" Steven said, as the hunters gave up on shooting the thing and took off. "You can't outrun it!"

But the hunters kept on fleeing, some of them dropping their weapons so they could move faster. And Steven found himself to be the last man standing before the snarling creature.

"Bro, it's cool," Steven said, stepping away from the bear. "You proved your point. We don't have to hunt anyone anymore."

The bear stood on its two legs, towering over the scrawny white guy.

"Look," Steven continued. "No matter how strong you are, you won't survive a 12-gauge blast to the face. Let's call it even and go our separate ways."

The beast did not back down, stalking closer to the hunter. Steven looked down at his double barrel shotgun. There were only two shots. He would have to use them wisely.

"You know how much money my family has?" Steven asked. "I could pay you. What is killing me going to prove? I could make you rich. You'd never have to worry about money ever again."

Even though the bear had Brian's thoughts, it also had its own animal urges. And what it wanted far more than money was blood.

"Bring it on, then!" Steven yelled with tears in his eyes.

As Steven fired his shotgun, the bear dropped down onto his four legs and charged. The blast barely grazed the beast's forehead.

"Motherfucker!"

With the last shot, Steven aimed for its face. The blast echoed through the forest.

Furries in pink bunny suits looked up from their hiding spots in the brush, twitching their ears and darting their eyes back and forth. The rich, fat hunters tripped and tumbled in the dark. One of them breathed so heavy he sounded like he was ready to have a heart attack.

Steven wheezed and coughed up blood. Lying on his back in the grass, he shuddered and squirmed as the bear chewed on his insides. The shotgun blast had hit the bear in the belly as he lunged forward, but it wasn't enough to kill the beast. The creature still had enough strength to rip Steven's stomach open and eat him alive.

"Piece of shit…" Steven said, his voice drifting away as his bladder popped in the bear's mouth.

When Steven was dead, Big Bear turned away and glared deep into the woods. Although he was badly wounded, he couldn't give up just yet. There were still plenty of hunters out there who needed to be dealt with. By morning, they would learn which of them was truly the most dangerous game.

THE
UNLIKELY
GUEST

Rachel heard her husband's voice pulling her out of a deep, warm, snuggly dream. The kind of dream a working mother only gets to experience a few times a year. She did not wake up happy.

"Come on, get up," Mike said.

He stood at the edge of the bed in his boxer shorts and t-shirt. She could hardly make him out in the dark.

"What time is it?" Rachel asked, rubbing crust from her eyes to see the clock read 3:27am. "Are you kidding me?"

"We've got an intruder," Mike said.

"What?"

"Somebody's in the backyard."

Rachel sat up. She put on her glasses. "Are you sure it's not just Amy sneaking out again?"

"Positive," Mike said.

She noticed her husband was holding a baseball bat.

"Just call the police if you think someone's really out there," Rachel said.

"I'm not calling the police," Mike said.

Rachel picked up her cell phone. "I'll do it myself then."

Mike grabbed the phone away from her and tossed it across the room. "We're not calling the police!" When he realized he was getting angry, he calmed his voice and took a deep breath. "Don't worry. I'll take care of it."

"Well, I'm coming with you," she said, putting on her robe.

Rachel took the flashlight and followed him into the hallway.

"What's going on, Mom?" Amy asked, coming out of her bedroom.

"Go back to sleep, honey," Rachel said. "It's nothing."

"Did someone break in?" Amy asked, looking up at the baseball bat.

The teenager was wearing only a t-shirt and panties. Mike, being her stepfather and not a blood relative, hated when she walked half-naked around the house.

"Go to bed, Amy!" Mike yelled.

He mostly wanted her to go to bed so he wouldn't have to look at her nipples that were clearly visible through her shirt's thin white fabric.

Amy, as always, didn't listen. She followed them down the stairs.

Before they entered the living room, an old woman jumped out of the hallway and cut them off.

"Where's everyone going?" asked the old woman.

Rachel screamed when she saw her. Mike nearly knocked off her head.

"Mom, what are you doing awake?" Rachel asked.

"I was just wondering where you were all off to so late in the evening," the old woman said.

Even worse than his stepdaughter, Mike hated how his mother-in-law dressed around the house. She walked with her robe wide open, laced granny underwear in clear view. Mike always wondered if there was something deeply wrong with his wife's family.

"Mom, go back to sleep," Rachel said. "It's nothing to worry about."

"Somebody broke in, Grandma!" Amy said.

"Shhh," Rachel hushed her daughter. "Nobody broke in. Mike thinks he saw someone in the backyard. It's nothing."

"There's definitely someone in the backyard," Mike said.

"Don't any of you worry, I'll take care of this," Grandma said. "You all go on back to bed."

"Mom, you're not going out there," Rachel cried.

"Nonsense," Grandma said. "This is still my house. I'm the one who should be responsible for scaring off the transients."

"We never said anything about transients," Mike said.

"Just let me get my shotgun..." the old woman said as she

74

hobbled back into her room. "Do you think I'll need more than two shells?"

"Let's just go," Rachel said, pointing her husband to the back door.

Mike led the way through the living room. His wife and her daughter followed.

"I'll take a whole handful of them, just to be safe," the grandma's voice echoed in the background.

Mike opened the arcadia door slowly, trying not to make too much noise. Then he pointed up at the treehouse. There was a light on in the window.

"I think Mom was right," Rachel said. "I think it's a transient."

She understood why the treehouse would appeal to a transient. It was as big as a hotel room and was fully furnished, with glass windows, insulation, and even electricity. Rachel practically lived up there when she was a teenager.

"Damn, I hope he doesn't mess with my stuff," Amy said.

By *stuff*, Amy meant she hoped he didn't find her weed.

"Go back inside," Mike said, waving his stepdaughter away.

Mike stepped forward and readied his bat, staring up at the treehouse window.

"Whoever you are, you're on private property," Mike yelled up at the vagrant. "I'd like you to leave the treehouse immediately."

There was movement in the window, then the light went out.

"We know you're in there," Mike said. "If you don't leave now we're going to call the police."

They waited for a moment, but nobody came out.

Grandma suddenly appeared behind them. "Should I fire a warning shot?"

Rachel moved the barrel of her mother's shotgun away from her husband's back. "That won't be necessary, Mom."

"We're armed," Mike yelled up at the treehouse. "We're not playing games. Come down now and you won't get hurt."

"I'm telling you, we need to fire a warning shot," Grandma said.

Rachel hushed her mother.

They waited a few more minutes. If there was somebody up

there, they weren't moving.

Grandma fired a warning shot in the air. The power of the blast nearly blew out Mike's eardrums.

She yelled, "Come out now, you bastard, or I'll blow a hole in yer belly the size of the Grand Canyon!"

The door of the treehouse flew open.

"Don't shoot," the intruder said. "I'm coming down. Just don't shoot."

The intruder stepped out of the treehouse, holding up his arms.

"What?" Rachel said, shocked by the vagrant climbing down the ladder.

"It's just a kid," Amy said.

The boy was wearing baggy pajamas and a raincoat, carrying a single briefcase.

"I'm sorry," the kid said. "I just needed a place to sleep for the night."

When the kid made it to the ground, he held up his hands.

"You've got to be shitting me…" Mike said, lowering his bat.

"I've got money," the boy said. "If you let me stay, I can pay you."

The boy tried to open the briefcase with his hands raised. When it unlocked, the case flew open and money came pouring out. That's all there was inside of it—just thousands upon thousands of bills, raining onto their backyard lawn.

"Holy crap," Grandma said. "The kid is loaded."

The others couldn't say a thing. They just stared at the boy, their mouths wide open. The last person they expected to be trespassing on their property was a small child carrying more money than any of them had seen in the past ten years.

"Your name's Elmore?" Rachel asked, giving the boy a cup of hot chamomile tea. "Where are your parents?"

When the boy sipped the tea, he seemed to relish the flavor.

Rachel thought it was odd he was more interested in chamomile tea than hot cocoa with marshmallows.

"Dead," Elmore said. "My dad died a long time ago. My mom more recently."

"Don't you have any other family?" Rachel asked.

"No, nobody," Elmore said. "I'm all on my own."

Mike pointed to the stacks of money on the table between them.

"Where'd all this money come from, bud?" Mike asked.

"It's mine," Elmore said.

"Did you steal it from somewhere?" Mike asked.

The boy shook his head.

"It's mine," Elmore said.

"How much do you have here?"

"It's *his*, Mike," Rachel said, when she realized her husband was getting a little too interested in the money.

"I'm just a little curious how a seven-year-old kid came across this kind of cash."

"It's eight hundred thousand dollars," Elmore said. "My mom left it to me the day she died."

Mike nearly wanted to cry. He picked up a stack of money and flipped it like a deck of cards.

"Gees, bud…" Mike shook his head. He didn't know what else to do but laugh with envy. "That's an incredible amount of dough for such a little dude."

"I figured it would be enough to last me until I reached a hirable age," Elmore said.

Mike nodded his head. "Yeah… Yeah, I'd say that's enough." Under his breath he added, "It's nearly a million dollars…"

Elmore continued, "I'm not sure what the job market will be like in the next ten to fifteen years, but I'm optimistic the economy will turn around by then."

"The kid's hilarious," Amy said from the entryway.

"I think he's cute," the old lady said, standing next to her granddaughter, leaning on the shotgun between them like an armrest.

Rachel started stacking the boy's money back into his

briefcase. Her husband hated to see all that lovely green disappear into the cold, black container, away from his eyes.

"Well, you can stay in the treehouse tonight, Elmore," Rachel told the boy. "But we'll have to figure out what we're going to do with you in the morning."

"I'd like to stay on as a boarder, if you don't mind," Elmore said. "I can pay rent in advance."

"I think that's a great idea," Mike said.

His wife gave her husband a dirty look. "We'll talk about it in the morning."

When Rachel stood from her chair, Elmore grabbed her by the hand.

"Thank you, Rachel," Elmore told her, staring deep into her eyes. "It means a lot to me."

Rachel pulled her hand away and half-smiled.

"Are you sure you're only seven?" Rachel asked the boy.

Elmore bowed at the family, took his briefcase full of money, and went toward the back door. He bowed again before taking his leave.

"He's so cute!" Grandma yelled, after the boy closed the door and returned to the treehouse.

"Are you crazy?" Rachel yelled at her husband.

Grandma and Amy went off to bed. It was just the two of them, arguing about what they should do with the boy.

"We could use the money," Mike said. "You know we can. I haven't been able to get work in almost a year now. Even with you working double shifts we're hardly able to pay bills, let alone all the debts."

"But renting a treehouse to a seven-year-old has got to be illegal," Rachel said. "We probably should call child protective services. He needs to be put in a foster home."

Mike paced back and forth in the dining room as he articulated his thoughts on the situation. "Normally, I'd agree with you, but what do you think's going to happen to all that money? They're not going to let him keep it. The police are going to take it or some foster family will spend all of it and leave him with nothing by the time he turns eighteen. What's best for him would be to stay with a family who'll look out for his best interests, who won't take advantage of him. A family like us."

Rachel looked into her tea and let out a sigh. She knew it was going to be difficult to help the kid without putting him at risk of losing all his money.

"Well, I agree that we can't just let him leave," Rachel said. "Out on the streets, he's going to be a target. Somebody's going to kill him for that money eventually."

Mike nodded his head rapidly in agreement.

"But we can't just let him stay here without telling anybody either," Rachel said. "He needs to be put in school. If anybody found him here we might be accused of kidnapping."

"What if we became his foster parents?" Mike said.

Rachel couldn't believe her ears. Mike proved time and time again that he wasn't very fond of kids, with the exception of Amy, of course.

"You've been talking about adopting for years now," Mike said, leaning his arms on the table.

"And you kept making excuses about why we shouldn't," Rachel said.

"But that was only because we couldn't afford to support another child," Mike said. "This kid has his own money. He'd pay for himself."

Rachel wasn't sure.

"Amy will go off to college in a couple years. It might be good for you to have another kid around the house."

"I don't think it's as easy as that," Rachel said. "We can't just claim a kid we found in our treehouse like we would a stray dog."

"Maybe not, but it's worth a try," Mike said. "We can talk to the kid in the morning, see how he feels about it. Then we can call whoever we need to call and see what we can do. Nobody has to know about the money. We can keep that part secret."

Rachel took a sip of her tea. It was long cold.

After a moment of silence, Rachel responded, "If we can manage it, I'm willing to give it a shot. But with all our debts and you being unemployed, not to mention your criminal record, I just don't know if they'll think we'd make a suitable foster family."

The little boy appeared behind them, stepping out of the darkened living room.

"I can hire a lawyer," Elmore said, as if he'd heard every word they were saying about him.

The adults looked back at him, surprised to see the kid lurking in the dark.

"It shouldn't be too difficult to get temporary custody," the boy continued. "I've read enough books on law to know there's a loophole for everything."

The boy didn't say another word. He just continued on his way to the bathroom, walking straight to the third door on the left, as if he knew the exact layout of the house without ever having been there before.

Rachel and Mike just stared at each other. Rachel couldn't explain why, but she had the sneaking suspicion that the strange kid had planned all of this from the start.

"Mr. Elmore Wormwood," Paul Underman said to the boy sitting across from him in his office. "Under the care of Michael and Rachel Heffington." Underman adjusted his glasses, looking up at Rachel and Mike standing behind the child.

"They've been my foster parents for the past three weeks," Elmore said, smiling up at Rachel. She returned the smile and rubbed his shoulders.

"And you say you've only been homeschooled up until this point?" asked the balding middle-aged man.

"That is correct," Elmore said.

Mr. Underman looked up at the foster parents. "Normally, it's a little difficult for a homeschooled child to adjust to public school. Now, my recommendation would be—"

"Oh, I have no intention of attending your school, Mr. Underman," Elmore said. "No offense. It's a beautiful establishment."

Rachel looked down at the boy, shocked by his rudeness. "Elmore!"

The boy ignored his foster mother.

"I've just come for a diploma," Elmore said. "I assure you there's nothing your educators can teach me that I don't already know."

Mr. Underman chuckled at the boy. He was used to pretentious little shits coming into his office from time to time, but nothing like this kid.

"Is he for real?" Mr. Underman asked the foster parents.

Mike shrugged. Rachel didn't know what to say.

Mr. Underman returned his attention to the boy. "We have placement exams if you'd like to skip the third grade and go immediately to the fourth."

"That won't do," Elmore said. "What's the highest grade available in your school?"

"We go all the way to the eighth grade here," said Mr. Underman. "The middle school and junior high are across the street."

"Very well," Elmore said. "I'll take the eighth grade placement exam."

"You're only seven," Rachel said, leaning over his shoulder to look him in the eyes. "You can't take an eighth grade placement exam."

"Trust me, kid," Mike said, leaning over his other shoulder. "You don't want to be seven in eighth grade. School is more than just what you learn in books. There's a social education you don't get when you're homeschooled."

"I understand the awkwardness of being a child in junior high," Elmore said. "I have no intention of attending the eighth grade, either. I would just like the diploma."

All the adults in the room couldn't help but groan at him.

"I'll tell you what," said Mr. Underman. "You take the fourth grade placement exam and we'll see how you do with that. Then, maybe, you can take the one for fifth grade."

Elmore held out his hand. "Just give me them all at once. It'll save everyone a lot of time."

Mr. Underman didn't even want to look at the boy anymore. He looked up at the parents. "Bring him back tomorrow and we'll have him tested."

"I can take them now, if that's okay with you," Elmore said. "It shouldn't take me very long."

Mr. Underman's teeth were clearly grinding. It wasn't the troublemaker kids who got under his skin the most; it was the smug little smartasses with an overblown sense of entitlement. Part of him wanted to see the kid fail miserably, while the other part wanted the brat to actually do so well that he'd never have to deal with him ever again.

"Well, your new brother's a certified genius," Mike said to Amy as they came home that evening.

The teenager hopped out of the couch, excited to hear the news.

"Did they skip him a few grades?" Amy asked. "I told you they were going to skip him a few grades."

"He didn't skip a just few grades," Rachel said, carrying two boxes of celebratory pizza.

"He skipped *every* grade," Mike said, taking the pizzas from his wife.

Amy high-fived Elmore. "I knew you'd blow them away!"

Elmore smiled, then blushed. He didn't feel comfortable getting so much attention.

"The school wouldn't even take him," Rachel said. "They recommended he go to a private school for gifted children."

"In other words, an *expensive* school," Mike said.

Mike didn't bother waiting to get the pizza into the kitchen. He pulled out a slice and lowered it into his mouth.

"Elmore can afford it," Amy said.

"I'd prefer not bother with school at all," Elmore said. "They're overrated."

"Overrated he says…" Mike shook his head at the kid's words while chewing on pepperoni and cheese.

"You have to go to some kind of school," Rachel said. "You can't just skip your education and go straight to a career."

"Maybe he should go to medical school," Mike said. "He could be Doogie Howser."

Elmore looked at Rachel and then Amy.

"I'd be open to enrolling in an art school," Elmore said. "I always wanted to learn to paint or play the piano. My mother never let me do anything too creative."

Amy's eyes lit up. "Hey, yeah! There's a charter school that focuses on the arts in the Ashland District. Sarah's little sister goes there."

Elmore looked over at Rachel.

"I guess we can look into that," Rachel said.

"It's settled then," Mike said, taking another slice of pizza from the box. "Now everyone dig in before the food gets cold."

Amy play-punched her stepdad. "Or before you eat it all!"

It was getting late. Grandma and Amy retired to their bedrooms for the evening. Rachel was straightening up the kitchen, getting ready to call it a night. Mike and Elmore were playing a game of Stratego on the living room coffee table.

"This is my game," Mike said. "Nobody's ever beaten me at this, not even come close." He took a sip from a can of Budweiser. "But here you are, creaming me at it."

Elmore was having a good time playing a more adult game. He'd only played kids games like Candyland or Tiddlywinks when he lived with his mother. A game that let him use his brain was much more stimulating.

"It's a fun game," Elmore said. "I can see why you'd like it."

"Have you ever played chess?" Mike asked.

Elmore shook his head and made his move.

"I think Stratego is far superior to chess," Mike said, thinking carefully over his next move. "It requires creativity as well as strategy, because you get to choose the formation of your pieces at the start of the game. In chess, the formation is always the same. You also have to read your opponent and try to figure out what his pieces are before you attack."

Mike moved his lieutenant piece into one of Elmore's, suspecting it to be his spy. But it was a landmine. His lieutenant was killed.

"What about poker?" Elmore asked, taking away the lieutenant piece. "How does that compare to chess as a strategy game?"

Mike took a swig of beer. "Poker is probably the most complex strategy game in the world. I didn't think so until I started playing Texas Hold'em. I used to always think it was based purely on luck, not strategy."

Elmore took Mike's spy with a scout.

"I hate games based purely on luck," Mike said.

Mike also hated games he wasn't very good at, like chess or poker.

"So which spell do you know?" Elmore asked.

Mike moved his sergeant slowly toward Elmore's scout, not sure exactly what Elmore was asking him.

"I'm guessing it's some kind of gambling magic, yes?" Elmore asked.

Mike removed his hand from his piece and looked up, staring the kid in the eyes.

"My mother knew a spell," Elmore said. He finished Mike's move for him, removing the fallen scout from the board. "She made quite a bit of money from it."

Mike looked back, toward the kitchen. Rachel was in there doing dishes. With the water on, she couldn't hear what they were saying.

He leaned in close to Elmore, and whispered, "Are you saying I know how to use magic?"

Elmore pointed at Mike's pupils. "It's in your eyes."

"My eyes?" Mike asked.

"Look in the mirror." Elmore nodded toward a mirror on the mantle. "You have a pair of dice inside your eyes."

Mike stood up and went to the mirror. He'd never noticed it

before, but there were dice in his eyes. They were like miniature tattoos right on his green irises.

"The more you cast the spell, the more your body will transform," Elmore said. "It starts out as just images on your body, but the images grow. If you keep using the magic, one day your eyes won't be eyes anymore. You will have nothing but dice in your eye sockets."

"These were never here before…" Mike said, still focused on the dice in his eyes.

"My mother used her magic so much that she was hardly human by the time she died," Elmore said. "Most of her body was glass. Just her head and limbs were still living flesh."

Mike turned to the boy, giving him a disturbed look.

"It's not actually the magic that changes you," Elmore said. "It's the universe that changes you." Elmore grabbed Mike's beer and took a swig from it, then relished the flavor. He hadn't had a beer since the last time he was a teenager.

"Who are you?" Mike asked. "Where did you come from?"

Elmore ignored the question.

"You see, when you use magic," Elmore continued, "you're actually breaking the laws of physics; you're *cheating* reality. This confuses the universe; it doesn't know what to do with you. So it finds a way to correct the imbalance. For instance, if you cast a spell that makes you fly, you will begin to grow wings. If you cast a spell that makes you strong enough to lift a tanker trunk with one arm, you will grow grotesquely huge muscles big enough to lift such a truck. It's just how the universe makes sense of magic, how it corrects the impossible."

Mike just stared at the kid, terrified of him.

"Go to bed," Mike told him.

Elmore took another sip of Mike's beer. "We haven't finished our game yet."

"I don't care," Mike said, his voice softer and higher than usual. "I'm your legal guardian. You have to do as I say. Now go to bed."

"If you wish," Elmore said, standing up from the coffee table.

"Now!" Mike yelled.

Elmore turned away from the man and went toward the back door. When Rachel entered from the kitchen, she saw the boy heading outside toward the treehouse. She also saw her husband visibly shaking.

"What's wrong?" she asked.

"Nothing," Mike said.

"You're shaking. Did something happen?"

"No," Mike said, still watching Elmore through the window. "Kid beat me at Stratego."

Mike and Rachel lay awake that night, deep in thought.

"There's something about that kid…" Rachel said.

Mike fluffed his pillow and rolled his eyes. "Tell me about it…"

"He reminds me so much of David."

"David?"

"Amy's father."

"Oh yeah, that guy." Mike hated hearing about his wife's previous lovers.

"If you'd have met him you'd know what I mean. They both had the same look in their deep, dark eyes. They were both smart. God, he was smart…"

Mike wanted to groan. Rachel rarely ever spoke of David, but whenever she did it was as though she were still deeply in love with the guy even though he abandoned her.

"He even lived up in that treehouse just like Elmore," Rachel said.

"He lived with you here?" Mike asked. "While you were still in high school?"

"I told you he was a runaway. Mom found him up there, nearly blew his head off with Dad's shotgun."

Mike laughed an *I wish she would have* laugh.

"She let him live up there for three years," Rachel continued. "I guess she felt sorry for him. He was a runaway and had an abusive home life."

Mike shook his head and chuckled. "Never in a million years would my mom let me have a live-in girlfriend at that age."

"Well, Mom didn't know we were hooking up behind her back," Rachel said. "Not until I was pregnant with Amy."

"That's when the loser left you, right? After he found out you were knocked up?"

"Not quite," Rachel said. "He proposed to me the second he found out I wanted to keep the baby. We were supposed to be married as soon as we graduated from high school."

"But he still changed his mind and hit the road, didn't he?"

Rachel shrugged. "One night, out of nowhere, he just disappeared and I never heard from him again. I don't really blame him. We were just kids. But still, it was a shock. I was *so* in love with that boy..."

"Do we really have to keep talking about this guy?"

"I remember having the weirdest dream the night he disappeared," Rachel said. "We were sleeping together up in the treehouse when this creepy-looking woman came into the room. Physically, she looked really young, but in her eyes she appeared to be a rotten old hag. When she took off her coat, I saw that her body was made of glass."

"Made of glass?" Mike asked.

"Yeah. She was like some kind of witch. She cast a spell on David, which shrank him down to the size of a football. Then she ran away with him."

"The size of a football?"

"I was in counseling for years because of that dream. My psychologist had all sorts of theories about what it meant, but I'm sure it was just my subconscious trying to come up with an excuse for why he'd actually leave me."

Mike was suddenly very quiet.

"Amy is so much like him, too..." Rachel said. "I wish she got a chance to meet him. They would have loved each other."

Rachel turned to Mike.

"Call me crazy," she began. "But I don't think Elmore came here by coincidence."

"Oh, yeah?" He knew she couldn't possibly be thinking

what he was thinking.

"I don't know why, but I have this feeling that Elmore is actually David's son."

"His son?"

"Just imagine it. David gets remarried and has a son, Elmore. Both David and his wife die, leaving Elmore all alone. Where is Elmore going to go? To the only family he has left."

"Who? You? You're not his family."

"Not me," Rachel said. "Amy. His long lost half-sister. It would make sense that he would come here. His father might have even left him this address."

"If that were the case, why wouldn't he have said anything?"

"I don't know…" Rachel turned away. "Maybe he's waiting for the right moment."

"Whatever you do, don't tell Amy about this," Mike said.

"No, of course not."

"I mean it. Unless you're one hundred percent positive, she shouldn't know."

Rachel nodded.

"If it's the truth, I'm sure Elmore will let us know when he's ready."

"So what was it like growing up here?" Elmore asked Amy.

They were in the living room, watching *Dancing with the Stars* while Elmore helped the teenager with her homework.

"Oh, I didn't grow up here," Amy said. "We moved in with Grandma once Mike lost his job and we couldn't afford the old apartment. Personally, I preferred the city over the suburbs."

Elmore couldn't take his eyes off of her. He tried to hide the smile on his face, but it kept creeping back on. He never thought he would get the chance to meet her, let alone actually live with her as part of her family.

"Has Mike always been a good dad to you?" Elmore asked.

"Mom went through a lot of boyfriends when I was young," Amy said. "Mike was the only one who stuck around. They got married a few years ago, but he's been kind of like a dad ever since I was ten."

"That's good," Elmore said. "He seems like a nice guy."

Amy laughed at the kid's weird questions.

"What about you?" Amy asked. "How was your dad?"

"I don't remember my dad."

"How about your mom?"

Elmore paused for a moment.

He said, "My mom loved me so much she squeezed all the life out of me."

Amy giggled. "Yeah, my mom's the same way."

"No," Elmore said. "I mean she literally stole my life from me. Until I came here, I wasn't actually allowed to live."

Amy didn't know how to respond to that.

"Um, okay…" Amy said.

Mike came home covered in blood.

"Dad!" Amy said, jumping up from her homework. "What happened?"

"It's nothing," Mike said.

His nose looked broken. Blood poured from his lips and nostrils. One of his eyes was swelling shut.

"Did somebody beat you up?" Amy cried. "Did you get jumped?"

"Yeah," Mike said, grabbing a couch cushion and putting it up to his face. "Somebody jumped me."

"Did you call the police?"

"No, it's fine," Mike said. "Can you get me some ice?"

His stepdaughter nodded and ran into the kitchen.

Mike looked down at Elmore.

"We need to talk," Mike said.

Mike and Elmore sat on the back porch

"I need to borrow some money," Mike said, holding the ice pack to his swollen eye.

Elmore nodded but wasn't agreeing. "For what?"

"To cover some gambling debts," Mike said. "It's important."

Elmore just watched him.

"Look, you were right about the spell," Mike said. "I didn't even believe in magic until I started using it. I found it in an old book last year. When I couldn't find work, I started doing odd jobs I looked up on craigslist, such as cleaning out garages and basements, that sort of thing. The book looked old. I thought it had value, so I took it. Once I figured out what it was supposed to be, I tried it out."

"And it worked?"

Mike paused a moment. Then he nodded slowly.

"Yeah," Mike said. "It worked. The spell is Control Dice. Basically, I can make a pair of dice come up any number I want as long as I'm within visual range."

"So you started gambling?"

"I never liked playing games that were based on luck," Mike said. "But when it's a sure thing? I'll play that. And I did."

"If the spell worked then why do you need money?" Elmore asked.

"I borrowed some money from some bad people." Mike wiped blood from his nose.

"Loan sharks?"

"I guess you can call them that," Mike said. "Anyway, I borrowed as much money as they could possibly give me. Then I used my spell and played some craps. In one hour, I won enough money to last me a lifetime."

"And what happened?" Elmore said.

"The casino wouldn't let me collect my winnings," Mike said. "They claimed I was a cheat. They showed me a pair of loaded dice, which they accused me of bringing into their casino. Obviously, it was complete bullshit. All my money was gone and they put my name and face on the blacklist. Now I'm not even allowed inside a casino without being escorted out by security."

"They also might have known you were using gambling magic," Elmore said. "If they saw the dice in your eyes they would have known."

"But how would they know gambling magic even exists?"

"If they didn't know gambling magic existed then all casinos would have gone out of business a long time ago, robbed by those with gambling-related spells."

"I guess so…" Mike said.

"So how much do you owe the loan shark?"

"A hundred thousand," Mike said.

"You could've turned a hundred dollars into a hundred thousand dollars yourself, without taking out a loan."

"You don't have to tell me what I could've done differently." Mike's good eye was tearing up. "I could've started betting small at the casino. I could have lost a few times. I could have made it seem like luck instead of winning big on every roll. But I wanted to get real rich, real fast." He kicked over the lawn chair next to him. "I fucked up, and now I'm fucked."

"I'll give you the money," Elmore said.

"Damn right you will," Mike said.

Elmore wondered what his new tone of voice was all about.

"The way I see it, you owe that money to this family anyway," Mike said.

"For taking me in?" Elmore asked.

"No, for abandoning Rachel and Amy," Mike said.

Elmore looked confused. Mike glared at him, blood dripping down the side of his face.

"That's right, David," Mike said. "I figured it out."

Elmore leaned his head back against the stucco wall.

"David?" the kid said. Then he chuckled and smiled. "I haven't been called that name in a long time."

"Your mother's spell made you young again, didn't it?" Mike asked. "She turned you back into a child after you ran away."

"Not a child, a baby," Elmore said.

"It clicked once Rachel mentioned the dream she had the night you disappeared," Mike said. "Like magic, a woman with a glass body shrank you to the size of a football and took you away."

Elmore exhaled deeply. "My mother murdered David that night. She left Amy without a father and Rachel without a husband. My mother was a very selfish, unreasonable woman."

"I don't want you here," Mike said. "You're a son of a bitch for coming here. But the rest of the family has grown attached to you. I wish I could kick you out, but I can't."

"You don't have to be jealous of me, Mike," Elmore said. "I'm only a seven-year-old. I'm not interested in Rachel anymore."

"Here's what we're going to do. You give me the money, just the amount I need to pay off my debts, and I'll keep your secret. I'll pretend you're just an overly smart seven-year-old until the day I die."

"That sounds perfectly fair," Elmore said.

Elmore was about to get up and head up to the treehouse, but Mike stopped him, grabbed him by the arm.

"One more thing," Mike said. "Rachel seems to think you're David's son from another woman, as well as Amy's half-brother."

Mike let go of Elmore's arm to wipe blood dripping from his eye. Elmore was surprised to hear Rachel had come to such a conclusion.

"I think you should go with that story," Mike continued. "It would make Rachel and Amy very happy."

Elmore nodded. As strange of a relationship as it would be, it made the most sense to him. He missed out on a life with Rachel, but he wouldn't miss out on a life with his daughter... even though she was now over twice his age.

A
THIRST
FOR
BLOOD

"What the hell do you mean you can't cure this shit?" Angry Eddie yelled at the paper-skinned hipster kid at the spell shop.

The kid's book-shaped body pulsed rapidly, pages flipping open and shut, as the man yelled at him. The shop was tiny and cluttered with old books, scrolls, and potions, all locked down tight with strong security magic.

"I'm sorry, Mr. Eddie," the hipster kid cried. "We don't carry any spells that can help you with that… problem."

The place was mostly empty of customers that day. The only other person in the shop was an old woman with stretchy arms, who was terrified of the language that was coming out of the angry man's mouth. She stared in shock as Angry Eddie shoved his hands into his pants and scratched his crotch with fury.

"Does such a spell even fucking exist?" Eddie asked.

"Not that I'm aware of."

Eddie looked over at the old woman as he scratched his junk.

"Jesus fuck…" he said, grinding deep into the pus-soaked cracks of his scrotal tissue.

The old woman turned away and hid behind a bookshelf in a corner of the store.

"With all this goddamned magic these days, you'd think they'd have something that could cure a simple STD."

"I don't think you've got a *simple* STD there, Mr. Eddie," the kid said.

"You think? My goddamned crotch has turned green with swirls of purple fungus. The lumps are the worst part, though. They itch like the chicken pox until they become volcanoes of pus. Do you want to see?"

The boy shook his head and diverted his eyes before Angry Eddie could take his pants down to show him his torment.

"I never should have fucked that frog bitch..." Eddie said, removing his hand to pay the kid for the painkiller potion. It was the only thing that even slightly relieved his suffering.

After taking the receipt, Eddie said, "Word of advice, kid. When you have a choice between a twenty dollar whore and a two hundred dollar whore, go for the more expensive one. It'll be cheaper in the long run."

The kid didn't know how to respond to that. His paper skin flipped open like a fan. "Um... Thanks?"

Eddie gave him a salute in response. As the weird customer left the store, the kid looked down at the money on the counter. He really didn't want to pick it up with his own hands.

He was called Angry Eddie because his face was permanently contorted into a pissed off grimace all the time. But he couldn't do anything to help it. When he was younger, he cast so many Pie Conjuring spells that it warped his human head into the shape of a chef hat from the scalp up. But the mutation also caused deep creases in his forehead, which gave him the appearance of having the pointiest/angriest eyebrows of any human on the face of the planet.

"Any word from Bee?" Eddie asked Big Strange as he stepped out of the spell shop.

Big Strange looked up from his newspaper. "Bloopa-bloo."

"Damn," Eddie said. "What happened to that woman..."

Then he took a swig of painkiller potion.

Big Strange's face went sad. "Bloopa-bloo..."

"I don't care how long she's been missing," Eddie said. "The Arachne didn't get her."

"Bloo—"

"Don't say it. She'll turn up eventually. Let's just get on with the job before the dolls get to the body."

Big Strange followed Eddie down the street, toward the

next victim of the blood-drinking killer. This was the eighth victim to be found, all with their eyes gouged out, tongue split open, and blood completely drained.

Eddie and Big Strange didn't have the heads for detective work. One was a pastry chef, the other a bouncer and janitor. They were just meant to be Bee's backup, but with her being MIA it was completely up to these two to figure out who was murdering the innocent people of Hell's Bottom.

"I fucking hate the people of Hell's Bottom," Eddie said, pushing his way through the crowd of filthy freaks and mutants.

Torko was already on the scene when Angry Eddie and Big Strange got to the body. Like the other victims, the corpse had been found in an alley.

"Hoggins wants us back as soon as possible," Torko said, the second they arrived. "You know, just in case we get hit by the Arachne tonight."

"Yeah, yeah..." Eddie said, leaning down to check out the latest victim. This time it was a woman. Mid-twenties. Long blond hair. Naked, but her nudity was mostly covered by the large white angel wings that grew from her back. "Whatever."

Torko didn't like Eddie's dismissive attitude.

"Just because they haven't hit us yet, doesn't mean they're not going to," Torko said. "Those freaks are crazy. Who knows what they're planning..."

Eddie never liked Torko very much. In fact, he didn't like him at all. The guy was too worried; always terrified that something bad was going to happen to him. He knew some powerful spells, like Lightning and Super Speed, but he refused to use them under any circumstance because he was scared that he'd end up looking like a freak. This didn't make a lot of sense to Eddie, since the guy was already one of the ugliest pricks he'd ever laid eyes on—with or without being deformed by magic.

"Relax," Eddie said. "Let's focus on the murders first. We'll deal with the Arachne when we have to."

Eddie touched the victim's feathered wing. It was soft. He'd never seen an angel before.

Torko wouldn't let it go. "But what if we have to fight them?"

"Then use your magic."

"I'm not using magic."

Eddie glared at the lumpy, saggy, crooked-nosed, big-teethed, zit-scar-covered asshole as if he were about to knock that stupid face off his worthless head. If Eddie had Torko's magic he would be far less worried about getting into a fight with the Arachne. There was only so much good that Pie Conjuring could do in a fight.

"I'm only a go-between," Torko said. "I don't even live in Hell's Bottom. Why do I have to fight Arachne?"

"Because it's your job, you prick. You'd rather just leave your boss to die? After everything he's done for you?"

Torko shut up. Eddie was not the kind of person who tolerated whiners, especially not when he had burning festering pains in his crotch.

"Bloopa-bloo…" Big Strange said, pointing at the victim's body.

Eddie had been too distracted by Torko to notice it. When Big Strange lifted the angel's wing, Eddie saw the bruising.

"She's not completely drained of blood," Eddie said.

Torko looked closely. "What does that mean?"

"The killer didn't finish the job."

Angry Eddie waved Torko and Big Strange in closer, as if he were showing them a clue on the corpse's body.

"Don't look," Eddie whispered to them, "but we're being watched."

Torko would have immediately turned around to take a look if Eddie hadn't grabbed him by the back of the neck just in time.

"Bloopa-bloo," Big Strange whispered.

"I don't know who it is," Eddie said. "It could be our guy."

Eddie looked at a reflection of the person in the glass of a half-broken window. The figure was black. He wasn't wearing black clothes. He was just black. His skin, his hair, his eyeballs. There was no color or features on his body whatsoever. He was like a shadow, peeking out from behind a trashcan on the other side of the street.

"We're going to jump him," Eddie said.

"What?" Torko cried. "Are you kidding me?"

"It's the best chance we've got of stopping this guy."

"What if it's not really our guy and just some random suspicious-looking person?"

"Could be." Eddie looked in the reflection again. The shadowy figure was shifting back and forth, watching to see if anyone was following him. "Actually, it's very possibly not the guy. But we're going to jump him anyway."

Eddie took a deep breath.

"Okay, here's the plan. I'll get him with some pies. Hopefully, it'll distract him from using whatever spells he might know. Strange, you bring him to the ground while he's distracted. Torko, you run at him like an idiot. You're good at that. It might confuse him for a few seconds."

"Are you serious?"

Eddie nodded.

"Let's do it."

When they turned around, the three of them charged. Angry Eddie conjured pies, sending them into the shadowy figure. One strawberry rhubarb, one pumpkin, one cherry cheesecake.

"Take him down!" Eddie yelled.

Instead of charging the suspect, Torko jumped behind a dumpster. Big Strange barreled through the street, knocking down a goat woman and a washing machine boy.

Before any of them got close, the shadowy figure was gone.

"Bloopa-bloo?" Strange asked, when he arrived to the spot the shadow had been standing.

There was no sign of him. He just vanished.

"What happened?" Eddie said.

"Bloopa-bloo."

Eddie scanned the streets and buildings around him.

"He must have had some kind of teleportation magic," Eddie said.

Then he noticed a trail of pie crumbs.

"Or invisibility…" Eddie said.

The crumbs went up the street and turned a corner. Though the suspect was somehow cloaked, he was still covered in Eddie's pies. And those pies were dripping all over the fucking place.

"Let's follow the trail, boys," Eddie said.

Torko came out from his hiding place and went after his co-workers. Eddie let him catch up.

"You know Torko, with your magic you could have taken that guy down within seconds… if you weren't such a pussy."

After nine blocks of chasing the pie crumbs, Eddie was beat. They took a rest against the wall of a tavern.

"Cast your speed magic," Eddie told Torko. "It would be so much easier."

"Hell no," Torko said.

"Come on? We're never going to catch up. This guy's way too fast."

"I'm not casting any magic. I'm not going to risk mutation or losing my job as a go-between."

"Then teach me the spell," Eddie said. "I'll cast it."

"Hell, no," Torko said. "That spell is worth a fortune."

"Cheap bastard. Tell that to the families of the people who die because we didn't stop this guy when we had the chance."

"I'm not taking responsibility for what some psycho does."

"Fine, let's just keep going. Fucking worthless shitbag."

Eddie didn't have time to argue. He'd have to kick Torko's ass later. Maybe Hoggins could talk sense into him.

Before they continued on, Eddie stuck his hands down his pants, scratched the hell out of the pustules that were flaring up again, then wiped the juice on Torko's shoulder.

The trail went cold a few blocks away.

"Bloopa-bloo," Big Strange said, scanning the area.

Eddie put his hands on his waist and nodded his head. "Yeah, I don't see anything, either."

"Maybe all the pie fell off already," Torko said.

"No way." Eddie held out his hand and pinched at the air. "My pies are moist and sticky. This guy's not getting all of that stuff off until he gets home and takes a shower."

"Bloopa-bloo!" Big Strange yelled from an alley to their right, pointing up the side of an old, crumbling warehouse.

Eddie went to him and squinted in the direction the big guy was pointing.

"What is it?" Torko asked, afraid to step off the main strip.

"Whipped cream," Eddie said. "A lot of it."

The pie trail continued up a ladder on the side of the building.

"He's on the roof."

"We can't go up there," Torko said. "What if he's waiting for us?"

"Grow some fucking balls."

Eddie went first, followed by Torko. Big Strange took up the rear. The ladder was covered in rust and squealed as they climbed it.

"Be ready once we get up to the top," Eddie said.

When they were halfway up, the ladder banged and rattled. Bolts broke, popping out of the wall and falling past their heads. The right side was wobbling loose.

"Damn shitty old buildings..." Eddie grumbled.

"We're going to fall!" Torko cried, holding the ladder tightly.

"Shut up, Torko." Eddie looked down at the big guy. "Strange, you're too heavy. This thing can't hold your weight. Climb back down."

"Bloopa?" asked the beetle-headed man.

"Just climb back down. Watch the street for us just in case he comes down on the other side."

Big Strange reluctantly obeyed and climbed back down the ladder. Torko tried to follow him.

"Not you, Torko. You're with me."

Once the big guy was on the ground, the ladder stopped rattling. They were able to climb up without tearing the ladder from the wall, though every rung wobbled them from side to side, knocking them off balance.

Before reaching the top, Eddie looked down at Torko and put his finger to his lips to keep him silent. Then he lifted himself up. A brick came loose from the ledge and fell past him, nearly hitting Torko in the head.

"This place is falling apart," Eddie said.

He looked down at Torko who was glaring at him with his bright red face. Eddie just shrugged at him.

"Nobody's here," Torko said, as they scanned the rooftop.

They followed the whipped cream trail, careful where they stepped on the water-warped surface. The floor was weak. They felt as if they might fall through at any moment.

"We should go back to Hoggins," Torko said. "This is useless."

"He probably went into the building." Eddie pointed at the entrance on the other side of the roof. "Come on."

"Are you kidding me?" Torko asked. "Shouldn't we wait for backup or something?"

"We are the backup."

Torko just stopped in the middle of the rooftop. He wouldn't go any farther. Eddie turned around and glared at him.

"If you get into trouble just use your magic," Eddie said.

Before Torko could respond, Eddie saw something moving behind the ugly kid. It was growing out of the shadow by the ledge.

"Look out!" Eddie yelled.

Torko turned around to see what was going on. The shadowy figure they were chasing didn't just *look* like a shadow; he physically *was* a shadow. He knew lurking magic and led them up onto the roof in order to set an ambush.

"Cast Lightning!" Eddie yelled.

But Torko did nothing. He just froze, hesitating about what to do next. He probably wanted to use his magic, but couldn't convince himself to do it.

The shadow lifted his hand and launched a flurry of magic darts from his fingertips. The thin metal needles created a high pitch whistle through the air, then pierced Torko's legs and lower abdomen. He crumpled to the ground.

"Torko!"

Angry Eddie charged toward his fallen partner as the shadow readied more magic.

"Cast the goddamned spell!" Eddie yelled.

The boy couldn't hear him. He didn't even know where he was anymore. He twitched and writhed, holding his wounds. One of the needles hit an artery in Torko's thigh and the blood shot out of him like a geyser. The only noise Torko could hear was the sound of his heart thumping in his chest.

"Get back," Eddie yelled at the shadow.

Eddie got between the killer and his fallen partner, blocking the psycho's attempt to finish him off. Then he raised his palms in the air, pulling all the magic energy he could collect from the center of his being.

The shadow man moved his fingers so they were pointing at Eddie, aimed directly at his throat.

"Not today," Eddie said.

As the shadow launched his darts, Eddie cast his spell of Pie Conjuring. But he put more energy into it than he ever had in all of his castings combined. Before the darts could come anywhere near Eddie, a mountain of pies two stories tall materialized between them.

"Pie Mountain!" Eddie yelled, standing before his massive still-steaming creation, his fists raised above his head, his voice echoing through the streets of Hell's Bottom.

It was like the Great Wall of China made of piping hot apple pies, completely separating Torko and Eddie from the killer. He didn't know how long it would keep the attacker back, but Eddie figured it would buy him enough time to help his friend.

"Why didn't you cast the fucking spell, you idiot?" Eddie said as he kneeled down to Torko. His words were critical, but the tone in his voice was that of panic. The boy was bleeding out too fast.

"Come on, Torko," Eddie said. "You've got magic that can cauterize this. Use it."

Torko shook his head.

"Goddamnit," Eddie said.

He realized he had to stop the bleeding without magic. He needed to make a tourniquet.

Eddie ripped Torko's shirt from his chest, twisted it into a rope and tied it as tightly as he could around the boy's thigh. While holding it in place with his left hand, he used his right to pull out his painkiller potion and poured the whole bottle down the boy's throat. Eddie's crotch screamed at him the second the bottle was empty.

The potion quickly took effect. Most of the pain drifted away and the boy was able to speak again.

"You fucked up my shirt," Torko said through his rapid breaths.

Eddie tossed the bottle over his shoulder and applied pressure with both hands.

"Of course," Eddie tried to joke. "I'm not messing up my own shirt for a worthless fuckup like you."

Torko smiled. Eddie looked down at the wound. No matter how tightly he wrapped the tourniquet, he couldn't completely stop the bleeding.

"Seriously, you need to use some magic here," Eddie said. "Cast a speed spell on me."

"No," Torko said.

"Come on. I'll be able to get you to the clinic within seconds."

"No."

"You'll die!"

"I don't care. I won't use magic, even if it kills me."

"You little shit…"

Then Eddie noticed the scars covering Torko's body. They were originally hidden in all the blood. There were electrical burn marks, gashes, puncture wounds, random dents and holes, and that was just what Eddie could see. The boy had hundreds of them.

With the kid refusing to cast a spell, Eddie had no choice but to keep applying pressure to the wound and hope the bleeding would eventually stop.

The shadow blocked out the sun.

Eddie looked up. Standing at the top of the pie mountain, the killer gazed down at them, preparing spells with both of his hands. Eddie couldn't do anything to protect himself. He'd used up all of his energy in his last spell, so he wouldn't be able to conjure up another pie for days. And if he let go of Torko's leg to dodge the attack, the dumb kid would surely bleed to death. He just had to endure the attack and hope his body could handle a few bolts of metal injected into his skin.

The shadow paused his spell as a cracking sound echoed around them. It was the sound of warping and bending. The wood beneath them was giving out.

"It's going to collapse," Eddie cried.

The weight of the pie mountain was too much for the roof of the old building. The shadow quit casting his spell and tried to leap from the mass of pies, but it happened too fast. The roof caved in, taking everyone with it.

"Hold on," Eddie yelled.

He huddled in close to Torko, holding onto the boy's leg as tightly as he could. As they fell through the warehouse roof, swallowed by the pie avalanche, Eddie wouldn't let go. They fell through floor after floor, blinded by the mass of apple syrup filling, but Eddie kept holding on. He wouldn't let another drop of blood spill from that ugly kid's body.

Even after Big Strange used his digging magic to get them

out of there and somehow found the communication skills to gather up a group of good Samaritans to transport them to Hell's Bottom Clinic, Angry Eddie gripped like a vice until the doctors got Torko into the operating room.

It was a few hours before Angry Eddie heard any news. He sat outside the clinic, smoking a clove cigarette, covered from head to toe in dried apple pie syrup that the flies were going crazy for. It was hard for Eddie to stand on one leg, but for the most part he had only suffered a few bumps and bruises in the fall.

"You doing alright?" Hoggins asked Eddie, stepping out of the clinic with an éclair in his chubby fingers.

"Fine," Eddie said. "How about the kid?"

"He'll live." Hoggins bit into the pastry and sucked out the crème filling. "They said he'll be conscious pretty soon. He almost didn't make it."

"He's a fucking idiot," Eddie said, flicking his cigarette butt across the street. "He could have saved himself at any time, but he refused to use magic."

"What makes you so sure magic would have saved him?"

"He could have tried."

"You know why he doesn't use magic?" Hoggins asked.

Eddie shrugged.

"He made a promise to his mother on her death bed that he wouldn't end up like his father."

"What was wrong with his father?"

"He was an asshole. You know, the violent kind."

"So was mine. So what?"

"So did your father know any telekinetic spells that could toss you across the room for knocking over his beer? Did he ever hold your sister down and make you watch as he filled her with so much lightning magic that her eyeballs burst?"

Eddie rubbed syrup from his nose and looked away.

Hoggins pointed at the hospital door. "That kid in there was tormented his whole life by a vicious son of a bitch who had the powers of a god. He'd rather die than become like that sick fuck."

"He very nearly did," Eddie said.

"Then he would have died a man," Hoggins said. He swallowed the rest of his éclair and licked his fingers.

Eddie watched his pig boss hobble across the street, heading back toward the restaurant. He always wondered why Hoggins took in that worthless little prick when there were so many more capable men out there in Hell's Bottom dying for work. Eddie guessed the fat man had a soft spot for pathetic sons of bitches.

"Damn frog bitch…" Eddie said, scratching his crotch with unrelenting fury.

"You're alive," Eddie said to Torko the second he was allowed to see him.

"Yes, I'm alive." Torko smiled. The kid looked even uglier when he smiled. He was in the hospital bed, his lower body covered in bandages, holding a plate of éclairs Hoggins must have brought him.

"All thanks to me," Eddie said. "And maybe Big Strange for getting us out of that pie oven."

Eddie noticed the doctor was still in the room. "Oh, and you too, Doc."

The wooden-faced doctor ignored him and walked out of the room.

"The doctors have some pretty powerful magic here," Torko said. "I probably would have died if this were a normal hospital."

Eddie chuckled. "So you're fine with other people using magic to save your life, but you're too good to use it yourself?"

The smile fell from Torko's face.

Eddie quit chuckling and looked away. Then he sat down in the chair next to Torko's bed.

"Big Strange found the body of the guy we were chasing," Eddie said. "He wasn't as lucky as we were, though. He broke both legs in the fall and was buried under that heap of pies.

Suffocated to death."

"Was he our guy? The serial killer?"

"Actually…" Eddie let out a sigh. "Hoggins did some digging on the guy and figured he wasn't exactly a serial killer. He was an arcanist who was using humans as test subjects to create some new spell."

"What was the spell supposed to do?"

"Who the fuck knows. Nothing good, I'll tell you that."

"We should destroy the research," Torko said. "Burn down the asshole's whole fucking lab."

Eddie snickered at the kid's enthusiasm. "Hoggins will handle it. The big problem is that we don't think this guy was working alone. There might even be a gang of these jerkoffs operating in Hell's Bottom."

"A gang?"

"Yeah…" Eddie shook his head. "Well, maybe this asshole's death will scare off the rest of them… or at least stop them from using our neighbors as test subjects."

"Are they going to come after us? Seek revenge for killing their friend?"

"I doubt it," Eddie said. "They kill innocent people in the name of science. I don't think they give two shits about their dead friend here."

"Well, if you decide to go after them, do me a favor."

"What's that?"

"Don't bring me along with you," Torko said.

Eddie laughed.

"I never want to go through anything like that ever again."

"Me neither, kid," Eddie said. "Let's hope Bee returns soon so we can go back to running errands and crafting desserts."

As they smiled and laughed together, Torko was amused by the angry expression on Eddie's face. No matter what emotion he was feeling, the guy always looked like he was pissed off to all hell. But the looks don't always make the man. Angry Eddie might have been the nicest meanest-looking guy Torko had ever known.

THE
LOST
GAMBLER

After the third knock, a man with thick black spectacles peered through the crack in the door.

"I'm here to see Frank the Head," Mike said, his voice kind of muffled through his swollen tongue and fat lip.

"What for?" said the man with the thick black spectacles.

The asshole knew exactly why he was there. He was the same guy who beat him down the day before.

"I'm here to pay him the money I owe him," Mike said.

"Hand it through the door then," said the doorman.

"I want to give it to him personally," Mike said. "I have a quick proposal I'd like to make him."

The man blinked. His eyes were gigantic within the lenses of his coke-bottle glasses. They were practically magnifying glasses. The guy's name was Odd Carl. Mike had met the man a few times before. With his thick glasses, receding hairline, horrible comb-over, and awkward social skills, Mike would have thought Odd Carl was the biggest nerd anyone had ever laid eyes on. But when he took his shirt off, Carl was the size of a garbage truck. He had more muscles than five gorillas.

"Just let him in, Carl," Frank's voice called from beyond the door.

The ogre-sized nerd let Mike pass inside the building. Then he escorted him through the warehouse to Frank, who was drinking a Spanish coffee in what would have been a lounge had there been walls around the couches and tables positioned there.

"Hey, Mike the Douchebag, how you been?" Frank said.

Frank was a scary little man who always had a scowl on his face even when he was happy. He was probably sixty, judging

111

by his dark leathered skin, but he tried to stay youthful by dying his hair jet black and wearing nothing but jeans, t-shirts, and whatever was the newest brand of Nike sneakers on the market.

"Mike the Douchebag?" Mike asked. "Is that my nickname now?"

"That's right," Frank said. "Anyone who's late paying me gets *douchebag* attached to their name." He pointed at Odd Carl. "If Odd Carl's late paying me, he gets the name Carl the Douchebag." He pointed at the man making Spanish coffees next to him. "If Jesus was late paying me, he'd become Jesus the Douchebag."

"I get it," Mike said.

"No, you don't get it," Frank said. "I don't like douchebags. They're not welcome around here."

"Well, I've got the money now, with interest," Mike said. "So you don't have to call me a douchebag."

Frank held out his hands to accept the cash. "I'll call you whatever I want to call you, douchebag. Now let me see it."

Instead of handing it over, Mike held onto the case.

"Let me ask you a question first," Mike said.

Frank was beginning to lose his patience.

"Are you a gambling man?" Mike asked.

"Am I a gambling man?" Frank leaned back on the couch. "Is this guy for real?"

"I want to make a bet with you," Mike said.

"Only douchebags are gambling men. I'm a business man. I only place bets when I know I'm going to win."

"Then you'll like this one," Mike said.

Mike set the case down and opened it, revealing the cash.

"I've got almost $800,000 here," Mike said. "If you win it's yours. If you lose I get to keep it and I owe you nothing."

Frank shook his head and laughed. "I already told you, I'm not a gambling man. I'm a business man. And the business man in me is thinking about cracking you over the head and keeping all your money."

"That would be cheating," Mike said.

"I like cheating."

"I thought you might say that…" Mike pointed at a small lens on the side of the briefcase. "That's why you're being filmed. Everything is being uploaded online as we speak and will be sent to the police if anything happens to me or my money."

"Bullshit, that's the stupidest thing I ever heard," Frank said. "There's no way you'd be dumb enough to try something like that."

"This isn't a bluff."

Mike really was bluffing. The lens was from an old digital camera Amy used before she upgraded to a newer model. Still, he figured Frank wouldn't risk it.

"Okay, fine, I'll consider it," Frank said. "What's your game?"

Mike pulled out a pair of dice.

"Just dice," Mike said. "If I roll seven or higher, I win. If I roll six or less, you win."

"No deal," Frank said. "I don't play when the odds are 50/50. I'll tell you what. You roll a seven, you win. If you roll anything else, I win."

"Okay," Mike said. "Let's do it."

Mike was about to roll the dice, when Frank held up his hand.

"Not so fast," Frank said. "You were too quick to agree to such shoddy terms. Nobody's putting that kind of money on the line unless they know they've got a sure thing."

"You set the terms," Mike said. "How can I cheat if you pick the number? We can do three if you like? Twelve? Pick any number. I've got luck on my side. I know I can't lose."

"Funny," Frank said. "I once knew a guy who could roll any number he wanted to roll. He trained himself how to throw them so they'd always land just right, every time, without fail. He was a pro at it. He made a living at it. I wonder if Mike the Douchebag has what that guy had."

Mike stayed silent.

"Here's what we're going to do," Frank said. "We use my dice. I get to roll. If I roll snake eyes, you win. If I roll anything else, you lose."

Mike looked away for a second, not agreeing immediately. He had to make it appear as if he didn't like this change of events.

"What?" Frank asked. "Don't like the terms?"

"Wait..." Mike said. "How can I trust your dice aren't weighted?"

"You can't. Tough shit."

Mike kept silent again. Frank opened a cabinet under the coffee table and pulled out a Monopoly board game.

"Monopoly?" Mike asked.

"Yeah, you got a problem with Monopoly? I fucking love Monopoly."

Frank removed the dice from the Monopoly box.

"So, how confident are you in your luck now?" Frank asked, holding up the dice. "Still want to make the bet?"

"Actually..."

"Still want to make the bet?"

Mike looked down and then nodded. He couldn't let on that things were still going perfectly according to plan. Even if he wasn't rolling the dice himself, he could still control what number they fell on.

"Ready?" Frank asked.

Mike nodded.

"Ready..." he said with an exaggerated sigh.

Frank raised his hand to roll, but then stopped himself.

"Wait a second..." Frank said. "One more thing."

"What?"

Frank took the monopoly box and lifted it up.

"I don't want you to see me rolling the dice," Frank said.

"What?" Mike cried, not at all hiding his alarm. "I mean, why?"

"You know, I just don't want you to jinx it," Frank said. "You might do some kind of Jedi mind trick on it or something and I want it to be perfectly fair."

"How is it fair if I can't even see the dice?"

"You'll see them a second after they land. I just don't want you to see them while I roll them. It's perfectly fair."

Mike didn't know what to do. If he lost all of Elmore's money his wife was going to kill him.

"Ready?" Frank asked.

"No, not yet..." Mike said.

Frank looked up at Mike and winked at him. It was a knowing wink, like he knew about Mike's gambling magic the whole time. Mike felt like he wasn't playing these guys. He was the one being played.

"Here we go," Frank said.

Just before Frank rolled, Odd Carl walked around the other side of the box to get a good look at the dice. Mike's eyes darted up just in time, looking at the dice in the reflection of the big man's glasses.

"Two," Mike said, as the dice hit.

It was all he had to say to make the spell work.

The monopoly box fell over and the dice were clearly visible. Snake eyes. Mike had won.

"Hell yeah!" Mike cried.

Then he looked up at Frank and said, "I told you I was lucky!"

But Frank wasn't there. The man had vanished. Mike looked around. Odd Carl was also gone. Jesus was gone. Everyone in the warehouse had suddenly vanished.

"Hello?" Mike asked, looking around, still wondering where everyone went.

It was like a reverse-rapture, where only the world's scumbags were spirited away.

Mike gripped his briefcase tightly and walked away. He half-expected someone to jump out at him, like it was some joke, but the place was dead silent. When he exited the warehouse, the silence was only greater. The streets were empty, devoid of life.

"Hello?" Mike yelled. His voice echoed through the downtown buildings. "Is anybody there?"

There was no one.

He was all alone.

The entire way home, Mike didn't see a living soul. There were no animals, no cars, no movement other than the wind in the trees.

"Hello?" Mike called out.

No answers at all.

He wondered if he was dead. He wondered if maybe one of Frank's men put a bullet in the back of his head the second he rolled the dice.

"Rachel?" Mike called out, as he ran through the front door of their house.

His home was empty. Dinner was cooking on the stove. Amy's homework was lying on the living room coffee table. It was as if they were here only a second ago, then suddenly vanished.

"Rachel?" he called out again. "Amy?"

They weren't there. Everyone was gone.

Mike saw his reflection in the mirror above the mantle. He approached it.

"What on Earth…"

Examining his reflection, he realized that his eyes had changed. They were no longer human. Just as Elmore had told him, his eyeballs had transformed into dice. It seemed impossible. He could still see through them. But they were dice. Two rounded cubes. Both sides of the dice were ones. Snake eyes.

When he touched the dice, they didn't hurt. They felt like normal dice. Elmore was right. The magic had changed him.

Then Elmore's reflection appeared next to him in the mirror, crossing the living room.

"See you later, Mike," Elmore said, as he left the room.

Mike paused. He thought it had to have been a hallucination.

When Mike turned around, Elmore was already gone.

"Elmore?" Mike yelled. "What's going on?"

He searched the house for him.

"Where did everybody go?"

He couldn't find him anywhere.

"Elmore?"

There was the sound of a car starting up in the driveway.

"Elmore!"

Mike ran outside just in time to see Rachel's car drive away, but he didn't see Rachel in it. He only saw Elmore in the passenger seat. The car seemed to drive itself.

"What the hell is going on…" Mike said.

He didn't know what else to do. Mike ran after the car, waving his hands, trying to catch up.

Mike ran down the street, but there was no sign of where the car had gone. He decided to keep going.

He wondered why he could see Elmore but nobody else. Were they still there? Did they all suddenly become invisible? He wondered if Elmore was responsible. Maybe the kid did something to him to make him disappear.

"I'm going to kill that little shit," Mike said. "*See you later, Mike?* What was that supposed to mean?"

Mike continued down the road. He heard cars from time to time, off in the distance. He went toward those sounds. Eventually, he found himself out of the suburbs, deep in the heart of downtown.

He walked through buildings, calling Elmore's name, demanding to know what he'd done to him.

"Elmore!" Mike cried. "Bring me back, you son of a bitch!"

As he walked past an alley, he got a quick glimpse of a woman smoking a cigarette.

"Who's Elmore?" It was a woman's voice.

Mike turned around. Standing in the alley, there was a woman. The strangest woman Mike had ever seen in his life.

"What are you doing here?" Mike asked.

She stood there as if she were a prostitute waiting for a customer. But she wasn't quite human. She looked like she was wearing a bee costume, only it wasn't a costume. She had black and yellow striped skin, insect wings, and antennae on her head.

"What am *I* doing here?" Bee asked, stepping toward the man. "I'm smoking a cigarette. What are you doing wandering around the dead zone?"

"The dead zone?" Mike said. "Look, I don't know what's going on here…"

The bee womancircled him like a buzzing insect.

"Let me guess," she said. "You cast one spell too many and the next thing you know everyone in the world's vanished. Am I correct?"

"Yeah," Mike said. "Wait, you mean Elmore didn't do this to me?"

"You did this to yourself," Bee said. "Just like I did it to myself many years ago."

"You're a spell caster, too?"

Bee nodded.

"Is that why you look…" Mike said, scanning her body up and down. "That way."

"I sure wasn't born looking like an insect."

"So how do I get back?" Mike asked. "How do I get back to my family?"

"I hate to break it to you, pal, but there's no going back. Once the universe gets rid of you, you're stuck in this limbo."

"Are you kidding me?" Mike asked. "I can't stay here. I have a wife and family."

"We all had wives and family once. This is your punishment for using magic. You didn't think cheating the laws of reality wouldn't go unpunished, did you? This is karma punching you in the face."

"So what do I do?" Mike paced back and forth, about to have a panic attack. "I can't stay here. Do I abandon my family? Do I just wander the empty streets forever?"

Bee went to him and grabbed him by the arm. "Relax. Don't think of it as the end of the world. It's more like the beginning of a new one."

Mike studied his reflection in a puddle at his feet. He wished he could rip his dice-eyes out and return to normal again. He gave up everything for a briefcase full of money that he couldn't even use anymore.

"What's happened to you has been happening to people for centuries," Bee said, lighting up another cigarette. "Everyone who uses magic ends up here eventually. We have our own cities, our own world."

"What do you mean by cities?"

"You'll see," Bee said. "We're just outside of Hell's Bottom. It's full of lost souls just like yourself."

Bee turned around and walked deeper into the alleyway. When she realized Mike wasn't following her, she turned around.

"Come on. I'll buy you a drink."

Then she led him into the darkness, toward one of the hidden entrances into Hell's Bottom.

Mike thought he'd been transported into an alien ghetto. The streets were thin, too thin to drive a truck through, and densely populated. All the people were mutated in one way or another. A dog boy urinated against the side of a building, a woman made of clocks tick-tocked across his path, a small girl that seemed to be made entirely of pink liquid splashed from one fire escape to another overhead. The people and the buildings all seemed to be withered, grease-stained, and ready to fall over at any second.

"People actually live here?" Mike asked.

"It doesn't look very pleasant at first, but you'll get used to it," Bee said, leading him through the filthy mob. "It's the very definition of a hellhole. It's even hot as hell due to the steam pouring up from the sewers."

"What's in the sewers?"

"Engines."

"Engines?"

"Machines. They're what keep Hell's Bottom running. Not just electricity, but the machines keep the citizens of Hell's

Bottom from disappearing completely. The universe wants to be rid of us for good. Too bad we refuse to go."

Mike could feel the steam coming up from the sewer vents. Sweat was already beginning to pool in the armpits of his button-up shirt.

"Follow me," Bee said.

She pulled him down a side alley, away from the main road. Then they ducked behind some trash cans.

"What's going on?"

"They're some friends of mine," Bee said, pointing at two men. One of them was muscular with a beetle-shaped head. The other was short with a head shaped like a chef hat.

"Are you in some kind of trouble?" Mike asked, hiding behind the bee girl.

"Yeah, you can definitely say that," Bee said. "That's why I'm avoiding my friends. I don't want to put them in any danger."

Bee's wings fluttered in Mike's face, tickling his nose.

"Are you putting me in danger?"

She looked up at him and giggled.

"Don't worry about it," she said. "I'll protect you."

Outside the bar, six people were pressed up against the windows. Their eyes were vacant, their mouths drooling.

"What's up with those people?" Mike asked.

Each of them had red spots in the center of their foreheads.

"We call them hollow-heads, or just *hollows*," Bee said.

"What's wrong with them?"

"Their brains are empty," Bee said, taking Mike through the entrance into the tiny bar. "Sucked dry. They wander the streets, searching for their lost memories."

There were only eight seats in the bar and half of them were taken by filthy vagrant wizards. They looked more human than most of the people outside, though one of them had skin made of diamonds.

"So they're amnesiacs?" Mike asked, as he took a seat.

"They're like babies," Bee said. "Everything wiped but their natural instincts."

The zipper-faced bartender didn't ask them what they'd like to drink before serving them. He gave them each glasses of red mushroom whiskey.

"How'd they get that way?"

Mike looked down at his glass. The fluid was peppery, cloudy, and pinkish-orange in color.

"Somebody did that to them," Bee said. "Somebody drank their memories like a vampire drinks blood."

"Why would somebody do that?"

"Lots of reasons." Bee took a swig of pink whiskey. "To gain wisdom. Within minutes, you could learn what other people have learned during their whole lifetime. Also, there's a pleasure in experiencing somebody else's life through memory."

"To learn new spells?" Mike asked.

"Good thinking," Bee said with a smile. "Maybe you should sign on as my new partner. We'd solve the case of the hollow-heads in no time."

"Are you a detective or something?"

"Something like that," she said. "Though I was joking about you being my partner. My boss wouldn't hire a newcomer with useless magic. In fact, you're going to have a tough time getting a job anywhere around here."

"So it's no different than the world I left behind?"

Mike laughed at his own joke, but then he was disgusted at himself for laughing. The fact that he really had left his world behind still hadn't fully dawned on him.

"Seriously," Bee said. "You'll need to learn some new magic if you want to get a job around here. Rolling dice won't make you any money among wizards."

"How do I learn new magic?"

"There are plenty of spell shops, but spells don't come cheap. Anything halfway useful will cost two year's salary."

"Is there any other way?"

"You can trade spells, but nobody will want to trade for a spell like yours. Plus, people are protective of their magic and usually won't give up anything rare. The more people who know a spell the less value it'll have to employers."

"Then what do you recommend?"

"Make friends," Bee said. "Make lots of friends. Charismatic people go far in Hell's Bottom. You never know when someone might give you a useful spell just because you gave them a little bit of companionship."

"So do you want to teach me one of your spells?" Mike asked.

"Not a chance in hell," Bee said.

She paid the bartender in cash. Two fives.

When he saw the Lincolns, Mike asked, "They take American money here?"

Mike realized he was still carrying eight hundred thousand dollars in cash. If the people in Hell's Bottom accepted American currency, Mike would be set.

"Yeah, we still consider ourselves a part of the United States," Bee said. "We even do business with the real world."

"How's that possible? We can't see them and they can't see us."

"Yeah, but there are go-betweens." Bee slammed back the rest of her drink. "Some people live in both worlds. These are the people who have used only a small amount of magic or have had magic used on them."

Mike wondered if that was why he saw Elmore back at home, but nobody else. Elmore's mother had used magic on him, but he didn't use magic himself. He was a go-between who lived in both worlds at once.

"There is also doorway magic that can be used to travel for brief periods between the two worlds," Bee said. "But it's not cheap."

"How much?"

"Forget about it," she said.

"I didn't get to say goodbye to my family," Mike said. "It might be worth any price."

"I think it's going for around $100,000 a minute these days."

Mike looked down at his briefcase. He wondered if it was worth trading all the money he had to spend just eight final minutes with Rachel.

"So now what?" Mike asked, as they got up from the bar to leave.

"Well, that's up to you," Bee said. "I can give you a floor to crash on for one night and one night only. Or we can part ways and you can explore your new world on your own."

"I think I'll take the floor," Mike said. "Thanks."

"You won't thank me once the dolls come out at night."

"The dolls?"

"You'll see."

"Somebody helped me when I was a newcomer," Bee said, showing Mike around her apartment. It was closer to a grubby hotel room than an apartment. "Now I help any newcomer I find, but just for one night."

"I understand," Mike said. "I wouldn't want to be a burden."

"You have to understand, there are a lot of newcomers. I usually have at least one a week in this place."

"Really? That many?"

"But one night can make a huge difference," Bee said. "It did with me. When all my family and friends disappeared, I was in such a panic I would have killed myself if I didn't run into Hoggins."

"Hoggins?"

"Yeah, he let me stay with his family my first night, gave me dinner, told me the basics of survival in Hell's Bottom. I still had to make my own way after that, but that one night calmed me down, gave me hope."

"Yeah, I can see that."

"So I try to do the same for others."

Mike smiled and nodded. Bee buzzed her wings.

"I have a question," Mike asked her. "How can I get an apartment?"

"You'll probably need a job before you can find a place to live."

"I have my own money," Mike said.

"No, you don't," Bee said. "Any money you had in the real world stayed in the real world."

"Are you sure?"

"You can't take money out of your bank account, you can't take money you stashed in your underwear drawer, you can't even pick up money you find on the streets. The universe won't allow it."

"Really?"

"The only money you can bring into Hell's Bottom is the money you had on you at the moment you vanished, which isn't going to be enough."

"I had plenty of money on me when I vanished." Mike blinked his dice eyes.

"How much? A hundred? Two hundred? That's not going to last."

Mike set his briefcase down on Bee's bed and opened it up.

"I was carrying this much."

The woman's eyes bugged open when she saw the money. She picked up a stack. It was more money than she'd ever seen in her life. Even Hoggins didn't have that kind of dough sitting around.

"You must be the luckiest newcomer I've ever met," she said, having difficulty letting the wad of cash go.

"It's not really mine, though. I was holding it for a friend."

"It's yours now. You couldn't give it back if you wanted to, anyway. Unless you hired a go-between."

Mike wasn't sure what to do. Because Elmore was a go-between, he thought about tracking him down to give him his money back. It would've been the right thing to do. Plus, Elmore could maybe somehow explain to Rachel what had happened to him.

"I don't know," Mike said.

He shut the briefcase.

"If you want to share the rent you can stay here for longer

than one night if you want," Bee said. "Hell, you can move in. We can be roommates."

The thought of bringing Elmore his money back was sounding less and less desirable to Mike as the night went on.

"We can get bunk beds, it'll be great!" Bee cried, raising her striped arms in the air.

Mike slapped his knee, chuckling. Three empty bottles of plum wine fell over and rolled off the table.

"I wasn't really cut out for suburban life anyway," Mike said. "I couldn't stand living with my stepdaughter and mother-in-law."

They'd been drinking for hours since dinner.

"Oh, I hate those people!"

Both of them were incredibly drunk.

"And Rachel made me feel old. She wanted me to be something I wasn't meant to be."

Bee chuckled, opening another wine bottle. "And what were you meant to be?"

"You know, somebody wild… somebody who lived danger-ously, you know?"

"You like danger?" Bee asked, leaning close to him with a wicked smile.

"Yeah," Mike said, raising his eyebrows

The drunker he got, the harder it was for Mike to take his eyes off of Bee's breasts. And the drunker Bee got, the more she liked having his eyes on her breasts.

"*I'm* dangerous," she said. "Do you like *me*?"

Mike laughed. "How are *you* dangerous?"

The bee woman stepped back and buzzed her wings. She flew up into the air, hovering above the table, looking down at Mike.

"I'm a bee," she said. "Aren't you afraid you might get stung?"

"Why should I? I'm not allergic to bees?"

"Are you sure?" She came closer, buzzing over his head. Her

face leaned down to his, staring him deep in his eyes. "You might be allergic to this one."

She closed her eyes and kissed him, wrapping her black lips around his tongue.

"Nope," Mike said, once she pulled away. "No allergic reaction at all."

"I'll give you a reaction," Bee said.

She flew into his arms and wrapped her striped legs around his waist, her shiny black fingers around his neck and cheeks. Buzzing her wings to hold up her weight, she kissed him deeply, sucking on his tongue and lips.

"Yeah, I think I'm feeling a reaction now," Mike said, as she sucked on his neck.

Mike realized at that moment that he didn't give a shit if he ever saw Rachel again. As messed up as it was, Elmore was Amy's real father. And even though it had been sixteen years, Rachel had never really gotten over him. Mike figured it was a fair trade—the money for his family. Elmore could keep that family.

"Your skin is so soft," Mike said, rubbing her black and yellow breasts. "And sleek."

Bee pulled off his clothes, rubbing her shiny fingers down his chest. "Your skin is so juicy and fresh."

They were naked in bed together. Bee's wings buzzed as she straddled him. The bug girl looked down on his body with her inhuman eyes.

"You need to leave," Bee said.

Mike sucked her nipples into his mouth.

"You need to get out of here, now," Bee said, louder.

"Huh?"

Mike didn't know how to react to her words. Although she told him to go, her body was telling him to stay. She rubbed herself against him, licking his neck and earlobe.

"Run!" Bee cried.

But as she said it, she pulled his penis inside of her and moaned with pleasure.

"You have to get out of here before it's too late," she said.

He was beginning to think there was something deeply wrong

with this girl.

"What are you talking about?" he asked.

"I'm losing control," she said, as she slowly fucked him.

She breathed heavily into his ear, kissed his neck.

"What does that mean?" Mike closed his eyes, enjoying the eggy alien textures inside of her.

"I'm going to sting you," she said.

"You what?"

As she fucked him faster, Bee became like another person. The look in her eyes changed. Her wings buzzed so loudly they drowned out the sound of her moans.

"Hungry..." she said, her voice twisted and warped.

"What?"

She looked at him with deep, black, predatory eyes.

"Hungry, hungry buggy bug..."

As Mike orgasmed, he closed his eyes and cried out.

He didn't see it when it happened. He just felt something blade-like pierce deep into his lung, stealing his breath away. When he looked down, he saw the stinger inside his chest. It was more like the tail of a scorpion than a bee, reaching out of the woman's lower abdomen, curled around her waist, pumping poison into his body.

Bee smiled at him as his eyes widened with shock.

"Hungry, hungry...."

Mike's head rolled back. He couldn't keep it upright anymore. He couldn't move his arms or legs.

"Drink the nectar..."

Bee hadn't cum yet, so she continued to fuck him while he was paralyzed. Mike was still erect, but couldn't feel a thing. He just watched as she finished herself off using his body.

"Suck it all up..."

She arched her back and widened her mouth as she reached orgasm. Then a long black tongue slid out of her lips.

"Hungry, hungry..."

She licked his neck and face with this fat sticky tongue.

"Don't..." Mike tried to say, but the words could hardly be released.

Bee pressed the slithering tongue down on the center of Mike's forehead. He then realized it wasn't exactly a tongue. It was more like a straw made of tongue-flesh. Bee injected it through his skull. Like a mosquito, she sucked. But instead of sucking blood, she sucked out his memories.

"Ra…" Mike tried to say. "Chel…"

Bee was ravenous, starving. She feasted on his thoughts, his dreams, his past. She was so hungry for them. She just couldn't stop herself. It was her weakness, her obsession.

"Sorrry…" he said, as his breath slipped from his lungs.

Like a glutton with a bottomless stomach, the bug gorged herself on the contents of Mike's mind. She didn't need to take it all. She could have just taken some, just a taste. But that wasn't in her nature. She wouldn't stop until she drank him all up.

When Mike awoke the next morning, he didn't know where he was. He didn't even know who he was. He didn't know how to speak, or write, or put on his own clothes anymore.

There was a bee woman lying on top of him, though he didn't know anything about bees or women. She shook him, as if trying to bring him back to life, back to how he was.

"Mike…" she said. He didn't understand what that meant. She shook him again.

"No…" she said. "I told you to run. Why didn't you run?"

Tears dripped down her yellow face. He felt them splash against his chest. They were warm and soothing. He liked them. He wanted her to cry on him some more.

"This wasn't supposed to happen," she said. "Why does this always happen…"

Drool slipped down his lips. He didn't know how to close his mouth properly anymore.

"You need to get out of here," Bee told the hollow-headed Mike.

She pulled him out of the bed and shoved him toward the door.

"Go."

He could hardly stand up, grabbing onto the back of a chair for balance, falling to one knee.

"Get out!" she yelled, tears filling her eyes.

Mike rolled over a giant pile of money on the way out the door. He didn't try to take the money with him as he went. The only thing he understood about the money was that it happened to be a very ugly shade of green.

THE
HOLLOW
WEB

"It was a shock that such a little bug would prove to be such a worthy adversary, Big Sister."

"I concur, Little Brother. But it will not be so easy for her to defeat the Viceroy."

The two Arachne siblings carried their dead brother's body through the catacombs, holding him upright as if he were just a drunk friend they were escorting home from a bar. The blanket of webs along the cavern walls cradled a row of glowing green orbs lighting their path.

"We will not let her get away next time, right Big Brother?" the female Arachne asked the dead body between them.

The corpse's head dangled at her. Slivers of meat dripped from the hole in its chest, sliding down its wilted legs. She waited patiently for the corpse to respond to her question, but it only leaked fluids and sagged closer to the ground.

"Your silence speaks volumes, Big Brother," said the female Arachne. "The bee woman will be paid back for the sins she has committed."

The catacombs opened up to a subterranean underworld that stretched deep into the earth. Spider webs zigzagged across the chasm, creating paths and canopies—the roads of the Arachne.

"But won't the Viceroy be displeased with our failure, Big Sister?" the younger sibling asked as they stepped onto the web bridge.

As they moved carefully across the web, their black pointed spider-leg boots gripping the glossy strings, the young Arachne stared down into the cavernous depths. Beneath them was a city of mammoth black machines that pumped and purred, spewing warm smoke through the spider domain. The machines were ancient, older than the Arachne, older than anything in the city.

"The Viceroy is wise, Little Brother. He will understand we did our best. Big Brother will explain it all to him. Won't you, Big Brother?"

She looked down at the corpse again and was answered with more silence.

"But remember how he reacted after we failed our last mission, Big Sister?"

"We did not fail our last mission, Little Brother. Our last mission failed us."

"But he was so angry when we decapitated that unarmed civilian, Big Sister."

They passed skeletons of dead cattle wrapped in the webbing along the bridge, their fluids sucked until they were just husks of dried meat and bone dangling in the web.

"Oh, Little Brother. It's not our responsibility if common peasants fail to get out of our way while we are on the hunt."

"That's not what the Viceroy said, Big Sister."

"That man got what he deserved, Little Brother. Remember that. We Arachne are a superior species. The bugs of Hell's Bottom are nothing but our livestock."

"Then why was the Viceroy so disturbed by the fact that we ate the victim after he was decapitated, Big Sister?"

"I'm sure he wasn't disturbed, Little Brother. Perhaps a little jealous, but not disturbed. That man proved to be quite a delicious meal even if he wasn't our intended target."

"Yes, Big Sister. Humans are filled with the tastiest fluids. I prefer them to the animal soup we usually consume."

The female Arachne licked her lips and widened her six red eyes at the thought of draining a human of his fluids. She thought the bee woman would be especially tasty. The dead cow carcasses they passed along the web bridge only made her sick.

"What happened to you three? Where have you been?"

The Viceroy sat on his throne of steel webbing, three pairs of arms draped over his lap, eying the two Arachne siblings as they dragged their dead brother across the red carpet. The Viceroy's palace was empty and still, but the shadows were full of soft whispers. Red eyes the size of fists bulged out of the walls and followed them through the grand hall.

"The Viceroy seems upset, Big Sister," said the young Arachne as they arrived at the foot of the throne.

"The Viceroy is always upset about something, Little Brother."

The Arachne lord brushed his waist-long white hair over his shoulders and glared at them with his six albino eyes. "Is it safe for me to assume you two failed to bring the bee woman to justice?"

"He's quick to assess the situation isn't he, Little Brother?"

"He has no idea how resourceful the bee woman was, Big Sister. She and her friends used such basic magic, yet were still able to defeat us before we could cast a single spell."

"So she's still alive?" asked the Viceroy.

"She won't be alive much longer, will she Little Brother?"

"Yes, Big Sister. She will not escape a second time."

The Viceroy rolled his eyes at the siblings and let out a long musty sigh. "That woman has drained the memories of almost a fifth of the residents of Hell's Bottom, leaving the city full of brain dead amnesiacs who can't even remember how to clothe themselves properly. This matter must be dealt with immediately."

"I am now certain the Viceroy is upset, Big Sister."

"Yes, Little Brother. He is not happy with the outcome at all, is he?"

"Tell me exactly what happened." The Viceroy was getting impatient with his three henchmen.

"Now he wants to know the whole story, Big Sister."

"How tiresome, Little Brother."

The Viceroy snapped. He slammed his six fists into the arm rests of his throne and yelled, "Show me the proper respect!"

The two siblings just stared at each other with blank faces.

"One of the five great Arachne lords is sitting before you. Stop talking to each other like I'm not a part of the conversation!"

"Very well, Big Brother," the female Arachne said to the corpse leaning against her. "If the Viceroy must know the whole story, you might as well explain it to him."

"Yes, Big Brother," said the younger brother. "You should be the one to enlighten the Viceroy."

"He's dead!" the Viceroy yelled, pointing at the corpse. "Your brother has a giant hole where his torso should be. Why are you still speaking to him?"

"I don't understand what the Viceroy is saying, Big Sister."

"Yes, he is especially infuriating today, Little Brother."

"Just tell me what happened or I'll feed you both to the hatchlings."

"Very well, Big Brother," said the female Arachne. "If you'd rather I tell the story I will do so."

Then she explained every detail of the encounter with Bee, Angry Eddie, and Big Strange. She mentioned how her older brother was killed, though she spoke of it as though getting one's guts burrowed out by a giant beetle-man was nothing fatal; to her, it was more like contracting a perfectly ordinary illness that caused people to temporarily lose all of their internal organs and leak body fluids all over the place.

The younger sibling said, "And that's when I escaped and you were captured, Big Sister."

"Yes, Little Brother. They brought Big Brother and me to a restaurant in the northwest quadrant."

"Which restaurant was that?" asked the Viceroy.

"You know the restaurant, Little Brother," said the female Arachne. "It's the one the pig man runs."

"I believe it's called *Le Petite Provence*, Big Sister."

"Yes, Little Brother. That's the one. The bee woman seems to be under the pig man's employ."

The Viceroy leaned back in his throne. "I know the place.

It is Mr. Hoggins' center of operations. He has been under our eyes for quite some time."

"We should eat the pig man for his insolence, Little Brother," said the female Arachne, licking her spider fangs.

"After we eat the bee woman, Big Sister," said the younger brother.

"You keep away from Mr. Hoggins," said the Viceroy. "I'll pay him a visit personally."

The female pouted at the corpse in her arms. "The Viceroy is no fun at all, Big Brother."

"I concur, Big Sister. I was so looking forward to tasting the pig's flesh."

"While I deal with Hoggins, you two must go see the Dollmaker."

"Who is this Dollmaker the Viceroy speaks of, Big Sister?"

"He is the man who makes the dolls, Little Brother."

"Just bring your brother to him," said the Viceroy. "If you hurry, the Dollmaker might be able to resurrect the poor fool."

"Yes, curing Big Brother should take priority, Big Sister."

"He has been in such an awful state, Little Brother. It would be nice to bring him back to his old self again."

"Be on your way," said the Viceroy. "We'll discuss what is to be done with the bee woman at a later time."

The Viceroy waved them off. He was done dealing with the irritating trio. They were intolerable. But it wasn't like he had a choice. All Arachne of their generation were pretentious little shits with a superiority complex and an overblown sense of entitlement. The only choice he had was to deal with them and hope they grow out of it someday.

The Dollmaker lived in the sewers under Hell's Bottom, but he didn't live in filth and scum as one would expect from a sewer-dweller. In fact, he was perhaps the cleanliest person in the city and very particular about everything in his perfectly-organized domain.

"So the Viceroy sent you, did he?" asked the Dollmaker.

The Arachne siblings stared blankly at the man in the doorway. The Dollmaker was in a bright white suit with black goggles over his eyes. He had bleached blond hair parted perfectly down the center, and his fingernails were glossy and neatly trimmed as if he gave himself a manicure each and every day.

"Do you believe this man can really cure our brother, Big Sister?"

"I don't know, Little Brother. He is not Arachne. His magic must be very weak."

The Dollmaker looked down at the corpse in their arms.

"I see," he said, leaning down to get a closer look.

When the neatly dressed man pulled on a rubber glove and slid it gently into their brother's torso cavity, their spidery eyes widened in horror.

"He's touching him, Big Sister! A human shouldn't touch an Arachne in such an intimate way."

"We must allow it, Little Brother. The Dollmaker is only investigating his ailment."

The human raised his gloved hand and examined the blood dripping from his fingers. With his clean hand, he adjusted the lenses of his goggles to view it on a microscopic level. Then he nodded his head.

"It's not too late," said the Dollmaker, carefully removing his gloves. "But we must hurry. Bring him inside."

The Arachne pulled their brother out of the damp, stench-filled sewer into a large underground bunker that was as sparkling clean as a brand new hospital.

"Step inside the evaporator," said the Dollmaker, pointing to a curtain-less shower stall in the entryway.

As the Arachne stepped into the tight space, the female said, "Do you think this machine will cure Big Brother, Little Brother?"

The Dollmaker flipped on a switch and the machine sucked all moisture from their bodies. It was as if they were being dry-cleaned.

"No, Big Sister. I think he just doesn't want us tracking sewage into his domain."

When the machine finished its cycle, the Arachne realized their clothes, skin, and hair had become just as clean as the Dollmaker's.

"Take him to that table over there," the Dollmaker said. "I'll call on the recyclers. They'll help repair your poor brother."

As the siblings carried the body, the young one said, "What is a recycler, Big Sister?"

Before she could answer, the Dollmaker said, "They are my dolls." He pulled a red lever on the wall which created a light hum vibrating beneath their feet. The humming quickly spread from the floor to the walls to the ceiling. It was soft and just barely noticeable to dull human senses, but the Arachne could tell it was powerful enough to vibrate through all the streets of Hell's Bottom.

"Here's one of them now," the Dollmaker said.

A living porcelain doll crawled out of an air vent next to them. It stepped through a miniature version of the evaporator the Arachne had been cleaned with, then it click-clacked across the tile floor toward the Dollmaker.

"The rats, Big Sister? How can the city's rats help our brother?"

"This man must be the one responsible for these detestable vermin, Little Brother. They infest Hell's Bottom like a plague."

The Dollmaker leaned down and allowed the tiny doll to climb up his arm and sit on his shoulder.

"Nonsense," said the Dollmaker. "My children perform a very important community service. They are the recyclers."

The banging of rats crawling in the air vents echoed through the sewers, rattling the pipes in the walls. Then dozens of the porcelain dolls entered the room, spilling out of the vents in their fluffy white dresses and painted-on faces.

"There was once a terrible garbage problem in Hell's Bottom until I introduced my dolls to the public. They eat all the city's refuse, then bring it back here for recycling." He pointed at the machinery in his bunker. There were cleaning machines, weaving machines, molding machines. "All of this was constructed using recycled materials from above."

"How can such little dolls recycle garbage into such large

devices, Big Sister?" asked the young Arachne.

"The dolls are infused with recycling magic," said the Doll-maker. "Everything they devour is repurposed. That is how they will heal your brother."

The man in the white suit stepped through the ever-growing sea of porcelain dolls that parted for him as if he were their Moses. From inside a storeroom, the Dollmaker wheeled out a dead body and pulled it up alongside the Arachne older brother.

"My dolls can even recycle old dead body parts into fresh new ones." The Dollmaker typed on a small computer that served as a remote control. Connected to a speaker system, the program sent waves of sound through the room.

The dolls responded to the humming sound that rumbled the floor. Like an army of ants, they crawled up onto the operating table and with razor sharp teeth they chewed on the cadaver, taking it apart one piece of meat at a time. The Arachne watched with both disgust and fascination.

"I can communicate with them through the vibrations," said the Dollmaker, wheeling out three more bodies to feed to his dolls. "They're very sensitive creatures. Although they are capable of speech, they do not use language as we do. They communicate by the texture of sound, rather than the use of words."

When the four corpses were stripped to the bone, the dolls went to the Arachne carcass. After seeing how quickly and easily the dolls dismantled the bodies, the Arachne siblings could not help but tremble with panic as their older brother disappeared into a sea of tiny porcelain bodies.

"What are they doing to him, Big Sister?"

"I don't know, Little Brother."

The dolls did not eat much of their brother's flesh. They only ate the rotting or damaged parts. When finished feasting, the porcelain recyclers puked up ropes of gray ooze into their brother's open cavity. The ooze was like clay that the dolls molded with their tiny white hands. The ooze quickly took shape, shifting from clay-like flesh to functional Arachne organs.

"They're rebuilding him, Big Sister."

"I see, Little Brother!"

The dolls worked quickly and meticulously. Although they didn't appear to have much intelligence, they were able to construct functional new organs out of the meat putty they took from the other bodies. Even the DNA was replicated to match that of an Arachne.

"Hmm…" the Dollmaker said, rubbing his chin as he watched his recyclers do their job.

"I can't believe it, Big Sister!"

The younger Arachne was nearly jumping with excitement as the dolls finished their work. When the creatures stepped away, the big brother was exactly as he was before the attack. It looked as if there never was a hole in his torso.

"He's completely cured, Little Brother!"

They wanted to run to their brother, lift him up and give him a big hug. But the Dollmaker interrupted them with a loud sigh that crushed their spirits.

"I'm sorry," said the Dollmaker. "The procedure was a failure."

The spider-fanged smiles fell from their faces when he spoke those words.

"What does the Dollmaker mean, Big Sister? Our brother has been resurrected. He is complete."

But then they noticed. The new flesh was smoking, then dissolving. It rotted from the inside out.

"His body is rejecting the magic," said the Dollmaker.

The Arachne siblings stared in horror as their brother's flesh fell apart before their eyes. Not just his new flesh, but his entire body melted and dripped.

"Quickly, we must save his brain," said the Dollmaker. "There's still hope if we save his brain."

The Arachne siblings were so panicked they didn't know how to help the human.

The Dollmaker typed on his keyboard with lightning-fingers, emitting a pulse from the speakers telling the dolls what to do. The recyclers rushed to the older Arachne and chewed through his neck, severing his head before the melting flesh disease could spread to his brain.

"What was that, Big Sister?" cried the younger Arachne.

"They turned him into soup, Little Brother!"

The dolls carried the head like a trail of ants toward the Dollmaker.

"I'm sorry..." the human said.

The siblings couldn't even hear his apology they were in such shock.

"What went wrong, Big Sister?" There were tears flowing from all six of the young Arachne's eyes. "Why did Big Brother melt away like that? He wasn't supposed to melt away."

The female couldn't even speak anymore she was so agitated.

"Some people are allergic to certain types of magic," said the Dollmaker. "Your brother had a bad reaction to it."

The older sister screamed and tossed all four operating tables across the room using a Force spell.

"It wasn't our brother's fault!" she yelled at the Dollmaker.

This time she didn't communicate through her brother. She spoke directly to the man in white.

She continued, "It was those *human* bodies you recycled that are to blame. They were too inferior to create flesh that could sustain my brother's form! He is of a higher species. He is of pure Arachne blood!"

Her face was soggy with tears. Her pale skin now beet red. Nothing was worse to an adult Arachne than losing a sibling. All they had in the world was each other. Her heart was weeping and screaming in her chest in a way she'd never felt before.

The little brother ran to his sister and wrapped his arms around her, spinning strands of web across her back and waist, sticking himself to her as if afraid that something horrible might happen to her if there were any distance between them at all.

"You're responsible for this," the spider girl screamed at the Dollmaker. "We never should have come to you. Your weak, inferior magic couldn't heal a fly, let alone a noble Arachne."

The Dollmaker just stood in place, knowing not to say a word until the siblings calmed down. He watched them as they cradled each other, sobbing and spinning web, cursing his name.

"Where are we going, Big Brother?" the little female Arachne asked, as they crawled through a cave of webs.

"As far away as we can, Little Sister."

They were only children at the time, just old enough to walk and speak on their own. The younger brother was so small he had to be cocooned all the way to his neck with spider thread and attached to the sister's back.

"I'm scared, Big Brother," said the girl, as they crawled deep into the darkness.

"Try to move in silence, Little Sister," said the brother, as he led the way. "We mustn't let mother hear us."

Arachne mothers ate their young. It was the spider in them. They couldn't control themselves. But the mother of these siblings was more ravenous than usual Arachne. Once she started eating, she couldn't stop. That part was the human in her. She just had to indulge herself, gobbling up the spider babies like her nest was a basket of chocolates.

The youngest sibling began to cry. He wanted to go back to their mother. He didn't understand why they were leaving her.

"I said keep quiet, Little Sister."

"It's not my fault, Big Brother," said the girl, pulling the baby from her back. "He's scared, that's all."

Infants of the Arachne were far from human. They didn't have the same cute-factor of human babies. They looked like basketball-sized spiders with baby heads growing from their abdomens. Known as hatchlings, these spider babies were born with insatiable hunger and ate everything that moved. If there was no living food near their nest they would eat each other, the stronger hatchlings feeding on the weaker hatchlings. And if there were enough of them, they would eat their own mother. One of the reasons Arachne mothers ate their young was to diminish their numbers, to prevent them from overwhelming her.

"Hush, Little Brother," the girl said to the spider baby. "It's not the time for sadness."

Less than half of the Arachne survived the hatchling phase and made it into childhood, and very few survived childhood and made it into adulthood. This was because the mother continued eating her children even after the hatchling phase. At birth, the mother ate the ones who were weak. During childhood, the mother ate the ones who were dumb, ugly, or just not very likeable. She chose which ones were to survive and which were to be food for the family. It was a horrifying experience to grow up as an Arachne. It was why the surviving Arachne formed such a close bond with their siblings.

"Where are you my darling?" their mother's voice echoed through the cave.

The female Arachne quieted the spider baby, but not in time. Their mother heard them, tracking them through the tunnel outside the nest.

"We need to move faster, Little Sister," the brother whispered.

They crawled on through the tunnel.

"You know how much I hate disobedience," said the mother. "Bring dinner back to me or you will be punished."

The little sister and baby brother were chosen to be food that day. It was why the older sibling was helping them escape. Because their mother was so gluttonous, she ate her children no matter how smart or strong or beautiful they might be. She ate them merely because they were so delicious. The older brother was the only surviving child from his batch of hatchlings. He knew if he didn't escape, all of them would eventually die.

"I won't let her get you, Little Sister," the big brother said, in response to their girl's anxious face. "Don't worry."

Arachne mothers lose their human-like appearance once they go through their first pregnancy. They become large spider-like creatures—humanoid from the waist up, but from the waist down they grow a massive arachnid abdomen the size of an elephant.

"This is the wrong way, Little Sister," said the brother. "I'm sorry. This won't lead us to the surface."

"Then where does it lead, Big Brother?"

"To the deep dark, Little Sister."

The girl's face quivered with panic. The deep dark was a scary place to Arachne children. It was the region beneath the catacombs that was without light, where no Arachne lived, where one could easily become lost within the complex maze of tunnels.

Once the mother crawled through the passage after them, the children could not turn back. They had to go straight into the deep dark, without light or supplies.

"But won't we get lost, Big Brother?"

"Yes, Little Sister. We'll get so lost that not even mother will be able to find us ever again."

For five years, the three siblings lived down in the deep dark, away from the rest of Arachne society. They lived as spiders, building large webs to catch bats and other subterranean creatures. These webs were their homes. They would spend most of their time in the web together, talking and dreaming, wrapping each other up in sticky threads so they would become a tight bundle of comfort.

All alone in the dark, the siblings created a whole world for themselves down there. It was *their* world, and it was a place that existed outside of the world where everyone else lived.

"Who is this, Big Brother?" asked the female sibling.

They looked down at a group of Arachne who were exploring the cave for mushrooms.

"They look like us, Little Sister."

The young one was not used to the light the explorers brought with them. He covered his face with his hands. "My eyes burn, Big Brother. Make it stop."

The Arachne mushroom-seekers stared up at the three paper-white teenagers standing in the giant web above them, wearing clothes sewn together using their own spider thread.

The girl licked her lips. "Perhaps we should taste them, Big Brother. Nothing so juicy has ever come through our cave before."

"No, Little Sister." The brother smiled. "They will be very useful to us. We should let them live."

"What are you three doing down here?" asked the head mushroom-seeker.

"But why, Big Brother?"

"Have you been down here since you were hatchlings?" asked another mushroom seeker.

"Because they are going to lead us back to our people, Little Sister."

"You mean back to mother, Big Brother?"

"Are you three even listening to us?" asked the head mushroom seeker.

"No, Little Sister. They will help us leave this cave so that we can join Arachne society, as we were destined to do."

"Why are you ignoring us?" asked the mushroom-seekers.

But the Arachne siblings were not ignoring the mushroom-seekers. They heard everything that was said. It was just that they were so used to being alone in their own world that they had no idea how to interact with anyone from the outside. For them, communicating with people in the real world seemed as absurd as trying to communicate with somebody you might watch on television.

The Dollmaker was the first person the female Arachne had spoken to directly since she was a child in her mother's nest. It was as if her brother's death cracked open the world the three siblings existed within, allowing her to peer outside through the hole and see the Dollmaker staring back at her.

They had been delusional about their brother's death because it was the only way they could cope with his loss. Their world required all three of them to hold it together. They didn't believe it was possible for him to die, unless they all died together.

"We can still save him," the Dollmaker said.

The Arachne looked at the man in white, but couldn't exactly believe him. Their brother was now just a pool of goo on the operating table.

"Come to my workshop," he said.

Bringing their brother's severed head, he led the Arachne into the next room. Inside, there were hundreds of doll parts.

"I can't return him to his old self," said the Dollmaker. "But I can give him a new body. He can be reborn as a doll."

"But our brother is not a doll, Big Sister..." said the crying younger brother, wrapping his eyes in webs so he didn't have to see.

"Of course not, Little Brother," the female said, then she turned to the Dollmaker, "What do you mean by giving him a new body?"

"All of my recyclers were once human," he said. "I am able to put the minds of living creatures into the dolls."

"But our brother is a noble Arachne sorcerer, who trained under the great Viceroy. You cannot turn him into one of your rat slaves."

"My dolls are not slaves. They have their own free will."

"But they live as vermin and they have no intelligence. It would not be our brother at all anymore."

"It won't look like your brother, no. But he will have the mind of your brother. He will be able to speak and use his magic. He will be the same person, just living inside of a small porcelain body."

The Arachne siblings looked at the dolls scurrying through the workshop, their feet tip-tapping across the floor. The older sister imagined what it would be like to have one as a brother, but she didn't like the idea one bit.

The Dollmaker continued, "These dolls act like this because their minds come from hollows." He pointed at the row of dead human bodies lying on tables on the far side of the workshop. "You see, the hollows are incapable of surviving in their human form. All of their memories have been sucked out of them. They no longer know how to live as humans. All they can do is eat and sleep—just what comes naturally to them."

The woman looked down at the dolls. "So this is what has been happening to all the missing hollows?"

"Their minds are much more suited to living as my recyclers," said the dollmaker. "Their doll bodies are much more durable. They don't need to worry about taking care of themselves. All they have to do is eat."

"But they are still your slaves."

"They are better slaves than dead."

"Perhaps such a life is good enough for hollows, but it is not good enough for my brother."

"Your brother will be different," said the Dollmaker. "He will still have his memories."

The woman shook her head. She refused to believe him.

"It's the only way," said the Dollmaker. "You can have your brother back as a doll or never see him again. What is your choice?"

The Arachne female lowered her eyes.

"Choose quickly," said the Dollmaker. "If we wait too long the process might not work."

She didn't give an answer, but the Dollmaker proceeded with the operation anyway. He saw it in her eyes; she wanted her brother back no matter what his condition, but as a proud Arachne pureblood she could not bring herself to agree to such a monstrous proposal. The very idea was an outrage. She prayed with all her soul the procedure would be a success.

The Arachne siblings couldn't believe how the operation worked. The Dollmaker removed their brother's brain from his skull and stuffed it into the doll's body. The brain was too large for the doll's head. Instead, the brain filled the doll's entire body cavity, spreading out into its arms and legs. The only part of the doll that wasn't filled with their brother's brain was its head, which contained an artificial stomach.

"So they're all filled with brains, Big Sister?" asked the younger Arachne as the dolls gathered by his feet.

"They seem to be completely made of brain matter, Little Brother... but with a porcelain exo-skeleton."

The Dollmaker closed the encasing on the toy and dressed

it in a tiny gray suit. Then he cast his magic on the device.

"He won't be allergic to this magic, will he Big Sister?"

"He better not be, Little Brother. It would be unhealthy for the Dollmaker to fail us a second time."

When the magic was completed, the doll began to twitch. Then it lifted its head and looked around the room.

"Is that really you, Big Brother?" asked the female, leaning close to the porcelain toy.

The doll turned its head from side to side.

"Why have you gotten so big, Little Sister?" asked the doll.

As he spoke, the toy grabbed at his neck. Its voice was high-pitched and metallic. It startled the doll. He couldn't believe that vocal tone came out of his throat. But upon touching his neck, he also couldn't believe his throat was his throat.

"You've gone through a transformation, Big Brother."

The doll looked at his tiny white hands.

"Why is my skin so hard, Little Sister?"

"You died, Big Brother. This was the only way we could bring you back to life."

The older Arachne looked down at the floor. He suddenly realized he was sitting on a table, dangling over it like a cliff. The Dollmaker held a mirror to the table.

"I'm a doll, Big Sister!" said the brother, as he saw his mirror image. "Why am I a doll?"

The girl smiled at her tiny brother. "Your old body was destroyed, Big Brother. You must make the best of this one."

Seeing him alive again brought tears to her eyes, even though he was getting very upset.

"But I'm so small, Little Sister! How can I live in such a small body?"

"Let me help you with that, Big Brother."

The female Arachne cast a spell of Growth on her brother. Then the doll expanded and grew, rolling off the table onto two porcelain legs, until he was the size of a human.

Now standing at equal height, the sister stood face to painted-on face with her porcelain doll brother. "How is that, Big Brother?"

"I'm still a doll, Little Sister…" His voice was still high-pitched and mechanical. He was not at all pleased.

"I know," she said, wrapping her arms around his porcelain skin. "Isn't it wonderful, Big Brother?"

Then the younger brother joined in and they both hugged the giant doll so tightly it nearly cracked.

"The bee woman will pay for doing this to me, Little Sister," said the doll Arachne. "We must hunt her down and finish her."

"Yes, Big Brother. We'll do anything you wish."

"She must suffer, Little Sister."

"Just shut up, Big Brother." The sister buried her face in his chest. "Hug me or I'll shatter you to pieces."

Although nothing felt right in his new body, the older brother put his arms around his two younger siblings and allowed them to embrace him with all their might. He felt a bit like a teacup as their warm spidery tears poured down his smooth white skin. It was going to be quite a long time before he'd be able to get used to life as a doll.

THE
HUNGRY
BUG

Zach had never been to one of the meetings before. He'd thought they were just for freaks who didn't have any self control, who were so far mutated from magic that they weren't even recognizably human anymore. But when he learned that Mia was part of this casting addiction support group, he wanted to attend.

Mia was the prettiest girl he'd met since coming to Hell's Bottom two years ago. She had short blue hair and piercing brown eyes that melted him whenever he looked directly into them. She was petite, curvy and had the cutest dimples when she smiled. From her style to her body type to her almost squeaky tone of voice—everything about her was perfect. She was exactly Zach's type. Only he hadn't the courage to speak to her for longer than two sentences. He figured that if he started attending the meetings with her, they'd have something in common to talk about. Maybe she'd even become his sponsor.

While sitting in a circle of chairs in the church basement, Zach watched every person who went through the door. He arrived extra early so there would be plenty of time to speak to Mia if she happened to recognize him, but she didn't come as early as he did. In fact, he wondered if she was going to show up at all.

As Zach watched each and every person walk through the paint-stripped door, he accidentally made eye contact with a woman he wished he hadn't. When their eyes met, she smiled at him and quickly approached.

"Hey, is this your first time?" said the woman as she sat in the chair next to Zach. Her smile was so electric that it was nearly bursting from her face.

She wrapped one arm around his shoulder as she shook his hand with the other.

"Yeah," Zach said. Then he broke eye contact and pulled his hand away. Zach didn't want this person sitting next to him. He was hoping to save that seat for Mia.

"Ohmygawd," the woman cried, rubbing him through his leather jacket. "This is my fifth time! It's so perfect that you came today. Are you coming tomorrow, too?"

The woman seemed more plant than human. Her skin was melon-green. Vines and leaves grew from her body instead of hair. Flowers budded from her cheeks and nipples. Crinkled edges of tree bark were beginning to form on her elbows and the back of her neck. But her appearance was not nearly as off-putting as her hyperactive personality.

"I don't know..." Zach said.

He felt her fingers weave into his hair. She inched closer to him, rubbing against him and fidgeting with his coat. He wondered if she was aggressively flirting with him or if this was how she usually communicated with people.

"My name's Janie, but you can call me Nymph. Everyone calls me Nymph."

"I'm Zach."

She closed her eyes and squeezed her shoulders together, repeating his name. "Zach? Yes, I can see that... Zach...Zachery..."

He realized the rumor was true. These meetings really were attended by complete freaks. And it wasn't only the twitchy-touchy plant lady. The room was filling with some of the strangest-looking people he'd ever met in Hell's Bottom. There was a man who was mostly computer. At first, Zach thought he was a robot, but he was a man who was quickly mutating into a machine. A teenager was made of paper and held a body-sized umbrella to keep the rain off of him. A woman had transparent plastic skin that exposed her internal organs and the blood pumping through her body.

"Everyone's really nice here," said Janie, nodding her head. "There's a really good vibe."

She thrust her chest in his face and Zach saw a honey bee crawling inside the flower that grew from her nipple. He struggled and pushed away from her. Zach was allergic to bees.

"I'm sorry," Janie said when she saw the look on his face. "Does it make you uncomfortable that I'm not wearing any clothes?"

With all the leaves growing from her body, Zach hadn't even realized she was naked.

"My vines are very sensitive," she said. "I can't put clothes over them. They'll get crushed."

"Okay…" Zach said.

When Mia finally arrived at the meeting, she couldn't see Zach behind the bushy plant woman. She darted to the other side of the room and embraced an older woman covered in cat hair as if they were old friends.

Zach didn't know what to do. He wanted to get Mia's attention, but the plant lady wouldn't leave him alone. She now spoke to him only inches from his face and appeared as if she were about to jump into his lap.

"Also, they need direct sunlight," Janie said, then she touched the flowers on her breasts. "And you wouldn't believe how much I have to water these suckers."

As she wiggled the plants, three bees flew out of her and buzzed around Zach's head. He gasped and thrashed his arms around.

"Janie," said the priest standing at the front of the room. "Come sit by the window here."

The priest pointed at an empty seat facing the sunlight.

"Okay!" Janie said, jumping off of Zach and rushing toward the window. The bees left Zach and followed her.

While Janie changed seats, the priest smiled at Zach and gave him a wink. The priest obviously realized the plant woman was bothering the newcomer. Zach mouthed the words *thank you* to the priest. But even with Janie out of the way, Mia still hadn't noticed him.

"Welcome to today's CAS group meeting," said the priest, quieting down the room of chit-chatting freaks. "For those who don't know me, I'm Father Harry. But this isn't a religious meeting, so please just call me Harry. Today marks my fifth anniversary holding these sessions. I'm happy to see some familiar faces today, as well as some new ones."

The priest's eyes oozed out of his head at Zach, who appeared to be the only newcomer in the room. His eyes were like those of a slug, only they could stretch almost two feet out of the sockets.

"I've seen many faces come into this room over the years," Harry continued. "A couple of you have even been coming since my very first gathering." He squeezed his slug-eyes at the cat woman. "I created this group as a haven for those who were weak to the temptations of the hungry bug. Life is hard enough in Hell's Bottom as it is without the constant seduction of sorcery. Maybe at first you might pick up a new spell so that you can get work. Then, once you can afford it, you pick up another to improve something that's missing from your personal life. Then, you don't even realize it when it comes. The hungry bug sneaks in and gets a tight hold on you, feeding on you like a parasite. After a while, the magic no longer seems voluntary. It becomes a necessity. You can't live without it. The bug eats you from the inside out."

Zach thought the speech was ridiculous.

The priest said, "I'd like to see a show of hands. Who has given in to the hungry bug within the past week?"

About seven of the twenty people in the room raised their hand, including both Mia and Janie. Zach was surprised to see Mia's hand up. He knew she had been going to the meetings for a long time and assumed she wasn't using anymore.

"Christian isn't raising his hand." The man with computer skin pointed at the teenager made of paper. "He used magic on me two days ago."

"I did not!" the paper man cried.

"Don't fucking lie, you emo piece of shit." The computer man was muscular and had probably been a bouncer at some Jersey Shore nightclub in his old life. Zach could almost hear his New Jersey accent through his electronic voice. "I can tell when you're inside my head with your bullshit."

"Dennis, let it go," the priest said, calming down the big man. "It's not your job to make accusations."

"It is when he's casting on me," Dennis yelled.

"He could be telling the truth," the priest said. "And if he is casting and doesn't want to admit that's something he has to deal with."

"I swear I haven't been using magic," Christian said, adjusting his brown horn-rimmed glasses.

"He used his magic on me as well," said a woman with lizard skin.

"And me, I'm pretty sure," Mia said, though she didn't seem as upset by it as the other people in the room.

The priest looked at the boy. "Have you been casting, Christian?"

The boy opened his mouth to deny it. Then he slunk back in his chair and shrugged. He was obviously guilty, but still wouldn't admit it.

"Maybe you should speak first," said the priest.

"I don't really want to speak today," Christian said.

"Everybody is speaking today. You might as well get it over with."

The kid groaned loudly, his paper body trembling. He obviously was uncomfortable speaking in front of a group of people.

"My name is Christian Southerland, MA," said the boy made of paper, "and I'm addicted to a spell called Dream Control."

Zach wondered if the kid actually did have a master's degree. He was probably only nineteen and couldn't possibly have gone through graduate school. It seemed like the kid was lying, just to seem more important.

"I was a novelist before I came to Hell's Bottom," Christian said, his voice shaky and awkward. "I wrote experimental postmodern literature. Kind of like James Joyce, Franz Kafka and Kurt Vonnegut all rolled into one. It was groundbreaking cutting-edge mind-blowing stuff. Three of my novels were released through Publish America and I've never gotten less than five stars on any amazon.com review. If I never used magic I would have been a legend by now. I would have been a bestselling author like Stephen King, only they would have been better than his books because they would have had more intellectual depth. They would have changed the way people look at literature... and the world."

Zach realized the guy was staring straight at him as he spoke. It sounded like Christian was trying to promote himself to Zach directly, as if Zach actually cared about what he did. Perhaps the kid was directing his attention at Zach just because he was a newcomer who never heard this story before.

"I found the spell in an old bookshop," Christian continued. "I always loved old books, especially leatherbound classics—their smell and texture, the way they feel in my hand, the sound they make when you crack them open. I think that's why I wanted to become a writer in the first place. I wanted to write the kinds of books that would one day be found in old bookshops. As a master of words, I was sure it would happen one day. Though it's kind of ironic that I set out to write books and now I'm turning into a book."

He laughed at himself, but nobody else laughed. The master of words didn't realize he misused the word *ironic*.

"I loved casting the spell once I learned that it was real," Christian continued. "Dream Control did just that. It allowed me to control dreams. I was able to live inside the worlds I created. My fictional universe had become a reality. Of course, as a man obsessed with his own visions, I couldn't stop casting the spell once I started. I just wanted to live in my dream worlds forever. I started sleeping twenty hour days. I had to take sleeping pills. I even flirted with the idea of inducing a coma so I'd never have to wake up."

Christian stood and exposed his torso to everyone. His legs were shaky as he stood, as if he couldn't believe he was actually showing this to everyone.

"Then I started turning into a book." He flipped through the torso-sized pages on his body, showing off all the over-worded sentences and illustrations. "I've become a story collection. Every time I cast Dream Control, that dream becomes a story printed in my body. The book has become so dense that I no longer have internal organs. From the inside out, I'm all book. It's kind of good because I don't have to eat or drink anymore, and my book-shaped body helped me get a job at the spell shop down the street, but without muscles I have a hard time getting around. I also have to watch out for water damage."

Zach couldn't imagine what it would have been like to have a book body. His pages would probably blow everywhere in the wind. Just a little water and he'd turn to a wrinkled soggy mess. Although he liked the idea of the Dream Control spell, he couldn't believe someone would continue to cast that spell knowing what would ultimately happen to them.

Dennis interrupted the kid, "Why don't you get to the point of how you keep casting your bullshit spell on us?"

"Dennis, please don't speak out of turn," said Father Harry.

"I'd have more sympathy for this hipster prick if he just cast it on himself." Dennis flexed his computerized muscles as he spoke. "But I'm sick of him making me dream his stupid fucking stories."

"I understand your concern," Harry said. "Let's just hear him out."

The kid took a while to continue.

"I'm sorry," Christian said, his paper skin turning red. "It's not my fault. I thought you'd like my dreams."

"How the hell could I like that garbage?" Dennis said. "The last one you gave me was just two people talking about their fucking boring lives while the furniture grew arms and played violin music in the background."

"You missed the subtext," Christian said. "There are many layers to my stories."

"But your stories suck."

"They *don't* suck. They just go over your head."

"Then why do you keep forcing me to dream them?"

Christian didn't like hearing negative feedback when it came to his art. He was so flustered that he almost broke into tears, but tried his hardest not to cry. If he cried, the tears would melt his paper skin.

"You don't understand…" Christian said. He turned to Harry. "Writing was my life before I came to Hell's Bottom. Without my art, I'm nothing. And since there're no fiction publications here, I'm not able to write anything that anyone will ever read. The only way people can experience my stories is if I cast my magic and control their dreams. I don't care if it mutates me. I'm willing to suffer for my art."

"But your stories suck," Dennis said. "Maybe if you added an actual plot to your stories they wouldn't piss us off so much."

Christian went silent again. The truth is he knew he wasn't the greatest writer in the world, but he thought he had the potential to one day be great. He just knew there was something special about him. If only he practiced and worked on his craft as hard as he could, eventually he would become a legend. But once Christian ended up in Hell's Bottom, he knew there was no hope. He thought his life was over. He'd never become the writer he wanted to be.

"I know I shouldn't do it," Christian said. "I know it's an invasion of your privacy and I know that it's destroying my body. But creating dreams for other people is the only thing that's kept me going all this time." He couldn't resist crying this time. The tears wrinkled his paper cheeks and the tips of his fingers as he wiped them away. "If it weren't for this magic I would have killed myself by now."

Harry handed him tissues to absorb his tears so that he wouldn't have to use his paper hands. "But if it weren't for the magic you wouldn't be in this situation in the first place. Casting isn't going to take your problems away. It only makes them worse."

"Then what do you want me to do? You want me to kill myself?"

"There are other ways you can create stories besides controlling dreams," Harry said. "Have you given more thought into the idea of starting a Hell's Bottom literary journal? You're not the only person in this community who likes to read and write stories."

Christian shrugged. "Yeah, but I don't know how to do that. How would I even get it printed?"

"Talk to the guy who runs the newsletter," Harry said. "He'd surely help you out."

"That guy's a jerk. I asked him to publish one of my stories in his newsletter once and he wouldn't even read it."

"But people don't read the newsletter for fiction, they read it for news. Talk to him about creating a literary version and he might help you out."

"But he's a pretentious asshole with a huge ego."

"So he's exactly like you?" Dennis said, chuckling to himself.

Harry glared at the computer man. "Dennis, since you like talking so much why don't you go next?"

"No, thanks," Dennis said, slinking in his chair.

"I insist," Harry said.

"My name's Dennis Ferreira," said the computer-skinned man. "I'm addicted to a spell called Electronic Telepathy. Basically, I'm able to speak to electronic machines, specifically computers. Before I came to Hell's Bottom, I learned the spell from my brother but who knows who he learned it from. Probably some tranny he was fucking. He died two months after he taught me the spell. I'm not sure what happened to him. They found his body behind some dumpster with a crowbar stuck in his head."

Dennis spoke the words as if they were matter of fact, acting out the motion of shoving a crowbar through a person's skull.

"The spell didn't really do much for me at first, outside of let me go on porn sites without paying for them," Dennis continued. "But then I realized just how powerful the magic was. I learned that I could talk to ATM machines and have them give me money without using a card. I could go online and access other people's bank accounts. For two years, I was rolling in dough. I was set for life. My wife quit her day job. My little girl was six years old and already had a college fund.

"We used to be strapped for cash. My car never worked. We couldn't afford heating in the winter. My little girl never even got a toy that didn't come from the Goodwill until I started casting."

Dennis stared off into space for a moment as a smile grew across the circuits on his cheeks.

Then he continued, "You should have seen the look on her face that first Christmas, when she actually got everything on her list. A new bike? Bam. It was hers, with a fresh custom hot pink paint job just as she wanted. Monster High Dolls? She got every single doll they made, even the rare collectible ones. A toy piano? I gave her a *real* piano, a baby grand just like you see in rich people houses. I'm telling you that Christmas morning had to be the highlight of my entire life. After disappointing my family time and time again, I was actually able to do something for them, you know? I was able to make them happy for a change."

Zach assumed the guy was an asshole by the way he treated the writer kid, but he suddenly felt sorry for him. He didn't realize the guy had family. It was hard for Zach dealing with the fact that he'd never see his mother or father ever again, but he couldn't imagine what it would be like to also be separated from a wife and child.

"But it wasn't worth it, of course," Dennis said. "Eventually, I cared more about buying stuff for myself than buying stuff for my family. I got myself a nice car, some sweet threads. I had women crawling off my nuts night after night. When my wife left me, I couldn't really blame her. I deserved it. The worst part was that I didn't even care. I figured I'd eventually be able to make it right with her, after I was done having my fun. But then it was too late. I disappeared and never saw them again."

Zach changed his mind. He decided he didn't like the guy after all.

"In Hell's Bottom, things weren't easy for me. They don't have ATMs here, so I wasn't able to get free money. In fact, with so few electronics my magic hardly has much use at all. But I am able to connect to the internet…"

Zach's eyes widened when he heard him say that last line. He hadn't heard of anyone getting on the internet in Hell's Bottom before.

"I'm able to pick up wireless networks in my brain. That's

when I really became addicted to casting. I always heard about people getting addicted to the internet but I didn't understand that at all until I came to Hell's Bottom. For the first few years I was here, that's all I did. I just read everything I could find online, reading news articles, checking out my old friends' Facebook profiles to see what they were up to. It was the only connection I had with the real world and I just couldn't stop."

Zach couldn't believe anyone had such a power. What he wouldn't give to go on the internet from Hell's Bottom. All the people he would contact, all the things he would do...

"Of course, I tried to get a hold of my ex-wife. She wouldn't respond to my emails. She never liked communicating through email anyway. She preferred talking on the phone or meeting in person. I wanted to tell her about what happened to me but I *knew* she wouldn't believe me. I knew it would only piss her off more."

If Dennis could write emails, Zach wondered if he'd write an email for him. There's so much he wanted to tell his parents. He'd pay anything for that.

"The longest I've ever gone without casting was 70 days," Dennis said. "This was almost a year ago. I probably would have quit completely, but then I got the email... It was from my daughter..." The big man had to pause for a moment. "I forgot how quickly that girl grows. She's ten now, old enough to go online without her mother's permission. I'm not sure if she got my email address from her mother or figured it out on her own. That girl was always smart. Much smarter than me."

Dennis was crying now. Zach didn't realize it at first, because you couldn't tell in his voice. He still spoke in that calm matter-of-fact way, even with the tears on his cheeks.

"When I read it, the thing broke my heart in two," Dennis continued. "*When are you coming home, Daddy?* That's all it said. No subject line. No signature. Just... *when are you coming home?* As if she didn't even know her mother and I were split up, as if this whole time she'd been expecting me to show up at the door and say, 'Sorry I'm late, sweetheart. I had a lot of overtime I had to do at work.' I mean..." He paused to rub his eyes. The water was causing his circuits to short. "I assumed she'd gotten over me years ago, before I even came to Hell's Bottom. I had no idea… She hasn't even begun to get over me yet. She's still waiting for her father to come home so she can get on with her life.

"Ever since then, I've been going online almost every day. Sometimes multiple times a day. And I just reread that message. *When are you coming home, Daddy?* I just read and reread those words, wondering if I should respond. And if I do respond, what should I say? I want so much to be a part of her life again, but I can't. I live here, in Hell's Bottom. We're not in the same world anymore. Would it help her if I were to send her messages? All I can do is write her. What would I do if she asked to see me, if she wanted me to be a part of her life again? I'd have to tell her I couldn't. Would that make her feel worse than not knowing what happened to me at all? Would she believe me if I told her I loved her after I refused to ever see her again?

"I've spent months trying to come up with a lie, with some kind of excuse that would make it okay for me to never see her again. I thought of pretending I was in another country. I even thought about pretending I was living in Antarctica or deep in the Amazon jungle, where she'd never be able to come visit. But how long could that lie last?

"The truth is, deep down I know that what's best for her would be to forget about me and move on as if I were dead. Maybe there's some other father figure who could give her what she truly needs from me, what I'm not able to give. She doesn't really need me. But the problem is *I* need her. *I* need her to tell me about everything in her life that I'm missing out on. *I* need for her to understand that it's not my fault I'm unable to be with her, even if that's a total lie. *I* need some kind of connection to her, because she's the only part of my life that actually means anything to me anymore."

The cat woman next to Dennis hugged him tight to her fuzzy body. Zach could tell she was also a mother who probably lost her children when she came to Hell's Bottom. In fact, a lot of people in the room seemed like they could relate.

"But I don't know what to do. I can't make up my mind. I just cast my spell and go online and reread that message over and over again. *When are you coming home, Daddy?* The words haunt me."

Dennis sat up straight and shook off his tears.

"So how long has it been since you last cast?" Harry asked.

"It's been four days," Dennis said. "I mean, after today it will be four."

"That's the longest you've gone since the email, isn't that right?" Harry asked.

Dennis nodded his head.

"Good job," Harry said with a smile.

The cat woman patted him on the back and whispered, "I'm so proud of you."

Zach didn't get it. He didn't know why the guy didn't just email his kid. That's what he would do in his situation, without hesitation. At least one last goodbye letter would have been enough. If he were the guy's kid he would have wanted to know what happened to his dad no matter how hard it was to hear, even if it was just to tell him he'd never see him ever again.

"So who's next?" Harry asked the group.

The plant woman jumped from her chair with her green arm raised as high as it could go. "Me! I'm dying to go! I've been waiting forever!"

The bees collecting pollen from the flowers on her body buzzed around her face as she hopped up and down.

"My name's Janie, but everybody calls me Nymph because you know I look like a forest nymph. Obviously."

The plant woman couldn't stop smiling. Her crazy eyes darted around the room, looking at each and every person individually as she spoke.

"I'm not really an addict, but my uncle makes me come here because he thinks I have a problem, but I *don't* have a problem at all. I just *like* casting, more than anything. The spell

I know is called Plant Growth, but I like to call it Green Love, you know? Because I love Mother Earth. That's why I cast. I like to go out into the woods and just cast all day, growing trees from little saplings to massive three-hundred-year-old oaks in the blink of an eye. There's something about pouring my essence into nature and watching it sprout and flourish around me. It electrifies my soul, you know?"

As the plant woman spoke, she rubbed her knees and tapped her feet lightning-fast. Zach could actually hear her grinding her teeth whenever she paused.

"Our planet's filled with so much love for us," she continued. "I don't know why people don't see that. I mean, if you just open your eyes… *Hello? Mother Earth calling, anybody home?*" She paused to giggle at herself. "Look at all the fruit and sunshine and beauty there is in the world. That's our planet expressing her love for us. No matter how selfish Man is, no matter how much we screw up the environment, she still loves us, unconditionally. Just like any mother would."

Some of the other people in the room seemed annoyed by Janie. Maybe it was because she had such a neurotic personality type or maybe they just didn't like how positive she was about casting while so many of their lives were ruined by it.

"That's why I cast. I want to show her my love. You know? I want to give back and make up for all the damage my kind has caused her. I'm going to save the world with my magic, I swear. I don't care that the magic changes my body. I think I look *beautiful*. I *hope* one day I completely transform into a tree and become one with nature. That only makes me want to cast even more."

Zach was getting bored with listening to the plant woman speak. He zoned her out and looked over at Mia, trying to make eye contact with her. She still didn't notice him.

"I feel like my life is going perfectly right now. Now that I fixed my bike, I'm getting a lot of exercise. I'm getting out of Hell's Bottom and going to the woods on a daily basis. It's so beautiful going to the woods in our dimension, because there're no people around to ruin it. I feel like I have the whole world to myself."

Trying to get noticed, Zach coughed and cleared his throat a couple of times. A few people looked over at him, but not Mia.

"I'm also really excited because I'm going to meet my soulmate tomorrow. That's what the stars told me. They said that tomorrow I'll meet the one I'll spend the rest of my life with. I can't wait to see who it is. He's going to be perfect. Obviously. If he doesn't know Green Love already, which he probably does, I'll just teach it to him. Then we can cast together every day. And eventually our bodies will grow together like vines and we'll become one massive tree in the heart of the forest. It's going to be beautiful. I swear. Just beautiful."

A woman with black and yellow striped skin and insect wings walked through the door and hid in the back of the room. She had guilt written all over her face, and it had nothing to do with the fact that she was running late.

"Bee, how have you been?" Harry asked the bee woman. "Come closer. Get involved. We haven't seen you in months."

Bee went to the circle and sat down in the empty seat next to Zach. Her wings fluttered in his face. He jerked as the wings tickled him, but she didn't seem to notice.

"I was worried about you," Harry said.

Bee just shrugged. She seemed obviously shaken up by something.

"I've been busy," she said. "That serial killer is still on the loose."

"Yes, yes," Harry said. "It's very unfortunate. While we're already talking to you, why don't you go next?"

"I don't know…" Bee said.

"Come on, Bee. We haven't heard from you in ages."

Bee was twitching, her wings buzzing like electricity. Being allergic to bees, Zach felt extremely uncomfortable sitting next to her. He wondered if his whole body would swell to the size of a wrecking ball if she stung him.

"My name's Bee." She paused for a moment to look back at the door. By the look on her face, it seemed like she thought she was being followed. "I don't like to talk about the spell I'm addicted to."

"You always neglect to tell us your spell, Bee," Harry said. "Hiding it only makes the hungry bug stronger."

"I'm sorry…" Bee shook her head. "I can't tell you. If you force me to tell you I'll just walk out that door and never come back again."

Harry raised his hands in defeat and let her continue.

"So this spell I'm addicted to…" Bee said, and then she thought about it for a minute. "Though I can't tell you what it is, I'll tell you this… My spell hurts people. In a bad way. A really bad way.

"For me, the hungry bug is alive. She's a real being that lives inside of me and completely takes over my body. I become something else when she takes control—a predator. A vampire who feeds on the life-force of young virgins."

Her eyes glazed over for a moment and her voice became low and grumbly.

"I become a hungry, hungry…buggy…"

Then she snapped out of it.

"I don't know how to control it," she said. "Yesterday, I used it on this man. This sweet, innocent man."

"What happened to him?" Father Harry asked.

Bee shrugged. "He's still alive… Mostly."

Zach then realized that many of the people in the room were absolutely terrified of the bee woman. He wondered what kind of magic she cast. He wondered if she was dangerous.

"It mostly happens when I'm sexually stimulated," Bee said. "Or really drunk. Or both. I want to stop. I *need* to stop. But it really isn't me when the bug takes over. How can I stop casting this spell if I'm not even able to control my own body anymore?"

"Maybe you shouldn't get so carried away with drinking and intercourse," the priest said.

"It's easy for you to say, Harry," Bee said. "But there's not much left in Hell's Bottom that makes life worth living. If I abstained from both sex and alcohol I'd have to shoot myself."

"But what about your victims?" Harry asked. "You cast on them when you're drunk and aroused. Do you warn them of the risk of doing these things with you?"

Bee shrugged. "I don't always cast on the people I get intimate with. It just happens sometimes. Half the time it happens when I'm not even with anyone. I could get turned on in my sleep and the hungry bug takes over my body. Before I regain consciousness, the bug will go out in the streets and hunt down some poor guy unlucky enough to cross paths with her. How do I stop something like that?"

"Maybe you should check into the institution," Harry said. "They'll do what they can to help you and you won't have to hurt anyone anymore."

Bee shook her head. "I feel bad for the people I harm, but I don't kill them. They're still perfectly fine. I'd rather fight the hungry bug on my own terms and try my hardest not to allow any more occurrences like the one from last night."

"Do you think that will work?"

"It has to," Bee said. "That institution is a pit. I'd rather die than go there. I'd sooner give up sex."

There was a pause. Bee didn't have anything more to say, but Harry wasn't through with her. She seemed as if she were Harry's special project... the real serious case that needed more attention than anyone else.

"You should start coming regularly, Bee," Harry said. "I think these meetings are exactly what you need."

The bee woman looked away from the priest and fluttered her wings in Zach's face. Then she lit a cigarette and stared Harry in the eyes until he turned his attention to somebody else.

While the priest called on the woman with the lizard skin to talk, Zach wondered if the touch of a bee wing against his lips would produce an allergic reaction. If so, he wondered if it would be fatal. His mouth was already starting to feel kind of itchy.

Scratching his mouth and leaning far away from the bee woman next to him, Zach waited for a break so he could get up and switch seats. But a break never seemed to come. People got up and went to the bathroom whenever they wanted, or poured themselves coffee whenever they needed caffeine. But the session continued nonstop.

The stories were getting so depressing that Zach started tuning them out. Some teenage girl told the story of how she accidentally cast her mother out of existence, an old lady explained her obsession with casting invisibility so that she could spy on other people's intimate conversations, a fat socially awkward guy explained how he was addicted to charm magic that compelled women go to bed with him yet he had no idea that what he was doing was basically rape. Zach couldn't relate to any of these people. He wasn't an addict himself, so their problems seemed ridiculous. He just wanted to tell them, "You want to stop casting? Then just stop. Learn some self control. It's that easy."

Then it was Mia's turn to speak and Zach sat up attentively. He hoped she would finally notice him as she spoke to the crowd.

"My name's Lisa and I'm addicted to a spell called Transfer Object," Mia said.

Zach wondered why she used the name Lisa instead of Mia. Maybe Lisa was an alias. Maybe she didn't want people to know her real name for some reason. Or maybe Lisa was her real name and Mia was the alias.

"I've gone two days without casting," she said. "Before that I had fifty days." She looked down and shook her head. "I can't believe myself... The last time I promised I'd never give in to the hungry bug again. But I couldn't help it." She broke into tears. "I'm such a horrible person..."

Zach felt so sorry for her. He knew she couldn't possibly be a horrible person. He saw the way she smiled in the hallway each morning, the way her eyes were so full of life. Those were not the expressions of a loathsome person. But standing there in front of him, she seemed like a person who loathed herself to the core. She appeared so exhausted, so depressed. Even the tone of her voice was a deep melancholy drawl instead of the perky squeaky voice he grew to love. It was as though she were a completely different person when she came to these meetings.

She composed herself and continued, "Before I came to Hell's Bottom I was a total kleptomaniac. With my spell, I can teleport any object in sight to any location of my choosing. I used to go to the mall and teleport things into my backpack. I didn't even have to go inside the store. I could just walk past windows. It was so easy…"

Zach didn't think that was so bad. So what if she stole from stores. He would have done the same thing in her shoes. She shouldn't beat herself up over stealing simple items from corporate mall stores.

"I wasn't really hurting anyone, so I figured *why not?* It was thrilling and there were so many things I wanted that I normally couldn't afford. I could wear any clothes or any shoes I wanted. But after a while, I didn't care about that stuff anymore. I could never have what I *really* wanted. I could never have a baby."

Mia looked directly at Zach and he smiled at her, half-waving his hand to get her attention. She broke eye contact the second he tried to signal her.

"The doctors said I wasn't able to have children and I guess it made me go a little crazy. When I learned that my spell could teleport a pregnant woman's fetus into my own womb, I thought I'd found the answer to my problem. I thought I found a way to have children. If I couldn't make a baby myself I could just take somebody else's. That's when the hungry bug hit me the hardest."

Zach was still smiling and trying to signal Mia. Then he paused for a moment once Mia's words processed through his head… *Did she just say she was addicted to stealing unborn babies?*

"I thought of all sorts of reasons to justify my actions. Those women were fertile. They could make more babies whenever they wanted, but not me. I *needed* their baby… *way* more than they did."

That's when it dawned on Zach that the girl he had a crush on was completely insane. She was the most fucked up person in the whole bunch of them, even more fucked up than that crazy plant chick.

"I still have nightmares about the first time I stole a fetus," she said. "The woman's scream was so piercing. She was absolutely horrified. I thought I'd be so happy the moment the fetus entered my womb, but I wasn't at all. There was so much pain… The thing felt like an explosion went off inside of me. My skin split open, creating stretch marks so deep they bled. Who knows what kind of damage it did to my insides. My whole system went into shock. But the physical pain wasn't the worst part. What I'm haunted by was the moment I looked into the woman's eyes and saw her soul crushed into tiny little pieces. I realized I had just done the worst thing I possibly could have done to another human being. I teleported the fetus back to her and ran home."

Zach didn't want to hear anymore. He just wanted to leave. This woman was a freak and he wanted nothing to do with her.

"After that, I vowed to never do it again. But that only lasted about a month. As I said, I was a klepto. I couldn't control myself. The next time I did it was the thing I regret most. I teleported the baby into me and ran away before I could see the woman's face or hear the woman's cries. I went home eight months pregnant, rubbing the new life inside of my belly. It was such a nice feeling I never wanted it to end. But by the time the sun went down, I was sick to my stomach. The baby inside of me was kicking like crazy. It was like he was rejecting me, totally aware that I wasn't his real mom. I didn't get a good look at the woman so I didn't know how to return the baby to her. I searched the hospitals and read the newspaper. There was nothing about a woman miraculously losing her fetus. I didn't know what to do. I couldn't keep it. I couldn't raise the baby as my own, knowing I stole it from his mother. I'd never be able to look him in the eyes… So I solved the problem the only

172

way I knew how… I teleported the baby into another woman's womb.

"For a while, I thought I did the right thing. But I have no idea what happened to the baby. The woman might not have ever wanted children. I wondered if she thought the baby was a miraculous conception, like the second coming of Christ, or maybe she thought it was some kind of demon or alien baby. My actions probably destroyed the lives of everyone involved, including the families of the mothers. I've never been so ashamed.

"I gave up on the idea of having a baby of my own, but that didn't stop me from casting my spell. I started teleporting fetuses into me for just a few minutes at a time, just to feel the child inside of me, just to pretend that I was pregnant if only for a little while. It didn't hurt the babies. It didn't hurt the mothers. It just gave them a little scare and then everything was back to normal, and I got to be a mother for a brief moment. I knew what I was doing was wrong, but I couldn't stop doing it. I didn't even call what I was doing *stealing* anymore. I was just *borrowing*. In my mind, it was no different than holding another woman's baby for a while.

"This went on for about a year until I came to Hell's Bottom. The shock of coming here kept me from casting for a short period of time, but the hungry bug crept up on me once again. Some people still get pregnant here, if their bodies haven't mutated too badly, so I still found fetuses to borrow. Then I had the delusion that if I kept stealing enough fetuses eventually I might transform into an actual pregnant woman, but that's not been the case. Beneath the clothes, my body has been mutating into a machine—a hospital incubator. Being unable to have children I felt like I wasn't entirely a woman. Now I don't have breasts or a vagina because of my incubator body. I'm not a woman at all anymore. Not only will I never have a child, because of my casting I'll never have a husband either…

"A few days ago, I was feeling lonely and depressed. Well, I'm *always* lonely and depressed but this time was even worse than usual. I wasn't planning on casting that day… it just sort of happened. I gave the fetus right back, though. It wasn't even in me for more than a minute. Still, I'm utterly ashamed of myself for it. The woman could tell it was me right away and nearly turned me into a frog as payback. I kind of wish she did. At least that would stop me from casting."

When Mia or Lisa or whatever her name was finally finished speaking, Zach could hardly believe this was the woman he'd been lusting after for so many months. He suddenly realized she wasn't attractive to him at all anymore. There was no excuse for her behavior. She didn't suffer from any addiction; she was just a horrible person who didn't care who she screwed over. Why didn't she just adopt a child? Why didn't she become a foster mother? It was obvious why—she was selfish. She wanted to give birth to her *own* child, even if it originated from someone else's womb. She was just a despicable, wretched excuse for a human being.

These thoughts raced through Zach's mind. All of this was too much for him. He stood up, ready to leave the room.

"You," Father Harry said, pointing at Zach. "Why don't you speak next. We haven't heard from a newcomer yet."

Zach froze in his place, then turned his head slowly to the priest. He wanted to bolt for the door, but with all the eyes on him he couldn't find the courage to run away. He found himself sitting back down in the chair, trying to figure out what he should tell them. At first he was going to lie, come up with a problem that people would empathize with, so that Mia would feel for him. Now that he doesn't have a girl to impress he decided to just go ahead and speak his mind.

"My name is Zach," he told them in an annoyed tone of voice. "And… I don't know why I'm here, really. I guess I was just bored and decided to show up. I'm not an addict. Look at me. You can't even tell I've mutated at all, unlike most of you. I don't know how any of you even became addicts in the first place. It seems so easy to me... If you don't want to cast then don't do it. All you need is a little self-control. "

Zach was expecting everyone to be offended by his words, but nobody gave him any dirty looks. Not even Dennis. They just listened with open ears.

"I don't just cast one spell. I know a lot of spells. I only use them when I really need them. Before I came to Hell's Bottom, I dated this goth chick who taught me these spells. She was obsessed with me. For some reason, goth girls were always obsessed with me even though I wasn't into that scene myself and they weren't really my type. Still, they were easy for me to get so almost every girl I ever dated was goth.

"She said she was descended from a long line of witches, if you can believe that. It could have been the truth. I mean, if magic exists then witches were probably real as well, weren't they? She had this old spell book she claimed was bound in human skin. My head nearly exploded when she cast that first spell and made us fly. It was so exhilarating and so... well, *magical* I guess. Once our relationship was serious she taught me some spells. She warned me not to cast any spell too many times or there would be major consequences. But being hardheaded, I didn't believe her. I cast the spells all the time. Then I woke up one day to find everything in the world had disappeared. I thought I was the last man on Earth.

"Maybe I went overboard a little before I came to Hell's Bottom, but I've still never been addicted. When I need money, I cast a spell that transforms pieces of paper into bills. I haven't needed a job in a couple years now. I'm also able to turn water into wine like I'm Jesus or something. I don't need to go to a bar to drink. I've got wine on tap in my apartment. I can also turn rocks into meat and wood into bread, so I can survive practically anywhere. They're useful spells, but there's nothing addicting about them. I only cast them when I need to eat or want to get drunk or have to pay for something. That's all.

"Sure, I guess I use my magic almost every day, but only because I have to eat every day. It's a lot easier than trying to find work around here. I had enough trouble trying to find employment back in the real world, but here it's virtually impossible, especially for somebody with no practical skills."

Zach paused for a moment to see everyone staring at him, just nodding their heads at every word he said. He didn't know what to say next, so he just kept talking, saying whatever came to his mind.

"I guess I cast more spells than just the ones I mentioned. Personal Illusion is one that I cast sometimes. It allows me to project my thoughts into a room like a movie… although I'm the only person who can see it. Still, it's a fun spell. Since there's no television in Hell's Bottom, I'll sometimes cast Illusion to amuse myself. Any movie I remember clearly enough I can watch in real 3-D. It's the best cinematic experience you'll ever get. And the spell can create porn that's a hundred times better than anything you'd watch back in the real world, I'll tell you that. It's like I've got a personal holosuite from Star Trek."

A few people laughed at the comment. He was surprised when even the old cat lady cracked a smile.

"I also cast that spell when I'm feeling lonely and don't have anyone to talk to. Sometimes I'll create an illusion of my parents or my friends I left behind. It really helps me cope with the fact that I'll never see them again. I don't really know anyone in Hell's Bottom. I don't have any close friends. So it's good that I can cast this spell whenever I have to. It's the best cure for loneliness I've ever had.

"Maybe I do cast on a regular basis, but I don't have a problem or anything. My life hasn't been ruined by magic. My life is just fine. I'm happy. I don't have any worries. I don't have to work. I don't have to leave my apartment at all anymore if I don't want to. In fact, I usually just sit in my room all day, drinking wine and hanging out with illusions of my old friends. It's fun.

"I can easily quit casting if I wanted to. You know, if I didn't need the magic anymore. I'm sure someday somebody will give me a job and I'll have real non-illusionary friends I can hang out with. Then I won't need to cast. But until then, I'll keep casting. You know, out of necessity…"

Then Zach just stopped talking. People kept staring at him, but he didn't know what else to say. He just shrugged. The expressions on their faces were as if they felt sorry for him, but he didn't understand why they were reacting that way. *They* were the addicts, not him.

Zach felt incredibly embarrassed after speaking and just wanted to leave the room. He stood up and aimed for the door.

Then Harry said, "Mia, we haven't heard from you today. You should go next."

Mia? Zach's ears perked up. He thought Mia called herself Lisa in this group. He wondered if it was just a coincidence that there were two Mias.

"Okay, I'll go," she said.

The girl named Mia spoke in a cute squeaky voice. It sounded exactly like the Mia he knew who lived across the hall. Only she didn't look like Mia. She looked like somebody else entirely. She was Latina with short dark hair.

"I'm Mia and I'm addicted to a spell called Mimic," Mia said.

Zach sat back down in his seat and stared carefully at the woman. Her voice was identical to the girl across the hall. While examining her carefully, he realized she also had the same eyes. Those deep brown eyes that made him weak in the knees, they were hers.

"I have the ability to physically turn myself into anyone I meet," Mia said. "I can't change my voice or my eyes, but other than that I can become anyone I want. All I need is to shake somebody's hand once and I'll always be able to turn into them."

Zach couldn't believe it. This woman really was the Mia that he knew. The other Mia was just some girl named Lisa that Mia must have mimicked. *His* Mia wasn't a baby-stealing freak after all. She was a shapeshifter.

"I don't cast very often. The good thing about my spell is

that once I cast it I'm able to remain in that body indefinitely. Sometimes I'll go a year or two without casting at all. But I do have an addiction to the magic. I can't undo the spell. I can't go back to being the real me.

"The first time I cast the spell was when I was fourteen. I was a late bloomer. I was flat-chested, my face was covered in zits, I was short and so skinny. People called me *Gelfling* back then because they said I looked like those elf-like Muppets from *The Dark Crystal*. When I learned the spell, I immediately transformed myself into Cindy Hanna. She was a senior and the most beautiful girl in school. I couldn't stay in my hometown because there already was a Cindy Hanna, so I ran away from home and started a new life for myself. But it was hard getting work so I transformed myself into a beautiful woman in her thirties that I met on a bus. Then suddenly I was a fourteen-year-old girl in a thirty-year-old body with a fulltime job, an apartment, and a steady boyfriend. Not bad for the creepy Gelfling that nobody would even talk to in high school.

"Whenever I got bored with a body, I'd switch it out for a better one and start a new life. It was pretty fun while it lasted, but then I cast the spell too many times and ended up here in Hell's Bottom.

"The biggest problem with my addiction is that I have no sense of self. The older I get, the more I realize that I'm not me. The real Mia does not exist. I'm just a series of temporary copies of other people. I've tried transforming back into my real self, but I just turn into that zit-faced fourteen-year-old girl again. That's not the real me either. I'm in my mid-twenties now, not an awkward teenager. But I have no idea what my original body would have looked like at age twenty-four, so I'm unable to transform into that person. That person never came to be.

"But I want to quit casting. I want to choose one body and stick with it, even if it's somebody else's."

Mia looked at Zach and their eyes connected. She blushed and diverted her sight as a smile crept on her face.

"There's this guy I like in my apartment building," she said. "He lives across the hall. I liked him for a whole year, but I couldn't get him to pay attention to me. Every week, I tried out a new body for him. I tried tall blonds with big boobs, redheads with freckles, Asian girls, tattooed punk rock chicks, but nothing seemed to get his attention. He didn't seem to care about any of the girls I transformed into."

Zach couldn't believe it. She had to have been talking about him. Once her eyes caught his attention again and a smile crept onto her face, he was sure of it.

"But for the last few months, one body I started mimicking has captured his attention. I could tell he liked her by the way he looked at her. She's kind of short and really cute, and I can tell why he's attracted to her. So I've kept it up. I've transformed into her as much as possible. It's been really fun. Her body feels right on me.

"I wasn't a hundred percent sure he liked me though, until today. I'm hoping he'll go out with me tonight, sometime after the meeting. That is, if he isn't too busy hiding in his apartment drinking wine and casting illusions to keep him company."

All eyes turned to Zach and his face went red. Everyone was giggling and smiling. He felt like the butt of a joke, but he was still thrilled by her words. He had no idea that Mia, *his* Mia, liked him the whole time.

"So I think I've finally found the one. I've finally found the body I want to be in for the rest of my life, so I can give up casting this spell once and for all. Who knows if it'll work out with this guy or not, but even if it doesn't I still want to keep this body. That is, if the owner doesn't mind…"

Mia looked at Lisa, raising her eyebrows as if asking a question.

Lisa shrugged. "Sure, use it all you want. It looks better on you anyway. You don't have the damn incubator parts when you use it."

Zach was surprised that Lisa already knew Mia had been mimicking her body. It seemed like something a normal person would hide. But for Mia it seemed normal to be honest about it, as if she were an abnormally open person.

After the meeting was over, Mia transformed from the Latina girl into the Lisa-clone that Zach had been crushing on for months.

"Do you need a sponsor?" Mia asked Zach as she approached him. "I know you're not *addicted* to spell casting, but maybe you might want to try hanging out with some non-illusionary people for a change."

Zach nodded. "Sure. I think I can cut back a little."

When Mia smiled, those cute dimples appeared on her cheeks. They made Zach's heart melt in his chest. Standing side by side with Lisa, the two women did not look at all alike even though one was a copy of the other. The original was hideous and the copy was beautiful. Zach had no idea that personality could have that much of an effect on beauty—not just inner beauty, but outer beauty as well.

Everyone came and said hi to Mia and Zach as they went out the door, as if congratulating them even though they still hardly knew each other. The two of them were treated almost like celebrities that night.

As Dennis was passing them, he went to Mia and said, "Did you tell this guy about the time you transformed into *him* and jerked off in front of a mirror?"

Mia's smile disappeared and her mouth dropped open, as Dennis laughed and walked away. She looked at Zach with embarrassment written all over her face.

"That did not happen," she told Zach. "I swear."

DEBT
COLLECTORS

"Where the fuck did he just go?" Frank the Head yelled at the empty space in front of him.

Odd Carl had no idea. One minute, Mike the Douchebag was standing there holding his briefcase full of cash, waiting for Frank to roll the monopoly dice. Then the next minute, he was gone.

"Did that piece of shit just disappear into thin air?"

Odd Carl shrugged his bulbous shoulders. He knew only as much as his boss.

"Did he get raptured? Is it the douchebag rapture today or something?" Frank was confused, and confusion pissed him off. "I'm gonna kill that son of a bitch."

Odd Carl looked around the room. There was no logical explanation for what had just occurred.

Frank got his gun. "Think you can disappear on me, you prick? I'll show you a disappearing act…"

"Are we going after him?" Odd Carl asked, as Frank tossed him the car keys.

"What do you think?"

Frank turned to Jesus. The old Hispanic guy looked like he'd just seen a ghost. "Hold down the fort until we get back."

"But wait…" Carl said. "What if he has other powers we don't know about?"

"What, you think he's Harry Potter now?" Frank led Carl out the door. "He's Mike the Douchebag. He's got only one power, and that's the power to give me a fucking headache."

"But he's going to be hard to find if he can disappear like that."

"That's why we're not going after Mr. Douchebag. We're

going to pay a visit to his family. He'll have to come to us."

When they got into the black Oldsmobile, Frank the Head put Mike's home address into his GPS. He was an asshole with very little patience, but Frank wasn't called *the Head* for nothing. His organization skills and record keeping ability were first class, and he had pages of notes on everyone he did business with, including Mike the Douchebag. Frank knew where he lived, the license on the car he drove, where his wife worked, where his stepdaughter went to school. He was always ready.

"If we're lucky we'll get to the family before Mike does," Frank said.

As soon as they pulled out of the garage, Odd Carl reached into his knapsack where he kept his sawed-off shotgun and took out some knitting supplies. He held the orange and brown balls of yarn between his massive thighs, pushed his glasses up on his face, and got to work with one needle in each hand.

Frank looked down at Carl's lap. Then back on the road. Then back at Carl's lap. Carl licked the tip of a frayed string of yarn.

"Are you fucking knitting?"

"I'm trying to," said Odd Carl. "The road's a little bumpy though."

"You want me to drive smoother for you, Martha Stewart?"

"I'll be fine."

Frank couldn't take his eyes off the knitting supplies.

"Are you going to explain to me why the toughest bastard in my employ is knitting a goddamn sweater instead of loading his fucking shotgun?"

"It's a dog sweater," said Odd Carl. "For Snacks, my mom's Scottish Terrier." Carl held up the tiny sweater. "She likes to dress him up sometimes."

"Well, do you have to do it now? Couldn't you just knit in the privacy of your own home and never tell anybody else about it, ever?"

Odd Carl shrugged. "I've got to get it done by my birthday tomorrow. It's a present."

"Wait a minute…" Frank's head was beginning to hurt. "You're making a present for your mom's dog to give to the thing on your own birthday?"

"The present's not for the dog, it's for my mom. I'm getting the dog a chew toy."

"I don't think you get the gist of what I'm saying. It's *your* birthday. People are supposed to give *you* presents. Why are you making a present for your mom?"

Carl focused on finishing the row he was knitting before he responded. "That's just how I was raised. My birthday's never really been about me. It's more about her. She thinks of it as a celebration of the day she gave birth to me."

"So she conned you out of your birthday so she could have two Mother's Days?"

"No, it's about both of us, not totally about her," Carl said. "We exchange presents. She chooses dinner and I choose dessert. But my birthday's always been far more important to her than it is to me."

"You fucking momma's boy."

"I'm not a momma's boy. I just love and respect my mom."

"Momma's boy."

"You wouldn't understand. I mean, didn't you kill your mom for her life insurance policy?"

"Hey, I loved my momma, too," Frank said. "She was a saint and raised me right." Frank took a left turn, nearly knocking all of Carl's knitting supplies on the floor. "She just made the mistake of telling me how much I'd get if anything were to happen to her. The temptation was just too great."

Carl straightened the dog sweater and continued knitting.

"That's cold, Boss."

"I don't regret it. I don't regret nothing." Frank kept a look out for Mike Heffington's place as he turned into the neighborhood. "I do miss her though."

The Heffington family was about to leave their garage when Frank the Head and Odd Carl arrived at the house.

"There they are," Frank yelled.

"Pull in behind them," Odd Carl said, removing his shotgun from his knitting knapsack.

Before Mrs. Heffington could pull out of the driveway, Frank parked the Oldsmobile behind her, blocking the exit. The two men leapt from the vehicle with their guns raised.

"Out of the car," Frank yelled at the woman behind the wheel. He pointed his .38 at the driver's side window.

"What do you want?" the woman asked, more surprised than scared.

There were two kids in the backseat. A boy and a teenage girl. When Odd Carl opened the back door and yelled at them to get out, they both just stared at him, wondering why he had so much yarn hanging off the end of his sawed off shotgun.

"Inside," Carl said, pointing his barrel back at the house.

The family did as they were told. Although the neighbors were out on the streets—walking their dogs, playing with their kids, mowing their lawns—nobody seemed to notice anything strange about the two men forcing Mrs. Heffington and her kids into the house at gunpoint.

"Hello, Mrs. Douchebag," Frank said to the woman. "We're here for Mr. Douchebag."

The two thugs sat the family down in the living room, keeping an eye out for Mike, though there were no signs of him.

"Who?" the woman said. "What do you want? I think you have the wrong house."

She tried to remain calm for the sake of her kids, but her heart was visibly battering her chest.

"You mean this isn't the Douchebag residence?"

"No."

"So your name's not Rachel Heffington, wife of one Mike the Douchebag who owes me 200k?"

The woman's eyes widened. It was clear she had no idea her husband was gambling again or that he was stupid enough to borrow that much money from someone like Frank the Head.

"And you must be little Amy," Frank said to the teenager. "I had no idea Mike had such a hot little stepdaughter."

The teenager didn't make eye contact with him as he stepped in closer. "Maybe if your dad doesn't show up you can help work off the debt he owes me."

Rachel stood up, but before she could tell him to get away from her daughter, Frank backed off. Carl pushed Rachel back into her seat.

Frank moved on to the boy.

"And who might you be, kid?"

"Elmore," the boy said.

"Last I looked, Mike didn't have a son. Are you his nephew or something?"

"Foster son," Rachel answered for him.

"A foster kid, huh?" Frank leaned down to get a good look at the boy. "I didn't see Mike as the sort to take in somebody else's kid. What the hell kind of Ghost of Christmas Past made him so damned charitable all of a sudden?"

Frank laughed and smacked the kid on the arm, but the smile quickly fell from his face when he saw something behind the boy's eyes. There was definitely something strange about the kid. Even with the gun pointed at him, the boy didn't flinch. It didn't worry him in the least bit, as if he'd had guns pointed at him his whole life.

Then the boy spoke. "I thought Mike paid you already."

Frank was a bit shocked to hear him speak, especially in such a calm and professional tone of voice.

"What are you talking about, kid?"

"I gave him the money to cover the debt he owed you."

"What?" Rachel said. "You knew about this, Elmore?"

"I'm sorry," the boy said to his foster mother.

Rachel was fuming. "Are you saying Mike convinced you

to give him two hundred thousand of your money to pay this guy back?"

If Mike was there Rachel would have slapped him across the face. Instead, she just visualized strangling him in her head.

"I'm sure he would have paid me back," Elmore said. "Besides, I didn't want anything bad to happen to the family."

"Well, he did happen to come pay me the 200K today," Frank said. "But then he vanished in thin air and took the money with him."

"What do you mean thin air?" Elmore asked.

"Like a magic show. Now you see me, now you don't—that kind of thing. He still owes me the money."

The kid broke eye contact and stared deep into his head, like he was pondering something. Frank wondered if the kid had any idea of what Mike actually did to make himself disappear like that.

"I have more," Elmore said.

Rachel shook her head. "Elmore, don't."

"More what?"

"More money," Elmore said. "Almost a million dollars in cash."

"Elmore, that's your money!" Rachel said.

"I don't care. It's just money."

"Where'd you get that kind of money, kid?"

"My mother," Elmore said.

"Was she rich?" Frank asked.

"Very."

"You got all that money here?"

Elmore nodded.

"Where?"

"The treehouse in the backyard," Elmore said. "Under the mattress in the corner of the room."

Frank looked up at Odd Carl and gestured to check it out. Carl nodded, then went for the back door. As the big man crossed the living room, Frank noticed the yarn tangled around his shotgun. It dragged behind him like a long multi-colored tail.

"Are you kidding me?" Frank said to Carl, pointing at the yarn. Carl looked down, uncoiled the yarn from the barrel and continued on.

"Next time, leave the knitting at home, ya homo," Frank said.

Carl held the mess of tangled yarn under his elbow as he opened the arcadia door and disappeared out back.

"You seem like an okay kid," Frank said to Elmore. "Not many people would dish out that much dough for a piece of shit like Mike."

Elmore shrugged.

"Mike's okay," the kid said. "He just doesn't think before he acts. He considers himself a brilliant strategist, but he really just relies on luck."

"You said it kid," Frank said.

"Just don't tell him I said that. He doesn't know he relies on luck."

Frank smiled. He was beginning to like the kid.

Rachel and the children weren't the only people in the house when the two men arrived. There was also Rachel's mom, who was in her bedroom watching *Walker Texas Ranger* just two doors down from where they were sitting. Rachel knew that at any moment her mom would come barging in with her shotgun and blow these guys' heads off, or at least disarm them long enough to call the cops. Rachel just waited, buying time, until it happened.

"Oh, I didn't know we had company!" Grandma said as she stepped out of her room, a big smile on her face.

Everyone looked at her. Rachel's mouth dropped open when she noticed her mom didn't have a shotgun in her hands—the one time in their lives they actually could have used that weapon.

"I'll go make some tea," Grandma said. "Does anyone want tea?"

Frank smiled at her. "Yeah, you go make us some tea, Grandma."

"I'll make a lovely pot of tea," she said, pinching Elmore on the cheek as she passed him. "And a side of Chessmen butter cookies for the kids."

"Mom!" Rachel yelled, trying to gesture with her eyebrows to get the old woman to notice the guy standing next to her had a gun.

"Oh, don't worry," Grandma said. "I'll only put Splenda in yours."

Then the grandma went into the kitchen to boil some water. When Odd Carl returned, he shook his head at his boss.

"There's nothing there," Carl said.

"You checked under the mattress?" Elmore asked.

"I checked everywhere."

"It should be in a black briefcase underneath the mattress." Carl shrugged.

"Wait..." Frank said. "You mean a leather briefcase containing $800,000?"

"Yeah," Elmore said.

"That was yours?"

Elmore nodded.

Frank let out a sigh and scratched the side of his head with the gun.

"I'm sorry to break it to you, kid. But your new dad swiped your cash."

"What?" Rachel said.

"I saw him with it earlier today," Frank said. "He must have grabbed your cash and skipped town."

"Are you serious?" Rachel cried.

Frank gave her a look of sincerity.

"That son of a bitch..." she said. Then she punched the couch cushion next to her. "That son of a bitch!"

"It's okay," Elmore said. "I don't mind."

"What do you mean you don't mind?" Rachel said. "That money was your life. Your schooling, your college education, your rent."

"He'll need it more than I will."

"So what are we going to do?" Rachel said, suddenly panicked, looking up at Frank the Head. "If he stole the money and ran off, what's going to happen? Shouldn't you leave us and go after him?"

Frank frowned at her.

"I wish it were that easy," Frank said. "But we can't let you go until we have the money."

"So what's that mean?"

"It means we sit here and wait until Mike the Douchebag shows up."

"But what if he doesn't show? What if he really took off for good?"

Frank scratched his head with his gun again. "We'll just hope it doesn't come to that."

When the tea was ready, they all moved into the kitchen. Everyone knew they had a long wait ahead of them and nobody liked it. They especially didn't like thinking about what was going to happen when the waiting was over and done with, but the money hadn't arrived yet. Not a single one in the room, apart from maybe Grandma, actually believed that Mike was coming back.

"Hey, can you help me with this while we wait?" Odd Carl asked the grandmother, holding up his half-finished knitting project. "Do you know how to knit?"

The old woman gave him a grumpy look.

"What do you think I am, an old lady?" the grandma said. Odd Carl bowed and apologized.

Then she smiled and lifted out her hands. "Bring it here. Of course I know how to knit!"

When she took the supplies, Grandma said, "Oh, how cute! A dog sweater!"

"For a Scottish terrier," Carl said, resting his sawed-off shotgun on his shoulder.

Grandma nodded excitedly as she began knitting. "I can tell!"

Elmore and Amy drank their tea and ate Chessmen. Amy wasn't talking at all. She seemed to be in shock. Elmore wondered if she took it seriously about having her work off Mike's debt. She'd seen a lot of documentaries on the sex slave trade.

"Want to cook us up some food while we wait?" Frank said to Rachel. "It could be a while and I skipped lunch."

Rachel didn't agree or disagree. She just got up and went to work.

The woman seemed broken, overwhelmed with shock. Not just because there were two strange armed men in her house, but because her husband wasn't the man she thought he was. She thought he'd left a life of crime behind him. She didn't know he still interacted with types like Frank the Head. She didn't know he was in serious debt with such dangerous people. She didn't know he was the kind of person to steal a seven-year-old's life savings, ditch town, and leave his whole family to the wolves. None of it possibly could have been real.

"What's going to happen if you can't get your money from Mike?" Elmore asked Frank.

"Elmore…" Rachel said, her voice soft and distant.

When he looked at his foster mother, she just shook her head. She didn't want the boy talking to the man with the gun. But Elmore turned back to Frank and stared at him until he got an answer.

Frank said, "Come on, kid. You don't really want to think about that, do ya?"

"Well, he's probably not coming back. We might as well figure out other ways of getting you your money."

"Like what? Are you going to take out a loan or something?" Elmore shook his head.

"How about you and me do a job together?" Elmore said.

Frank chuckled. "What the hell are talking about?"

"I know how we can get our hands on a lot of money." Elmore leaned in closer, as if he didn't want his foster family to hear. "I can cut you in for thirty percent. I just need a couple of guys to help me get it out of there."

Frank shook his head. "Stop playing around, kid. You watch too many stupid movies."

Elmore leaned back. "Where do you think I got that $800,000

from? That was just all the money I could carry from the place. There's a heck of a lot more where that came from."

Frank looked at Rachel. "Is this kid for real?"

"Leave him alone," Rachel said.

"No, I'd like to know," Frank said. "Where did a kid his age get that kind of money?"

"From his mother," Rachel said.

"His mom left him $800,000 in cash?" Frank asked. "Couldn't she have left it in her will? In some bank account?"

"She has millions of dollars in her house," Elmore said. "Maybe billions. It's far too much to count."

"So you stole this money?" Frank asked.

"I deserved it after what she put me through," Elmore said.

"Your mother?"

"My mother."

"Is she still there?"

Elmore looked at Rachel for a minute. Her eyes were glued on him, her mouth slipping open. He didn't want her to hear all of this.

"Her body is," Elmore said.

Frank the Head and Odd Carl were in the living room, talking it over. They kept the family in sight, just in case they tried to run away, but they didn't want anyone to hear their plan.

Grandma continued knitting, smiling away at her progress. Rachel continued making dinner, but she didn't really have any idea what she was doing—boiling spaghetti noodles, meatballs, and ketchup all in the same pot. Amy didn't speak, but her eyes darted around the room like a cornered animal.

Elmore heard someone burst through the front door and into the living room.

"Rachel?" a voice called out.

It was Mike. He'd come home. Elmore looked at Rachel and Amy. They didn't seem to hear anything.

"Rachel?" Mike called out again. "Amy?"

"Do you hear that?" Elmore whispered to Amy.

She didn't respond, but he could tell by the look on her face that she couldn't hear Mike's voice. The two men were still talking in the living room. They didn't notice Mike was in the same room with them.

Elmore hid behind the counter when Mike went racing through the kitchen, wondering where his family was. He saw the food cooking on the stove, but he didn't see Rachel cooking it.

"Okay," Frank said, returning to the kitchen. "We're going to check it out. But the kid better not be lying."

As Odd Carl came in behind him, Mike passed right through the big man's body like a ghost. Elmore knew exactly what happened to Mike, as he suspected when Frank said that he vanished in thin air. Mike was no longer a part of their world.

Elmore felt bad for Mike. He felt bad for Rachel and Amy. Mike would have no choice but to move to Hell's Bottom, the city of sorcerers that his mother always told him about. He knew Hell's Bottom was a harsh place, filled with crime and sorrow. He hoped the briefcase of money Mike had with him would help him find his way. It would be hard, though. Mike would never see his family ever again, and Rachel would live for the rest of her life thinking that he betrayed her.

Elmore heard Mike's voice in the living room. "What on Earth…"

"Come on, let's go," Frank said.

Elmore didn't want Mike to see him. As a go-between, Elmore existed in both worlds. It would be hard to explain to Mike what was happening in Rachel's world, and it would be hard to explain to everyone else how Mike was stuck in the sorcerer's dimension. He decided he just had to get out of there as quickly as he could.

While everyone was leaving the house, Elmore waited in the back of the group until the last minute and then darted for the door. As he crossed, Mike was staring at his new dice-shaped eyes in the mirror over the mantle. Elmore's image flashed through the reflection. He couldn't avoid it, Elmore had to say something.

"See you later, Mike," Elmore said. Then he jumped out the front door.

"Elmore?" Mike yelled. "What's going on?"

Rachel, Amy, Odd Carl, and Elmore were in one car.

"Grandma, you're with me," Frank said.

Rachel drove. Elmore was in the passenger seat, giving directions. Odd Carl was in the back, holding his sawed-off shotgun on the teenage girl.

By the time Mike ran out of the house, they were already on the road.

"This is the place," Elmore said, as they pulled up next to his mother's house.

He never expected to go back there. On the outside, it looked like such a nice suburban home—old, but well taken care of. He didn't really get a good look at the exterior when he made his escape the previous month. He hadn't seen the outside for a very long time. Most of his horrific memories of the place were generated within.

"Let's go," Odd Carl said, taking the family out of the vehicle and regrouping with Frank and Grandma.

"So nobody else lives here?" Frank asked Elmore.

"Nobody."

"We'll see about that." Frank turned to his partner. "Carl, go around back. See what you can find."

Carl hopped the fence and went toward the backyard.

"He won't be able to get inside back there," Elmore said. "The place is like a fortress."

Frank moved the group away from the street. "He's not going in. He's checking to see if you're lying about the place being empty."

When Carl returned, he shrugged. "The lights are on. Nobody's home."

"Let's go," Frank said.

Carl led the whole family toward the front door.

"You used to live here?" Amy asked.

195

"It's nice," the grandma said.

Elmore looked over at the grandmother. "It's not as nice as you'd think."

"You have the keys, kid?" Frank asked. When Elmore shook his head, he said, "I thought not." He waved his assistant ahead. "Carl."

Odd Carl stepped forward and kicked the door in. Even with seven locks, he didn't have much trouble getting it open.

"Everybody inside," Frank said.

One by one, they all shuffled into the old home. But Elmore had difficulty going through the doorway. The others wouldn't be able to see her, she didn't exist in *their* world, but he knew his mother's corpse would be right inside the door where he left her.

"Are you coming or not?" Frank asked.

Elmore didn't say anything. He wondered if there was a way he could stay back in the car.

"Let's go," Frank said.

He grabbed Elmore by the shoulder and pulled him inside. The kid stared straight ahead as he stepped through the door. He didn't want to see his mother's body anywhere except maybe in the corner of his eye.

"What a nice place you had, Elmore," Grandma said.

After Frank closed the front door, everyone spread out, looking around the place. The two men were interested in the money. The rest of the family was just curious about where Elmore came from.

"Okay, where do we look?" Frank asked. He closed the front door.

"Master bedroom," Elmore said.

Although Elmore didn't want to look around too much, he was wondering why he couldn't see his mother's body in the corners of his eyes. She should have been right near his feet. There was nothing.

Elmore lowered his eyes and looked around the room. His mother's body wasn't there. He stepped forward, looking down the hallway. Nothing.

"This way?" Frank said, stepping into the hallway behind him.

But instead of replying, Elmore ran in the other direction toward the dining room and kitchen. His breath quickened. His mother's body wasn't anywhere, which could only mean one thing.

"We have to get out of here," Elmore cried.

"Why?" Frank asked.

Rachel put her hand on his shoulder, "What's wrong?"

"My mother," Elmore told them. "She's not dead."

Elmore was in a panic. He wanted to get out of there, but Odd Carl blocked the exit. The big guy wouldn't let him out.

"What do you mean she's not dead?" Frank said. "She's still in here?"

"I locked her in," Elmore said. "She wouldn't have been able to leave. She's definitely here, somewhere."

"I didn't see her," Carl said. "I checked all the windows. There was no sign of anyone."

"You wouldn't have seen her," Elmore said. "She doesn't exist in this dimension."

Frank grabbed the kid by the arm. "Let's just get the money and go, kid. Lead me to it."

Elmore resisted. "No, I can't be trapped here again. I'll die before I'm trapped here again!"

"Let go of him," Rachel said.

Before the foster mother could get close to Elmore, Odd Carl pushed her back.

"Wait here," Carl told her.

"You two aren't being very nice," the grandmother told them.

"Shut it, Grandma," Frank said, pointing his gun at her face.

No matter what he did, Elmore couldn't stop himself from being dragged deeper into his mother's house.

"It's in there," Elmore whispered to Frank the Head, pointing at his mother's bedroom.

The door was closed. Although there was no light shining through the cracks, Elmore knew she was inside. He could hear the distant sound of sand passing through glass.

"I can't go in," Elmore said. "The money is through the door on the left hand wall. You won't miss it."

Frank pushed Elmore toward the door as if he didn't hear a word he'd said. "Come on."

As the light switched on, Elmore saw the bulge of blankets on the bed. His mother was sleeping.

"It's through here?" Frank asked, pointing at the wall on the other side of the bed.

Elmore nodded. He tried to be as quiet as possible. His mother wouldn't be able to see or hear Frank, so it didn't matter what he did. But if Elmore made any noise at all he could wake her up.

The lump in the bed shifted and rolled. A light snoring sound issued from beneath the covers. Elmore prepared himself to duck under the bed the second his mother opened her eyes.

"What the hell is this?" Frank said, as he opened up the door. "It's just an empty closet."

For a second, Elmore didn't know what the man was talking about. The closet was so full of mountains of cash that it was about to cause an avalanche across the bedroom. The reason Frank the Head couldn't see any of it was because it was, like the woman asleep on the bed, located in the sorcerer's dimension. It would require a go-between to transfer it into the human world.

"You better not be playing a game with me, kid," Frank said. "I'm not a patient man."

Elmore couldn't explain it to him out loud. He just had to show it to him. As he stepped carefully across the room, his mother tossed and turned. Elmore didn't take his eye off her.

"Why do you keep looking at the bed?" Frank asked.

To Frank, the bed looked like it hadn't been slept in for a hundred years. He didn't see Elmore's mother or even the bulge in the blankets.

Elmore shook his head. He refused to respond to anything the man said. He went to the mountain of cash inside the closet and picked a stack of bills from the top of the pile.

Frank's eyes lit up as the money appeared from thin air. "What the hell?"

As Elmore took more stacks of cash from the closet, the debt collector looked closely. He put his hand into the closet, waved it around. There was nothing in there. Just open space. But still, the kid pulled thousands of dollars out of there like a rabbit from a hat.

"You gotta explain this to me, kid," Frank said. "Where is all that money coming from?"

Elmore just shrugged in response. Then he stroked his hand down the stack of cash, revealing one side of the mountain of money. The two-foot stack hovered in midair. Frank couldn't believe his eyes.

"You should come work for me, kid," Frank said, not taking his eyes off of the hovering money. "I could use a sorcerer in my employ."

Elmore just shrugged again, pulling more and more cash out of the empty closet.

As the money disappeared from the sorcerer's dimension, it created a large hole in the center of the mountain stack. The cash was tilting over, about to collapse in on itself. Elmore reached up to stop the avalanche, but wasn't able to catch it in time.

A loud crashing noise echoed through the room as the mountain of money spilled out of the closet.

"Elmore?"

The boy didn't turn around.

"Elmore, is that you?"

The sound of her voice rattled his nerves.

"What's wrong with you, kid?" Frank the Head asked, noticing the boy trembling in his shoes. "You look like you've seen a ghost."

Elmore turned slowly to his mother.

"You've come back," she said.

She looked like a corpse lying in the bed. Her face was pale, her skin clammy and shriveled without makeup.

"I knew you'd come back."

Frank tapped the kid on the shoulder. "Keep pulling the money out of there. I'll get the others to help carry all this."

"No," Elmore told Frank. "Don't bring them in here."

"Why not?"

"We need to get out of here," Elmore said.

The mother looked at the money missing from the closet, then looked at her son.

"Is someone in the room with you?" she asked.

"No, no one's in here but me," Elmore said, waving his hands at his mother.

"Is somebody in here, forcing you to steal money from me?"

"No, no, it was just me," Elmore said.

"Who the hell are you talking to, kid?" Frank asked.

The mother stepped out of her bed and grabbed her robe.

"It's my mother." He flinched when his mother stood up, but she didn't go to him. She went for a drawer on the other side of the room. "We have to get out of here. Now."

"Nobody's here, kid."

"You can't see her," Elmore said. "Just like the money, she's invisible to you. We have to get out of here or she'll use her magic on us."

Elmore went for the door. Frank tried to grab him, but he ducked under the man's arms.

The mother pulled a potion out of the drawer and took the tiniest swig. It was the potion of Dimensional Doorway, which she often used to go between worlds to sell her magic ability.

Frank saw the woman materialize.

"What the hell?" he asked. "Where the hell did you come from?"

"You…" the woman said.

She ran toward him. "You corrupted my baby boy!"

"What are you talking about, lady?"

Frank pulled out his .38 revolver, but she grabbed him by the wrist before he could pull the trigger.

"It's your fault he turned against me," she screamed in his face.

Her fingernail dug into his skin. "Let go, you crazy bitch."

"You won't take my baby away from me again. I won't let you."

She turned over the hourglass on her body and cast Age Reversal. Frank could feel his body weakening. His flesh loosened and sagged. He became smaller, fragile. His body reverted in age one year per second.

At eight years old, Frank's hand was so slender that it cracked in the woman's vice-like grip. His fingers tightened around his gun, forcing down the trigger on his .38.

"My baby means the world to me," the mother yelled as the gunshot reverberated through the room. "I would do anything for him."

The bullet passed through the mother's robe, but didn't hit her hourglass body. She held Frank until he was so young he couldn't stand anymore. He fell to the ground, his head resting on his shoulder. He was in too much shock to react at that point.

Elmore waited in the doorway. He wanted to help Frank, but he was too scared to go anywhere near his mother. His eyes shivered at the sight of her.

"Crazy bitch," croaked the toddler in her arms.

When Frank was small enough to be killed by a woman's bare hands, the mother snapped his neck, dropped his tiny body and turned to her son.

"My baby…" she said.

Her glass body had been glued back together piece by piece, every grain of sand returned to the container. Although her body looked weak and spider-webbed with cracks, she had managed to survive.

The woman outstretched her arms. "Come to me."

Elmore closed the door and ran.

"We have to get out of here," Elmore yelled as he came down the hall.

Rachel, Amy, and Grandma jumped to their feet as Elmore rushed toward the exit.

"She's coming," Elmore yelled. "We have to get out of here!"

But Odd Carl wouldn't let him through the door.

"Where's Frank?" Carl asked.

"He's dead," Elmore said. "Let's go."

Carl pushed the kid away from him. "We're not leaving unless Frank says we're leaving."

Rachel took Elmore away from the large man and brought him toward Amy. "What do you mean he's dead? What happened in there?"

Elmore looked around the room for another way out, but it was locked up like a fortress. The only escape was behind the wall of a man standing behind them.

"My mother's here," Elmore said. He turned to her. She came down the hallway toward them. "Right there."

"Where?" Rachel asked.

Elmore's mother was in the sorcerer's dimension again. Because the potion was so expensive, she usually only used it for a few seconds at a time.

"Elmore, my darling…" His mother came toward him, holding her arms out. "Be my baby forever."

Elmore ran to Carl, looking back and forth at his approaching mother. "We need to get out of here. Please!"

Odd Carl didn't know what to do. He looked down the hallway and saw nothing but the dim light shining from the master bedroom.

"Frank?" Carl yelled down the hall. "What's the hold up?"

There was no answer.

"You there?" Odd Carl gripped his shotgun. "Frank?"

"He's not coming. We need to go."

The mother saw her son interacting with invisible people. She didn't like it.

"There are more of them in my house?" the mother asked. "They're all trying to take my baby away…"

The woman pulled the vial of magic from her robe pocket and took the tiniest sip. For one second, she appeared within Odd Carl's reality and locked eyes with him.

"Get away from my son," she said in a cold, crooked voice. Then she vanished.

"What the hell was that?" Carl said.

All of them saw her.

Rachel's eyes widened. "Elmore, that woman…"

"She was a ghost," the grandma said.

"She's not a ghost," Elmore said. "She's my mother. She just lives in another dimension."

Rachel looked at the boy, her eyes quivering. She wasn't sure, but she thought she'd seen that woman before.

"Where did she go?" Carl asked.

Elmore watched his mother in the sorcerer's dimension as she circled around the man with a shotgun.

"She's still here," Elmore said. Elmore pointed his finger at her. "She's trying to get behind you."

Carl looked behind him, but there was no one there.

"Follow my finger," Elmore said, pointing her out. "You can't see her, but she can't see you either."

Carl fired his shotgun where Elmore pointed. The blast ripped apart the family pictures on the wall in front of them.

"Don't shoot yet," Elmore said. "Wait until she appears."

When she heard Elmore speak, the mother stopped and stared.

"Are you helping *them*?" she asked. "Do you want them to hurt your mommy, after all she's done for you?"

Elmore kept pointing at her. "Just let us go."

"No…" His mother's eyes burned red. "I will never let you go. I made you. You belong to me."

She screamed and ran at Odd Carl. She didn't know exactly

where he was, but knew the general area.

"She's charging you," Elmore yelled. "Get ready!"

Carl had a hard time aiming his weapon at the same time as watching where Elmore's finger pointed. When the mother appeared, she was only in their world for a fraction of a second. It was enough time for her to locate Carl's position, but not enough time for him to aim and shoot.

"She knows where you are," Elmore said. "Move."

As Carl stepped out of the way, toward the center of the room, Elmore went for the door.

"Run for it!" he yelled at Amy and Rachel.

As the hostages tried to make their escape, Odd Carl felt he'd been had. He ran back toward the door and pointed his shotgun at them.

"Get away from the door," he told them. "We're not leaving without Frank."

Elmore's mother appeared behind the large man and grabbed him by the back of the throat. Rachel only saw the woman for a second, then she disappeared. But as the spell of Age Reversal was cast on Odd Carl, he became part of both dimensions. The large man turned to face the woman, her hands still around his throat. He tried to push her away, but she was too strong. He didn't understand why she was growing so tall before him.

"Let him go," Elmore cried.

Carl turned to Elmore to see he was the same size as the boy. Although he'd become ten years old, Odd Carl was still bald with a comb-over. The thick glasses were enormous on his face.

"What's happening?" Odd Carl said.

As he tried to raise the suddenly-too-heavy shotgun, the glass woman smacked it to the ground. Then she shrunk him even younger.

"Let go," Elmore yelled at his mother.

"I'll shrink you until you're no threat to my family," the mother said. "I'll shrink you until you're sperm."

Elmore grabbed at his mother's hands, trying to pry her

fingers open, but she would not let go. She strangled the now-boy-sized man as she reversed his age. Even though Odd Carl was a scumbag, Elmore knew what it was like to have his age reversed. He wouldn't wish that fate on anyone. When he was unable to pull her off, Elmore went for the shotgun on the floor.

"After I'm finished, I'll do the same to the women you brought with you," the mother said to the man as he shrank down to the age of a toddler. "Nobody will take away my little boy again."

Elmore lifted the shotgun and fired. He aimed for the center of his mother's hourglass body, where it was the thinnest. The glass shattered across the carpet. His mother broke into two pieces. She fell to the ground, her sand pouring out of her. This time, she wouldn't be able to glue herself back together again.

As Elmore dropped to the ground, staring at the invisible body on the carpet, Rachel went to him. She pulled him away from the shotgun, away from Odd Carl who was now baby-sized and could no longer walk unassisted.

"That woman…" Rachel said. "I've seen her before."

Elmore looked up at his foster mother.

"When I was in high school, my boyfriend…" She looked at the size of Odd Carl, then at the size of Elmore. "I thought she was just a dream. She came and shrank him to the size of a football. She took him away…"

Elmore let out a sigh.

"You're him…" Rachel said. "You're David."

Amy was in more shock than anyone in the room. She was catatonic, until the name David came up.

"David?" Amy said. "You mean the David that…"

Rachel said. "Yes, that David."

Amy couldn't believe it. "So Elmore's… my father?"

"I'm sorry I lied," Elmore said, staring up at the teenage girl. Then he turned to Rachel. "I wanted to tell you, but I didn't think you'd believe me. My mother never wanted me to grow up. She stole the life we could have had together."

"How can Elmore be my father?" Amy said.

Before the baby version of Odd Carl could go for his shotgun, Grandma picked him up into her arms.

"Well, aren't you the cutest thing," Grandma said to Carl, kissing him on his bald head.

Elmore looked at his mother, lying in two halves on the ground. She reached out for him, wanting to hold him.

"How could you do this to your mommy?" she asked her son. "I only kept you young to protect you."

"Protect me from whom?"

"There are people who will hurt you if they knew you were alive," she said. "They would recognize you in your adult form."

"Tell me who."

"That's why you can never be an adult. You must always stay a child."

"Why won't you tell me who?"

The mother just shook her head, staring right through him.

"I want you to see what you took from me," Elmore said.

He retrieved the vial of magic from his mother's robe pocket and dumped all of it down her throat. The woman shifted into the real world, so that she could see Rachel and Amy.

"This is the life you stole," Elmore told her.

He pushed his mother's face in Amy's direction.

"This is Amy," Elmore said. "She's your granddaughter."

The mother looked up at the teenage girl.

Elmore continued, "Rachel was pregnant with her when you found me in her treehouse sixteen years ago. They could have been my family if you hadn't turned me into a baby and taken me away."

His mother looked at her son and then back at the girl. "I have a granddaughter?"

"You could have had many grandchildren if you had let me grow up," Elmore said. "Because of you, Amy didn't have a father. Rachel didn't have a husband for another thirteen years. Your selfishness ruined more lives than just mine."

The mother could see the girl's resemblance to Elmore. She could see the resemblance to herself. They really were of the same blood.

"My granddaughter…" the mother said to Amy. "Come to me, my granddaughter."

Amy went to the broken woman.

"Stay back," Elmore said to the girl.

"It's okay," Amy said.

"I just want to hug my granddaughter," the mother said.

When she wrapped her arms around the teenage girl, the mother broke into tears.

"I'm so sorry, Elmore," his mother said. "It's all my fault. Because of me, you never got to see your daughter grow up."

"That's enough," Rachel said.

"Mom, let Amy go," Elmore said.

But the mother wouldn't let go.

"Let me make it better," said the mother. "Let me give all those years back to you."

"What are you doing?" Elmore yelled.

Amy screamed and pushed away.

The mother used her magic, spreading it through Amy's body.

"Don't!" Elmore cried.

But it was too late. Amy was getting younger by the second.

"I'll give you your baby back," the mother said, her tears dripping onto Amy's soft cheeks. "You'll get to see what it's like to have a child of your own."

By the time Elmore and Rachel separated Amy from the mother, the teenage girl was no longer a teenager. She was Elmore's age. She would have to go through puberty all over again.

"What happened?" Amy cried. "What's wrong with my voice?"

Then she looked down to see how baggy her clothes were. She was a child again.

"Do you have any idea what you've done?" Elmore yelled at his mom.

But the mother didn't hear him. The last grains of her sand

fell to the carpet. She closed her eyes. Her hollow body collapsed into glass dust. Elmore covered her face with Carl's coat, which was now far too big to be of any use to the baby-man.

Rachel and Amy gave Elmore the most evil look he'd ever seen in his life.

"I had a date on Saturday," Amy cried, looking down on her pre-pubescent body. "How am I supposed to do that now? I'm just a kid. He's going to hate me."

"Nevermind that," Rachel said. "How are they going to let you back into high school?"

"I'll fix this," Elmore said.

"How?" Rachel asked.

"With magic," Elmore said. "We need to find somebody who has aging magic."

"Where are you going to find someone like that?"

"In Hell's Bottom," Elmore said. "It's a city of sorcerers. I've never been there, but my mother used to go there to get work all the time. If anyone can help us we'll find them there."

Amy and Rachel looked at each other. They were at a loss.

"Fine," Rachel said. "We should leave as soon as we can."

"You can't go with us," Elmore said. "Amy and I will have to go alone."

"You're only children," Rachel said. "You can't go alone."

"We don't have a choice. The city exists in the dimension of the sorcerers. Only those who use magic or have been affected by magic can go there."

Rachel didn't like the idea, but she didn't seem to have any choice.

"How good are your chances of finding somebody who can help you?" Rachel asked.

Elmore said, "Fair, as long as we take a lot of money with us. The magic won't be cheap."

"Do you have money?"

"We have lots and lots of money."

Rachel looked at Amy. The girl nodded at her mother.

"And with any luck, we might find Mike there," Elmore said.

As the women's eyes lit up at the mention of Mike's name, and Elmore went on to explain what had happened to Amy's stepfather, Odd Carl stared out from Grandma's arms at the vast living room landscape. He wondered what his mother was going to think of his birthday present to her. Instead of the knitted dog sweater, his mom would be receiving the gift of having to raise her son all over again. Unfortunately, this was a present she would not be able to return, whether she liked it or not. But perhaps this time she'll do a better job of raising her son. Because she's already gone through it before, maybe this time he won't turn out to be the criminal scumbag she'd originally produced.

NYMPH

Janie's teeth were grinding, her knees bent like knotty twigs, her eyes wild with green glowing light. She cast Plant Growth across the forest and moaned in pleasure as trees erupted from the ground, twisting upward like waltzing giants, stretching so high in the clouds that they blocked out the view of the smog-choked city.

"Yesss…." she cried out. "*Yes!*"

The sun was like a drug on the back of her neck, seeping into her plant-like flesh and vibrating her nerves into orgasmic bliss. It was better than sex to her. It was an orgy of the elements.

"Grow for me, my lovelies… Get *big* for me."

She stepped through the woods, casting her spell at every clearing that had been cut down for lumber. A forest would instantly appear, exploding from the earth like monster wooden worms. She grew the trees until they were massive gnarled pillars, larger than any trees in that forest, trees so old they would have existed in the dinosaur age if they'd grown that size naturally.

"So powerful…" There were tears in her eyes. "So magnificent!"

Up ahead, she saw a large house in the middle of the forest. Her eyes grew cold. She didn't think it belonged there. Houses were for the city. Only the trees should live out in nature.

"Ugly," she said.

Then she cast her spell at the house. Weeds, vines, and trees burst from the soil beneath and ripped the house apart, curling through the walls, impaling the roof, twisting it up like it were caught in a tornado of vegetation. When the spell was finished, all that was left of the building were strips of wood and plaster dangling from branches.

As she watched the destruction, Janie tickled the flower

petals on her nipples and licked her dark green lips. Seeing nature obliterate man-made buildings was such a thrill to her. Her mind was intoxicated with the ecstasy of it all.

"Oh, yeah…" she whimpered. "That's the stuff. Give me more."

She ran deep into the woods, creating a trail of car-sized mushrooms as she went. Then she prepared a spell so potent it would have been an atomic explosion of plant life, but one second before it went off Janie saw something ahead of her. A wounded animal lay shivering in the undergrowth.

"Ohmygawd…" Janie said.

She rushed over to the animal to see that it wasn't a beast at all. It was a man who had animal-like features. His shoulders and chest had a thin layer of bear fur. His mouth was in the early stages of transforming into the jaws of a beast.

"Help me…" the beast man said, rolling in and out of consciousness.

Janie saw him clutching his chest. He had several bullet holes in his body, but for some reason the bullets hadn't embedded any deeper than thorns. However, one wound was pretty bad—a shotgun blast to his stomach had turned him into a bloody mess.

"What happened? Are you okay?"

"My name's Brian Nelson," he said. "The hunters… there's still more hunters… Call an ambulance."

Then he faded out.

"You poor thing," Janie cried. "You were hunted?"

Brian did not respond.

It seemed as if this man had only just now flipped between dimensions. He spoke of an ambulance, but there were no ambulances in Hell's Bottom—only pushcarts big enough to move a body.

"Wait a minute…" Janie said as she brushed his hair out of his eyes.

She saw that he was Native American, and because he was part animal she assumed he was a creature of Mother Nature.

"You're the one, aren't you?" she asked. "The stars told me

that I'd meet my soulmate today. It's you, isn't it? It has to be you. Obviously. Fate brought us together."

Brian's eyes rolled around in his head.

"It's so romantic…" Janie said, leaning back and smiling as she thought about it. "I find this wild wounded beast in the woods and nurture him back to health… then, to repay this debt, he stays by my side as my protector… and then we fall in love."

She looked down at the man whose wounds continued leaking blood all over the forest floor as she spoke.

"Isn't it such a perfect love story?" she asked. "We were destined to be together. Me and my brave Native American man-bear…"

Brian grumbled as he faded in and out of consciousness.

"The other furries…" he muttered. "They got away… right? They ran away…"

"Yes, of course we will," Janie said, having a conversation with him in her head. "Come home with me so you can meet my uncle."

Eventually, Janie cast her spell and a thin thread-like vine curled through Brian's flesh and stitched up his wounds. By the time she was finished, much of the bleeding had been stopped but now Brian's wounds were filled with weeds.

Brian was too heavy for her to carry. She had to use her magic so that tree limbs would lift his body off the ground and pass him from branch to branch until he was safely out of the forest.

"I'll get you to my uncle in no time," Janie said.

She cast her spell again to create a passenger car on her bike made of plants and wooden wheels, which grew into the shape she commanded of them. Although she was not able to communicate or control plants, she was able to manipulate the directions in which they grew. This enabled her to transport bodies through branches or sculpt passenger cars. It was a skill that took her years to master.

"My uncle's just going to love you," Janie said, as she rode them down the mountain trail. "He's a great man who's always overflowing with love for his fellow man."

"Why the hell did you bring him to me for, Janie?" Hoggins yelled at his niece.

"He's my soulmate," Janie said. "I wanted you to meet him."

"You should have taken him to the clinic," Hoggins said. "This is a restaurant. He's bleeding all over the floor. It's unsanitary."

"But Uncle, he's the one I've been telling you about all week," she said. "He's the one the stars said I'd be spending the rest of my life with."

"Yeah, good," Hoggins said. "Just bring him in the back before we lose any more customers."

"Isn't he beautiful?" Janie said.

"Yeah, just beautiful... whatever..."

Hoggins moaned and complained as he pulled the twigs out of Brian's wounds and cast a cleaning spell to kill the bacteria. Once the bullets were removed and the area was sanitized, Hoggins stitched him up properly.

"Damn kid..." he grumbled to himself. "She could have killed this poor sap..."

"Hey Boss," Angry Eddie said as he entered the kitchen. "The blood's all mopped up. You think it's a good idea letting your niece sit out there with the customers? She tends to make people uneasy, you know. It's bad for business."

Hoggins wasn't offended by the comment. He just laughed.

"Tell me about it," he said. "But I want to keep her away from this guy until I get a chance to talk to him. She thinks she's found her soulmate again."

Angry Eddie laughed. He remembered when he first met Janie and she thought *he* was her soulmate, because of how much she liked the taste of the pies he conjured. It happened around

216

the same time every year. That woman was all kinds of crazy.

"So what happened to him?" Eddie said, leaning over the bear man.

Hoggins washed his hands with a wet cloth. "Janie didn't say. She found him out in the woods. Looks like somebody shot him up pretty good."

"You think he's dangerous?"

"Not as dangerous as Janie's going to be once he explains to her that they're not soulmates."

Eddie chuckled. "But what if they are soulmates this time?"

"That'll be the day…"

Janie was in the bar sitting next to Big Strange as he guzzled beer from a bowl big enough to fit his beetle-shaped head.

"I want the wedding to be out in the forest," she said. "It'll be a pagan Celtic druid fairy wedding with a Navajo theme, obviously. My dress will be made completely out of white flowers. I'm not sure what kind of flowers though. White roses would be perfect but with all the thorns it would be too poky. I can't wait for you to meet him. His name's Brian. He has shape-shifting magic and so he's part bear. A noble brown bear…"

"Bloopa-bloo…." Big Strange said with a sigh.

He didn't like having to listen to the woman speak. She just prattled on about marrying this guy. She wouldn't give it a break for even a second.

"My apartment's kind of small for such a large man, but we'll make it work," she said. "It might be cozy with just the two of us in there. Do you think he'd wear matching pajamas? I love matching pajamas. Although I can't really wear pajamas anymore… Do you think bears and nymphs are perfect for each other? I think we'll be perfect for each other. Usually nymphs fall in love with satyrs and centaurs, you know, creatures that are half-man and half-goat or half-horse, but that's just mythology. Real nymphs like me would be fine in a relationship with half-man and half-bears."

Big Strange looked around the room for some kind of excuse to get up and leave.

"Bloopa-bloo," he said.

"You're right," Janie said. "Nobody really appreciates bears for their beauty but they totally are beautiful creatures. They're not really as ferocious as people say."

"Bloopa-bloo…"

"Don't worry, I'll make sure to invite you to the wedding. Hey, maybe if you make friends with Brian he'll make you a groomsman… though I don't know if it'll be the kind of wedding that has groomsmen. You can still come though."

"Bloopa-bloo?"

"Oh, I think the wedding will be in April. The middle of spring. I love spring weddings. Let's say April 27th. I lost my virginity on April 27th. "

Although she couldn't understand a word Big Strange was saying, she thought she was having a normal conversation with him. She loved speaking to a guy whose comments were completely up for interpretation.

"Bloo…"

Big Strange dropped his head onto the bar and closed his beetle eyes. It was no use. She was never going to shut up.

"Keep calm, you're safe now."

Brian's eyes opened to the sight of a pig-faced man staring down at him. At first, he thought it was somebody in a pig costume, one of the furries he helped save. But then he realized the man was really part pig.

"Whoa, man…" Brian said, snickering as he rubbed his eyes.

"Careful, you're wounded," Hoggins said.

But Brian didn't care. He was more interested in knowing why he hadn't completely reverted back to his human form. As he rubbed his face, he realized his arm was still furry, his mouth was part bear.

"What's going on? My face is all fucked up."

"You're in Hell's Bottom," Hoggins said. "It's a place where spell casters go when they've overused their magic abilities."

"Spell casters?"

"I guess you could call it some kind of purgatory. We live between dimensions."

"You know how to shapeshift?" Brian asked. "Do you transform into a pig like I transform into a bear?"

"No, not exactly. My Bottomless Stomach spell is what turned me into a pig. Everyone here has been corrupted by magic in one way or another. The more you cast your spell the more you will turn into a bear."

Brian groaned as if his hangover was more irritating to him than his gunshot wounds. "Oh man… Grandfather told me that would happen… I'm such an idiot. I need to go talk to him. Can you give me a ride?"

Hoggins took a deep breath.

"I hate to break it to you, but you'll never be able to return home. You're stuck here like the rest of us."

"Huh? Oh, yeah… He said that, too…"

Hoggins handed him a wet wash cloth to clean his face.

"Do you need a drink?"

"Hell yeah I do," Brian said.

Hoggins looked up at Angry Eddie, "Get this guy a whiskey."

"A double," Brian said.

"A double," Hoggins repeated.

After Eddie returned with the drink and Brian had a few moments to calm down, Hoggins pulled up a chair and put a serious expression on his face.

"Look," Hoggins said. "I'm sure you've just gone through a major ordeal with…" He pointed at his wounds. "Whoever did this to you." Brain looked down at his stitched up chest and said , "Huh?" As if he had only just realized the state he was in.

"You're also about to go through a major ordeal trying to adjust to life in Hell's Bottom and trying to cope with the loved ones you left behind. But none of that's important right now." Hoggins looked back at the door. Eddie went to the knob and locked it. "What *is* important is that you're in terrible danger."

Brian continued drinking. He seemed relaxed and not bothered by the situation at all, but Hoggins piqued his curiosity.

"The woman who found you in the woods…" Hoggins said. "Her name's Janie. She thinks she's my niece, but we're not really related. I helped her out when she first came to Hell's Bottom and I guess she got a little attached to me. Anyway, she's not right in the head. She has it in her mind that the two of you are soulmates and are destined to be married. She's even planning out your wedding as we speak."

"Is she hot?" Brian said, and then chuckled.

Hoggins didn't think it was funny.

"This isn't a joke. That woman is incredibly dangerous. She's a powerful sorcerer, yet she's mentally unstable. That is a lethal combination here. Normally, Janie's a really sweet kid, but when it comes to men she can get a little nuts. She becomes unpredictable. If you break her heart there's no telling what she might do."

"Who is this person again?"

"The last guy she had her sights on was nearly crippled for life. You're going to have to be very careful with her. Let her down in the gentlest way possible. Actually, your best option would be to sneak out the back door and never come back. She'll have her sights on another guy in no time."

"Hold on a minute…" Brian said. "I think I want to meet her before making a decision. If she's hot I might as well give her a chance."

"Dude…" Angry Eddie said. "You don't understand. The broad is fucking psycho."

"Yeah, but I kind of like crazy chicks," Brian said. "I like a girl with a little fire in her spirit."

"She doesn't just have fire in her spirit," Hoggins said. "She has a goddamned volcanic explosion in her spirit."

"Even better."

"She's expecting you to move in with her tonight," Eddie said.

Brian shrugged. "I don't have anywhere else to go. It sounds better than sleeping on the street."

"But it's not normal," Eddie said. "You haven't even spoken to each other, yet she acts as if you've known each other for years."

"If you actually move in with her things *will* end badly," Hoggins said. "Trust me. She's not somebody you can reason with."

"She sounds like a trip," Brian said. "When do I get to meet her?"

Then he chuckled out loud and downed the rest of his whiskey. Hoggins and Eddie couldn't tell if he was sincere or just fucking with them. He didn't seem like the kind of person who took anything too seriously.

The restaurant's power went out and the customers were left in the dark.

"Bloopa-bloo?" Big Strange asked, as darkness fell over them.

Janie didn't seem to notice anything happened and kept talking, "You should have seen the look on Brian's face when we first met. I swear it was love at first sight. He wasn't completely awake at the time, but you could still see it in his eyes…"

In the back of the restaurant, Hoggins looked around, wondering what caused the blackout.

"It's not the fuse box," Eddie said, wandering through the kitchen with his lighter leading the way. "The electricity's still functioning."

"Then what caused it?" Hoggins asked.

"I think it's some kind of… darkness spell."

"Shit…" Hoggins said. "It's the Arachne!"

"Who's the Arachne?" Brian asked, licking the remaining drops of whiskey from his glass.

"Get Big Strange," Hoggins yelled.

But before Angry Eddie could leave the room, a tall figure appeared before them. He was a man with long albino white hair, six arms with long gray fingernails, wearing the royal attire of an Arachne nobleman.

"They're here," Eddie cried.

He raised his hand to cast a pie, attempting to take down the Arachne lord as he did the three siblings. But the Arachne just flicked one of his fingers, casting a web at the pastry chef. Eddie found himself plastered to the wall, covered in threads as strong as steal.

"You son of a bitch," Hoggins yelled, throwing a pan of sizzling sausages at him.

The Arachne just stepped aside and it went over his shoulder. Then he sprayed Hoggins' feet, sticking him to the floor.

"Get the fuck away from him!" Eddie cried out when he saw his boss captured, but there was nothing he could do to help. He couldn't move his arms or cast his magic.

"Gentlemen, please…" said the Arachne lord. "I have come only to talk."

The Arachne didn't seem to notice Brian. He walked right past him and faced the restaurant owner. When the intruder's back was turned, Brian rolled underneath a table and watched from safety.

"What do you mean *only to talk?*" Eddie yelled. "The last Arachne we encountered tried to kill us."

"That was an unfortunate misunderstanding. I apologize for the actions of my underlings."

Eddie and Hoggins looked at each other. They couldn't believe they were still alive.

"Mr. Hoggins, Mr. Eddie…" the Arachne began. "It is an honor to meet the both of you. I am well aware of the services you provide for your community and find them both commendable and virtuous. You are looking out for the greater good and I deeply respect that. As the Arachne Viceroy, it is also my job to assist the citizens of Hell's Bottom. We are like peers, you might say. However, my efforts tend to be a bit more discreet."

Hoggins looked him up and down. He couldn't tell if he should trust a single word the creature was saying.

"I have come to ask for your assistance," said the Viceroy.

"What do you mean?" Hoggins asked.

"It is about a colleague of yours that we are hunting. You know her by the name of Bee."

"What about her?"

"My people have been after her for quite a while now. She is a serious threat to the citizens of Hell's Bottom."

"Bee? A threat?" Hoggins scoffed at him. "She's helped keep the peace around here for quite some time."

"I understand you might see things that way," said the Viceroy. "But in reality she is more of a demon than a savior."

"How so?"

"She is responsible for creating the mindless husks you call *hollows*," said the Viceroy. "She has a spell she casts that drains the memories of the people she encounters, leaving them as empty shells. There is no way to reverse this magic. She must be stopped immediately."

Hoggins shook his head. "You've got to have the wrong person. Bee's a good kid. She's the best. I've never met a more self-sacrificing person in my life."

"I assure you she is the one," said the Arachne. "I don't believe she has control over her actions when she does it. But that doesn't matter. The important thing is that she is stopped."

Hoggins thought about it for a second and then shook his head.

"I can't believe it. Not Bee. No way."

The Viceroy just stared at him. He couldn't convince a man who refused to see the truth.

"Boss..." Eddie said. "What if he's right?"

Hoggins snapped at his underling. "Are you fucking kidding me, Eddie? You're actually going to believe Bee is the one responsible for the hollow-heads this whole time? We've been working on that case for years."

Eddie shook his head. "Think about it. The second the Arachne showed up, she disappeared. An innocent person wouldn't run like that."

"Not necessarily," Hoggins said. "If the Arachne were after you wouldn't you run, even if you were innocent? I know I would."

"But she would have said something to us," Eddie said.

"You don't know the whole story. Have a little faith in your friends."

"But what if she really is the one turning all those people into hollows?" Eddie said. "She has to pay for that even if she's our friend."

"Maybe if she were the one responsible, but she's not. I guarantee it."

"There is no doubt," said the Viceroy. "The one you call Bee is most definitely to blame. I need your help to bring her in peacefully."

"If you think we'd actually help you catch our friend you're a complete idiot," Hoggins said.

The Viceroy folded one of his three pairs of arms. "If you don't help us there's no telling what will happen to her. I cannot ensure she will survive until trial."

"I don't care," Hoggins said. "We won't hand her over to you."

The Viceroy paused for a moment. "I expected better from you, Mr. Hoggins. I thought you cared about the greater good of Hell's Bottom."

"I do care about my community. I take care of my own. That's why I'll never betray a friend like Bee."

"Very well," said the Viceroy. "If you do not wish to assist us then we will take her on our own. Just stay out of our way. If you interfere, you will be considered an accomplice and will be treated accordingly."

"Is that a threat?" Hoggins asked.

"It's a warning," said the Viceroy. "I won't hesitate to kill you if you get in my way."

"Then you better kill me now," Hoggins said. "Because I won't let you have her. If Bee truly is responsible for the hollows then I'll be the one who brings her to justice."

Hoggins couldn't believe he'd just stood up to an Arachne lord like that. Just a week ago the word *Arachne* would have had him soiling his pants.

"Very well," the Viceroy said.

The Arachne raised his six hands and began chanting a spell, conjuring bolts of electricity that shot between his fingers like webs of lighting.

"If that's what you want…"

But before the Arachne could use the spell, Brian leapt from beneath the table and transformed into a bear. The massive beast attacked the six-armed man, biting into the back of his neck. The Arachne had no choice but to turn his spell on the animal.

"No!" Janie cried, as she entered the kitchen.

The bear was tossed across the room, electricity pulsing through his fur. When Janie saw the twitching body of her husband to be, her eyes glowed a deep green color.

She screamed like a banshee, "Don't you lay a finger on my soulmate!" and then cast her magic at the Viceroy.

Trees exploded from the tile floor and twisted around the Arachne, flipping him upside-down and pinning his arms behind his back as the branches grew together in a tight compressing squeeze.

Just before Janie finished the spell and tore him limb from limb, the Viceroy vanished into a cloud of smoke. Her piercing scream faded away and the trees stopped growing.

As the cloud of smoke traveled out of the kitchen, the Viceroy's voice boomed through the restaurant. "Stay out of my way, Mr. Hoggins. You won't be warned a second time."

The nymph ran to her fallen lover and wrapped him in her arms.

"You're safe now, my love," Janie said.

Brian was back in human form. He could still feel the current vibrating through his system, but he was fine. The voltage was not nearly enough to kill a bear.

Hoggins and Eddie pulled the webs off each other. They were both shaken up.

"We need to find Bee before the Arachne do," Hoggins said.

"Do you think she's really innocent?" Eddie asked.

"I don't know. We'll worry about that once we find her. If the Arachne beat us to her she's not going to get a fair trial. They've already made up their minds."

Hoggins looked at Janie as she kissed the bear man all over his fuzzy face, then he looked at the trees that have practically destroyed his kitchen.

"Go find Big Strange and get him to clean out these trees," he told Eddie. "I'll try to pry Janie off of our guest."

Angry Eddie smiled at the two lovebirds. "I don't know. When I see them together, they kind of make a cute couple."

As Eddie left the kitchen, Hoggins stared at his niece and her new boyfriend. He wondered if it were possible that she could have actually found somebody who could like her for who she was, despite being a completely psycho.

"You know what," Brian said to Janie. "You totally remind me of the chick on the Supreme Desolation album cover. They're this awesome Norwegian fantasy metal band. Ever heard of them?"

"Yeah, definitely!" Janie said, though she had no idea what he was talking about.

"The art on the cover had this half-naked goddess of the forest with green skin and vines growing all over her. It was totally hot. I love that album."

She smiled at him. The only words she heard him say were *goddess*, *hot*, and *love*. Her heart melted out of her chest.

"Do you listen to heavy metal?" Brian asked. "I'm all about heavy metal."

"I love to run naked through the woods and swim in the sky through the twinkling stars."

"Yeah, I do that all the time, too. When I'm drunk."

As Hoggins watched the two of them talking, he couldn't help but smile. Brian was obviously not her soulmate, but it was nice to see her happy for a change. It's difficult to find love when you're a fucking lunatic.

SPELL
FARMING

Mia didn't realize her arms were tied to the chair until she tried to scratch her nose. She was in a concrete room, scrapes marred her cheek and forehead, her chair bolted to the floor.

"What…"

She had no idea how she got there. The last thing she remembered was saying goodnight to her boyfriend, Zach, and then going back to her apartment to sleep.

"Was I kidnapped?"

There were two other people strapped to chairs in the room with her. She recognized them both from her support group. They were casting addicts, like her.

"Dennis, wake up," she yelled at the man with computer skin.

He was snoring. She had to yell three times before he woke up. When he came to, a look of shock spread across his face. He was the kind of person who always woke up angry, even when he wasn't tied to a chair against his will.

"What the fuck," Dennis yelled, fighting against his bonds. "Who the fuck did this? Where the fuck am I?" When he saw Mia, he said, "Lisa? What's this all about?"

"Not Lisa, it's Mia," she said. "I don't know what's going on. I don't remember anything."

Dennis paused for a moment. He didn't remember anything either.

"This is fucked!" he cried.

The third person in the room moaned.

"Will you both keep it down?" Bee said. "I'm trying to sleep."

"Bee!" Dennis yelled. "Do you know anything about this?"

Bee opened her black eyes and lifted her head. She looked around the sterile room, then looked at her hands tied to her chair, then she sighed and leaned her head back.

"Shit..." she said.

"What?" Mia asked. "Do you know anything?"

"I really hope it's not what I think it is..." Bee said.

"What?"

"Nevermind... you'll figure it out soon enough. Let's just focus on finding a way out of here."

The others looked around the room. They struggled against their bondage, but they were strapped down tight.

"How?" Mia asked.

"There's got to be a spell we can cast to get out of here," Bee said.

"I can communicate with electronics," Dennis said. "That's pretty much useless here."

"I can only change my appearance," Mia said.

"Hmm..." Bee said. "Try transforming into somebody small."

"Okay," Mia said.

The girl used her spell and transformed into her original self—a petite zit-faced girl with a bony frame. She slid her arms out from the bonds, stepped out of the chair and transformed back into the blue-haired woman she was before.

"Hurry," Bee said.

Mia went to Bee, untied her bonds, and then moved onto Dennis.

"Whoever did this is going to die once I get my hands on them," Dennis said.

Bee went to the door and examined its frame. It was bolted shut from the outside.

"You can only manipulate electronic machinery," Bee said. "Good luck getting in a fight with these people."

"You think my magic is weak?" Dennis said. "I'll go Maximum Overdrive on their asses!"

Bee pushed on the door. It didn't budge. Then she looked around the room, but there was nothing. They were trapped.

"It's locked," Bee said. She turned to Mia. "Are you able to cast the spells of the people you transform into?"

Mia shrugged. "It depends. I don't copy anyone's memories, so I don't know their spells. However, if somebody has a mutation caused by magic, such as your wings, I would be able to fly… although not very well without practice."

Bee went to her and grabbed her by the shoulders. "Think. Is there anyone you've met who was strong enough to break through that door or had some kind of digging ability?"

As Mia thought about it, Bee wished she had Big Strange with her at that moment. That guy would have been able to break them out of there within seconds.

"Hello?" Dennis said. "You still haven't untied me yet."

Mia shook her head. "No, nobody. I have to touch people in a specific way to absorb their DNA in order to transform into them. Most people I choose tend to be beautiful women, not grotesquely muscular men."

"Shit…" Bee said.

"Hello?" Dennis said, annoyed that he was still tied to his chair.

When they heard the door unlocking, Bee and Mia looked at each other.

"Back to your seat," Bee said.

As the two women pretended to still be bound to their chairs, a lone man stepped through the door and stared at the prisoners.

"Father Harry?" Mia asked. "Is that you?"

He poked out his snail eyes and smiled at the girl. "Yes, Mia. It's me."

Mia sighed with relief at the sight of Harry. He was the person who put together the casting addiction support group. She assumed this must have been some kind of extreme measure to help them with their problems. Although, Mia thought it was kind of odd, since she wasn't one of the bad cases. She wondered why she was chosen for this.

Dennis was pissed. "What the fuck is going on, man? Why are we tied up?"

"I'm sorry," Harry said, stepping into the room with his hands folded. "But we need the three of you."

"Why?" Mia asked. "What for?"

"It's for the greater good," Harry said. "You'll be used for the betterment of sorcerer-kind."

"You're arcanists, aren't you?" Bee asked.

Mia and Dennis looked at the bee woman. They wondered what she knew that she wasn't telling them.

"Very good, Bee," Harry said. "We call ourselves the Brotherhood of the Arrow. The most brilliant minds in all of Hell's Bottom work with us. Our mission is to create new, stronger magic. The ultimate spell we wish to create would be the one that allows us to permanently return to the real world, so that we can use our magic to guide mankind into a golden age of peace."

"But why do you need us?" Mia asked.

"Spell farming," said the priest. "Each of you can cast spells that we need for our experiments. That is why I created the support group in the first place. In fact, all the CAS group meetings in town are run by members of the Brotherhood such as myself. It makes it very easy for us to catalog who knows what spell, so that we know where to find them when we need them."

Harry went to the bee woman.

"It took me quite a long time to figure out your secret spell, Bee," he said to her. "But it was worth the wait. It's quite a rare one."

"I never told you my spell," Bee said.

"I figured it out in our last session," Harry said. "I already suspected, but there were certain things that tipped me off. I'm now positive that I know your secret spell."

"What spell?" Dennis asked.

The priest explained, "Bee here has a spell called Memory Theft. It enables the caster to suck memories out of human brains, like a bee taking nectar from flowers."

"You mean?" Mia began.

"Yes, she's the one responsible for the hollows. They're the victims of her weakness to the hungry bug."

Dennis and Mia stared at her. Bee turned away, couldn't

look them in the eyes. She had nothing to say to defend herself.

The priest rubbed his hands together. "Without further ado, we must get on with our work. Your spells will be extracted shortly."

"So you only need our spells?" Mia asked. "Why didn't you just ask us for our help?"

"You would have voluntarily sacrificed yourself for our work?" Harry asked. "We've not encountered anyone who's been that charitable."

"You're going to kill us?" Mia asked.

"It's not as though we want to kill you," Harry said. "Death is just a side effect of the procedure. Now shall we begin?"

Bee leapt from her chair toward Harry, buzzing at him stinger-first. Harry cast Telekinesis and tossed her across the room. Then Mia transformed into Bee and copied her attack, only she was hardly able to fly or work her stinger. Harry easily flung her over the chairs at the wall.

"Clever girls," Harry said. "But I'm a prime arcanist. I know over a hundred spells. You have no chance against me in a fight."

Mia tried to lift herself up but her bones felt twisted and stiff. She fell back to the floor. Across the room, Bee was knocked unconscious. Dennis was still in his seat, struggling against his bonds.

"We'll start with you, Dennis," Harry said to the seated man.

"Fuck you," Dennis said.

He spit at the priest, but Harry wouldn't give him the satisfaction. The wad of saliva froze in midair, turned around and went in the other direction. Dennis cringed as it splat against his own forehead.

"Bring in the extraction beast," Harry said to the doorway.

Two arcanists wearing yellow canary beaks entered, pushing a cage into the room. Inside the cage, a bear-sized creature that was half mammal and half insect gurgled and squealed like a bat. Its eyes were like those of a spider. Its mouth like a mosquito's. It had six legs and a furry white blob-like body.

"What is that?" Dennis cried. "What the fuck are you going to do with that thing?"

Harry looked back at the creature. "It's been genetically engineered to extract spells from human beings. You see, when you use magic, the spell becomes a part of your DNA. It infuses itself with your genetic makeup. In other words, the spell becomes a part of you. We have been able to learn any spell we want from people, whether they're willing to teach us their spell or not."

"I'll teach you my spell," Dennis said in a panic. "If you want it you can have it. You don't have to take it by force."

"We already have your spell," Harry said. "This isn't about learning your magic. It's about creating a new spell."

The arcanists opened the cage and let out the massive six-legged creature. It moved slowly toward Dennis.

"You see, the extraction beast doesn't only remove spells from people," Harry continued. "It also combines spells together, to form something new. Like a man and woman mating to create a baby that's a hybrid of them both, this beast creates a hybrid of spells. Up to three spells can be mixed together to form a hybrid spell. The results are often very surprising."

"You have to kill three people just to get one spell?" Mia asked. "That's horrible."

Harry smiled at Mia. "It is unfortunate, but so many new spells have been discovered this way. If we found a spell that could cure all diseases, wouldn't that be worth a few lives? So many people die every day. With a small number of sacrifices, we can create magic that could change the world."

"But how many hybrid spells are actually useful?" Bee asked.

Harry and Mia looked at her across the room. She'd just regained consciousness, standing to her feet.

"I bet most of the spells you discover are useless crap," she continued.

"The ones that prove useful more than make up for the ones

that aren't," Harry said.

"Keep telling yourself that," Bee said. "I call bullshit."

"And who is this passing judgment on me?" asked the priest. "You have wiped the minds of countless people in Hell's Bottom. And for what purpose? Pleasure? Addiction? You're far worse than any member of the Brotherhood. At least we make use of our victims."

Bee didn't have a response to that. She had no moral high ground to stand on. She was not in control of herself when she sucked the minds out of people, so it wasn't exactly her fault, but she understood she was still the one responsible even if it was out of her control.

"I won't let you do this," Bee said, marching straight for Harry, unafraid.

The priest cast a spell and an invisible barrier appeared between them. Bee slammed into it and fell backward.

"There's nothing you can do," Harry said.

As Harry turned around, the extraction beast crawled onto Dennis and wrapped its six limbs around his chair.

"Get this fucking thing off me!" he cried.

The creature opened its jaws and closed them around his face. Its fangs dug into Dennis' eyes and split open his tongue as a long tube went down his throat. Dennis gurgled and thrashed as his blood was drained. The creature's blubbery flesh rolling and vibrating as it consumed him.

"Harry..." Mia said, tears pouring from her eyes. "How could you..."

The priest glanced at her for a second, but wouldn't hold eye contact.

"She's next," Harry told the arcanists.

Once Dennis' body went limp beneath the wriggling creature, the two men grabbed Mia. Her wings buzzed at them as they pulled her into a chair and strapped her down.

An explosion shook the warehouse.

"What was that?" Harry asked.

The other arcanists looked back at the clouds of dust entering the room.

"Check it out."

As the two men left the storeroom, a bolt of smoke hit them in their faces. Their skin cracked, their clothing crumbled, then they turned to stone.

"What the heck…" Harry said.

Through the doorway emerged the silhouettes of three intruders.

"These arcanists are not as powerful as we suspected, Big Sister," said the first intruder.

"They were pathetic opponents, Little Brother."

Bee laughed out loud at the priest. She recognized the voices of the Arachne siblings.

"It looks like the Arachne found me," Bee said.

Harry looked at her in shock. "The Arachne?"

The priest had never seen an Arachne before. He thought they might have been a myth.

"Let us go," Bee said. "We can help you fight them. There's no way you can defeat these people alone."

Harry shook his head. "I am a prime arcanist. I don't need your help."

The priest cast Force Field around his body and left the room. He would not allow the Arachne to interfere with his plans, even if he took them on single-handed.

Mia and Bee could see the interaction between the priest and Arachne from the doorway. They did not cast on each other right away. They sized each other up. As Bee watched, she realized that the older Arachne sibling that had been killed was now alive again, only he did not look at all like he did before. He looked more like a human-sized doll.

"This must be their leader, Big Brother," said the female Arachne.

"He doesn't look like much, Little Sister."

Father Harry said, "What do you want? My people are not afraid of the Arachne."

The Arachne smiled their fangs at him.

"I am a prime arcanist in the Brotherhood of the Arrow," Harry continued. "I know over a hundred spells. If you attempt to fight me you will be obliterated."

The Arachne looked at each other.

"He acts as if a hundred spells is a lot, Big Sister."

"Yes, Little Brother. But even a thousand spells wouldn't be considered a lot to an Arachne."

Harry took a step back. He wondered if the siblings were bluffing. Nobody knew a thousand spells. It was impossible. Not even an Arachne could memorize that many.

"If you don't leave now, it will mean war between our factions," Harry said. "I'm sure neither of us wants a war."

"Did he call this a war, Little Sister?" said the doll brother.

"I believe he did, Big Brother. He must be unaware this is not a war, but an extermination."

"Yes, Little Sister. We have allowed this little group of spell-makers to go unchecked for far too long. It is time they paid the penalty for their actions."

"I'm sure they'll be delicious, Big Brother."

"This is our chance," Mia said. "We have to get out of here."

Bee put out her hands. The invisible barrier was still there, blocking her from Mia's side of the room. "I'm still locked in. Any ideas?"

"Don't you know more spells?" Mia asked. "You should know tons of spells."

"I only know three. Why should I know tons?"

"Because you can cast Memory Theft. If you've sucked out the memories of all those hollow-heads, you should know everything they know, including all their spells. You probably know hundreds of them."

Bee shook her head. "It's not like that. I become somebody else when I cast that spell. I don't remember anything when she takes over."

"But the spells have to be in your head somewhere. Think of something."

Bee turned away from Mia. There was nothing she could do. The only possibility was for her to let the hungry bug take over, but that would be too dangerous. There's no telling what she would do.

"Maybe this barrier spell will fade soon…" Bee said.

The battle only lasted for a few minutes. In the end, Father Harry was nothing more than a burnt skeleton on the concrete floor, smoldering like a man-shaped lump of charcoal.

"You burned our food, Little Brother," said the female Arachne.

"I'm sorry, Big Sister. I wasn't thinking."

"I was so looking forward to eating an arcanist, Little Brother. He would have been a good appetizer before the main course."

The older sibling nodded. "Yes, Little Sister. The main course is waiting in the next room."

"It was very convenient for the arcanists to capture the bee woman for us, Big Brother. We're able to eradicate two enemies in one excursion."

The Arachne siblings stepped over the charred corpse and entered the room with Mia and Bee. Their spider eyes noticed the one in the seat, then the one behind the barrier. There were two bee women. They didn't understand why.

"Which one is she, Big Sister?" asked the youngest sibling.

"I don't know, Little Brother. I guess we'll have to eat them both."

As the female Arachne approached Mia, drool dripping from her fangs, a large figure appeared behind them.

"Nobody's eating anybody," said the Viceroy.

The three siblings looked back. Disappointment spread across their faces.

"It appears as though the Viceroy caught up to us, Little Sister."

"I'll never get to eat my bug now, Big Brother," the female

said with pouty lips.

The Viceroy did not have the patience for them.

"Take them to my palace," said the Viceroy. "We'll deal with them there."

No matter how much they wanted to eat the bug girls, the Arachne siblings obeyed.

Cocooned in webs, the two bee girls were strapped to the backs of their Arachne captors, carried through the streets of Hell's Bottom.

"Why didn't you change back?" Bee asked Mia.

"I thought it would buy you time," Mia said.

"Buy me time for what?"

"To transform into your other self so that you'll remember all those spells you've obtained from your victims."

The Arachne siblings separated and the bee women weren't able to communicate for a few minutes. When they came back together, Bee said, "You're an idiot. That side of me is dangerous. I'd never voluntarily let her take control."

"You have to," Mia said. "It's our only chance."

"I don't even know if that version of me has remembered any spells," Bee said. "She only cares about drinking people's minds until they're empty."

"But it might be your only hope," Mia said.

Before the Arachne arrived at the entrance to the underworld, a mob of citizens blocked their path.

"Let them go," Hoggins said, leading the pack.

It was Hoggins' entire crew. Angry Eddie, Torko, and Big Strange were there, but also all of the pig man's employees and his entire support network. Even Janie and Brian were there, making out in the background.

"Go home, Mr. Hoggins," said the Viceroy. "I don't wish to

litter the streets with so many bodies."

"It's your bodies that will litter the streets," said Angry Eddie.

"She's a criminal who has created grave sins against your people. Are you all really willing to die for her—the person who created the hollows?"

Hoggins nodded his head. "She's one of ours. Hand her over."

Bee was shocked that Hoggins knew her dark secret and still risked his life to save her from the Arachne. She's done such horrible things to people in her community. She assumed even Hoggins would have killed her himself if he found out she was the one sucking heads dry.

"I think they want to fight, Big Brother," said the female Arachne, bouncing the cocooned Mia on her back.

"I hope it's more of a challenge than the last one, Little Sister."

As the giant doll spoke, Angry Eddie and Torko looked at each other, confused by the transformation of the Arachne. The porcelain body and smiling painted-on face made the man even creepier than he was within his old spidery form.

"Don't do this," Bee told Hoggins and her friends. "It's not worth it. Just go home."

"Shut the fuck up, Bee," Hoggins said. His words were filled with venom. Even though he was coming to her rescue, he was obviously not happy with Bee. Not in the slightest.

"You are all fools," said the Viceroy, raising his hands, electricity popping from his fingertips.

Bee shook her head. "A crowd of fools is the scariest kind."

Hoggins raised his hands like a boxer, his fists turning to iron. Eddie, Big Strange, and the rest of their gang prepared magic from their hands and eyes, staring down the Arachne. There was fear in their hearts, but not nearly as much as they thought there would be. These were the Arachne they were facing. The Arachne were supposed to be dangerous. That's what the rumors said. But just how dangerous could they possibly be?

The explosion of magic was so bright that Mia lost her ability to see. The flash—a collision of a hundred spells—hit the crowd with such force that everyone was thrown back. The street split open. The buildings cracked and crumbled.

It was over in less than a minute.

When Mia's vision faded back into focus, she saw everyone on the ground. Only the Arachne were still standing. Hoggins' people were burnt, bloody, bruised, beat up, knocked out, and covered in rubble. Most of them still seemed to be alive. A couple of them were clearly decapitated.

Mia and Bee were still cocooned in web, but had been separated from their Arachne captors. They were tossed across the street, away from the explosion.

"Bee?" Mia called out to the other web cocoon.

Bee was thrown further than Mia. During the explosion, she collided with the wall, headfirst. Her web bondage was torn open. Blood dripped onto the cracked pavement.

"Are you okay?"

The bee woman jerked and twitched, her head rolling on her shoulders.

"Hungry, hungry…" Bee mumbled, half-conscious.

"What?" Mia asked.

The Arachne turned and faced the two women. They finally realized which of them was the real Bee.

"Buggy, buggy…"

Bee stood up, strings of web hanging from her body. Her eyes were glazed over. It wasn't her anymore.

"Now's your chance," Mia said to Bee. "Use all the spells you've learned from your victims." But Bee wasn't listening. She was in a daze.

The younger Arachne leaned toward his siblings and said, "She seems different, Big Sister. Did she hit her head too hard?"

"Drink your nectar…" Bee staggered toward the Arachne. Blood streamed down her face.

"I think she wants to fight us, Little Brother. All by herself."

"How absurd, Little Sister. All these people failed to put a scratch on us. What magic can possibly come from a little bee?"

"Bee, bee, bee…" said the hungry bug as it came to life

within the staggering woman. "I am not just bee..."

"What is she babbling about, Big Brother?"

"She thinks she's more impressive than a mere bee, Little Sister."

Bee raised her arm and twitched her fingers in the air. "I am the queen bee, bee, bee..."

"End her, Big Brother," said the female Arachne. "Put her out of her misery."

The Viceroy stepped in. "No, just restrain her—"

But the Arachne lord wasn't fast enough. The older sibling cast his magic, shooting a fireball from his porcelain hand.

"No!" Mia screamed, watching as the fire engulfed the bee woman.

The fire extinguished itself immediately after impact. Someone cast a force field spell. It wasn't Bee. Mia looked out to the crowd of Hoggins' wounded men, but it wasn't them. They could hardly move.

"Who cast that, Big Brother?"

"I think someone else has joined the fight, Little Sister."

A figure stepped out of the shadows. His shoes tapping on the pavement, his arms outstretched, electricity pumping through his fingertips.

"Who is that, Big Sister?"

"I have no idea, Little Brother."

The figure came into view. He was a homeless man with a blank face. His mind was empty.

"Is that a Hollow, Big Brother?"

"Yes, Little Sister. It is a Hollow."

"It doesn't make sense, Big Brother. What is a Hollow doing casting magic to save the bee?"

The Viceroy cast Paralysis on the Hollow and the homeless man fell to the ground. Then another Hollow came out of the alley and cast Lightning Bolt. The blast hit the oldest sibling in his chest and his porcelain body shattered into pieces. Red slime-covered brain matter the size of a human being slipped from the shattered husk and plopped onto the street. When the other siblings saw their brother die all over again, they froze in shock.

"Queen bee, bee, bee, bee..."

From all over Hell's Bottom, the empty-headed hollows came to the bee woman's aid. They crept out of buildings, alleys, up from the sewers. Each of them preparing spells to use against the Arachne.

"She's controlling them, Big Sister!"

"Run away, Little Brother!"

There wasn't enough time for them to react. The younger Arachne turned to flee and was immediately vaporized. His body turned to ash before his sister's eyes. The female Arachne opened her mouth to scream, but before a sound escaped she fell to the ground. Her severed legs were walking away from her.

Like ants, an army of porcelain dolls came up from the sewers and swarmed the Arachne woman. They crawled up her thighs and arms, chewing her flesh away. Because the creatures were once hollows, they too were under Bee's control.

"Help me, Big Brother!" she cried to the blob of twitchy brain matter in the street. "Don't let her eat me! You said you wouldn't let her eat me!"

She was quickly taken apart by the recyclers. Not a speck of her was left by the time they returned to the sewer.

"Hungry, hungry bee, bee, bee…"

The Viceroy lasted only a short time longer than his three henchmen. He knew over a thousand spells, but he could only cast one at a time. His opponents were many and could cast a thousand spells at once. The Viceroy cast Web around five of the hollows, but the others kept coming. The Arachne lord had to turn his attention on one person—if he killed Bee, the hollows would surely quit their attack.

"Hungry, hungry…"

The Viceroy cast Lightning at Bee, but the force field spell still protected her. Then one of her minions cast Create Water, pouring ten gallons of water over the Arachne's head. The lightning spell curled back on the Viceroy, carrying the current through the water covering his body.

As the Viceroy was electrocuted, Bee licked her lips, saying, "Hungry queen bee, bee…" Her voice a deep, sinister grumble.

Queen Bee's opponent hit the ground a charred corpse,

his six arms twitching. She smiled down at his body, her neck curling to the side at an inhuman angle, drooling and gurgling with delight at the damage she caused.

Mia couldn't believe it. The bee woman didn't remember the spells from her Memory Theft victims, but she was able to control her victims as a queen bee controls her drones. The hollows didn't forget their magic when their memories were drained. They still had it in them, hidden deep inside their DNA.

"Hungry, hungry…"

Bee crawled on top of Mia, drooling and licking her lips. Mia squirmed and tried to wiggle away, but she was still cocooned inside the webbing. Bee had her like a bug trapped by a spider.

"You can change back now, Bee," Mia said in a shaky voice. "The Arachne are dead. Go back to normal."

"Thirsty bug…" Bee said.

A long black tongue slipped out of her lips. Mia cried as it licked across her face.

"Bee, don't!" A man yelled, staggering to his feet.

It was Hoggins. His skin coated in black ash. He coughed and gasped. Then he staggered closer.

"Please, Bee. Let her go."

Bee cocked her head at him. She was perched on top of Mia like a lion guarding her prey, growling at Hoggins as he stepped closer. Her wings buzzed in short bursts like a warning to stay back.

"Look deep inside yourself," Hoggins said. "You're not a monster. You're a good person."

The bee ignored him and looked down at Mia. Her tongue licked the girl's forehead. Gurgling as she said, "Hungry, hungry…"

"Snap out of it, Bee," Angry Eddie said, crawling out of the rubble.

"Yeah, snap out of it," Torko added, holding Eddie up by his waist.

But Bee kept looking at her meal. "Hungry…"

"Bloo," Big Strange said to her. "Bloopa-bloo."

Bee stared into the girl's eyes. She was crying. Mia said, "Please, Bee. Let me go."

Then the bee woman leaned away from her.

"You need help, Bee," Hoggins said. "I know it's not your fault. I know you wouldn't hurt all those people if you had control of your actions."

"Hungry..."

Bee looked out at all the hollows surrounding her, staring at her like zombies. She was no longer controlling them, but they stayed where she left them, crowding around her like an audience. When she saw their lack of emotion, their empty faces, something cracked inside of Bee. She started to cry.

"Let us help you," Hoggins said.

As Bee sobbed, Mia squeezed out of the web cocoon and ran away, behind Angry Eddie and Big Strange.

"You don't have to go through this alone."

Hoggins reached out his hand to Bee. When she looked up at him, the hungry bug was vanishing from her eyes.

"I'm sorry..." said the hungry bug in her twisted, curdling voice. "I'm so sorry..."

Then she was back to the old Bee again. Hoggins lifted her to her feet and wrapped his pudgy arms around her.

"We'll get you through this," Hoggins said.

"All those people..." Bee said, her cries becoming wails as the hollows stared empty-eyed at her. "What did I do to all those people..."

Angry Eddie and Big Strange wrapped their arms around her as well, holding her tightly as she cried at the top of her lungs. She didn't notice the handcuffs being put on her. She wanted their embrace to become tighter and tighter until she forgot all about the ugly creature that lurked deep inside of her.

LOST
CHILDREN

When eleven-year-old Amy got home to their tiny, crumbling apartment—which was actually considered a luxury apartment by Hell's Bottom standards—she crept past Elmore while he was busy reading old books, desperate to find the spell he was looking for, and hid inside her room. Closing the door quietly, she went to the bed and pulled out the tiny scroll she'd purchased from the magic shop around the corner.

"Activate Glider..." Amy said.

She read through the spell, memorizing how to cast it. Spells were like secret codes in video games. You had to say certain words in a certain order, and wiggle or move your body parts in a certain way, in order to unlock them. Once the magic became a part of your body, the casting became easier, saying the words might even become unnecessary.

"This is an easy one," Amy whispered.

She removed the bottom drawer from the dresser and hid her spell inside the open compartment, on top of all the other spells, then returned the drawer to its proper position. The words repeated inside of her head as she climbed up to the top of the dresser. Then she put her two thumbs together, blinked twice, and the magic flowed through her body.

"Eek!" Amy cried, giggling at the tingling sensation that crawled up her spine. The feeling was ticklish, yet it felt good, soothing. She almost liked the feeling of casting more than using the magic itself. Her teeth clenched, her eyes glazed over. Then she jumped from the dresser.

Her body didn't fall straight to the floor. She glided across the room, slowly, like a paper airplane. Her new spell, Glider, gave her the ability to float through the air like a gliding squirrel.

It would come in very handy when she wanted to sneak out. All she had to do was jump out the window and she could glide five stories to the street below. Getting back up wouldn't be as easy, but at least she had a method of escape when she needed it.

Amy clapped her hands and laughed with glee, then she went back to the dresser and tried it again.

"Did you buy another spell, Young Lady?" Elmore yelled, as he walked into Amy's bedroom.

The kid looked at her with piercing eyes. Amy wouldn't look in his direction, climbing down from the dresser, and going toward her bed.

"Yeah, so what…" Amy said.

Elmore marched up to her. "How many times do I have to tell you how dangerous magic is? You do realize that it will mutate your body, right? You do realize that if you keep casting you'll be stuck in Hell's Bottom and never see your mother again."

Amy wouldn't listen to him. She hated his stupid lectures.

"You're so annoying, Elmore," she said to her 8-year-old father. "I liked you better when you were just my little brother."

"I promised your mother you'd be safe. She's going to kill me if anything happens to you. Hell's Bottom is a dangerous enough place as it is; I don't want to have to also worry about you getting addicted to casting."

Amy snapped at him for saying that. "I'm not going to get addicted to casting!" She glared at him. "Meeting you was the worst thing that ever happened to me. You *ruined* my life. I was a teenager and now I'm a stupid kid again. I can never see my boyfriend or any of my friends ever again. It's like I died and have to start all over again."

Elmore lowered his head. He felt so guilty for what his mother did to her. Having gone through the experience several times in his life, Elmore knew exactly how she felt. It was incredibly depressing to have everything you've worked for, everything you've built for yourself, completely erased. It made you feel empty inside. And it was easy to want to fill that emptiness with something.

"Learning magic is the only good thing to come out of this,"

Amy said. "It makes it all worthwhile. If I can't cast, then I'm just a stupid kid going through puberty again."

"But you're going to cast too much," Elmore said. "Then you'll be lost, forever."

"I don't cast that much."

"Sometimes it only takes five times to trap you here, depending on how powerful the magic. The next spell you cast might be the one."

"But what are the odds of that?"

"Pretty good, actually. Trust me. Look at all the people around you in this city. The people here are just like you. They believe they have nothing left to live for, no hope, no future, so they just use magic all the time. That is their escape. That is what they live for now. And they just mutate away, becoming less and less human every time they cast. Is that what you want for yourself?"

Amy wouldn't look him in the eyes anymore.

"I promise you I'll find the spell to transform us to our proper ages," Elmore said, sitting down next to her on the powdery mattress. "I just found a lead that might be the answer."

"Oh yeah?" Amy said, her spirit suddenly shifting.

"It's a spell called Mimic," Elmore said. "It allows you to turn into anybody you want."

"But I don't want to turn into anybody else. I want to be myself."

"That's the thing," Elmore said. "If you cast the spell, you'll be able to transform back into your old self. It'll be a lot cheaper and easier to get a hold of than an age-controlling spell."

"Okay," Amy said. "I'll try it."

She nodded her head in agreement, but she wasn't getting her hopes up. This was probably the twentieth spell they'd gone after with no luck. The magic shops didn't sell many useful spells and people in Hell's Bottom usually refused to sell their magic no matter how much you paid them. Their spells were what defined most of these people. It was what made them special. Amy was pretty sure she was never going to get out of Hell's Bottom.

The two children walked through the Hell's Bottom streets, staying close together. Elmore made them hold hands so Amy felt incredibly stupid. They looked like victims, just waiting to be mugged or taken advantage of.

"So where are we going to find this person exactly?" Amy said.

"The man made out of paper I met yesterday said she just got a job at a restaurant nearby," Elmore said.

"He was made out of paper?"

"Yeah, like he was turning into a book. At the spell shop, he said he was in a support group with a girl who had the spell we're looking for. She's supposed to be really nice. I'm sure we'll be able to buy it from her."

The restaurant was just around the corner. They saw the sign, Le Petite Provence, and ducked out of the crowd of scum-covered mutants into the building. Although it was Hell's Bottom, the restaurant looked quite a bit nicer than any other place to get food in town. There were table cloths on the tables, the dishes were clean, and there weren't bugs and dolls crawling across the floor. It actually seemed like a real restaurant.

"What can I do for you, kids?" a pig man in a nice suit said to them, stepping out of the kitchen area. "I'm Hoggins, the owner of this fine establishment. May I seat you?"

"Sure," Elmore said. He hadn't had anything decent to eat for a while and decided to try the place out while they were there.

"Are your parents here? Do you have money?"

"I'm eighty years old," Elmore said. "She's my teenage daughter. Somebody used Age Reversal on us and we're trapped in the bodies of children."

"Tough break, kid," said Hoggins. "So you do have money?"

It appeared as though the pig man had a rough time keeping vagrants out of the establishment.

"Yes, money won't be a problem."

In fact, Elmore had more money than he knew what to do with. He had mountains of cash that he took from his mother's bedroom closet. There was enough to support them in Hell's Bottom for several decades. Unfortunately, because they had so much excess cash, Amy had all the money she needed for buying any spell she wanted. Elmore wondered if they would have been better off if he'd only taken a little cash with them.

Hoggins escorted them to a table in the corner of the room, away from the creepy plant lady who spoke a million words a minute at her large hairy date who seemed to have no idea what she was talking about.

"Is Mia working today?" Elmore asked.

"You know the new waitress already? She only just started."

"No, we've never met her, but I heard she knows shape-changing magic. As you can guess, my daughter and I would like to return to our old forms."

"Stop calling me your daughter, Elmore," Amy said. "It creeps me out."

"She thought I was her half-brother until recently." Elmore didn't know why he had to explain that to Hoggins, but he did anyway.

"Mia has the day off today," Hoggins said, handing the two of them menus. "She went through a rough experience the other day and is still dealing with it. She'll be in the day after tomorrow, though."

"Okay, we'll come in again then."

"Are you still going to eat here today?" Hoggins asked.

"Of course," Elmore said.

The pig man left them to review the menus. Amy didn't seem very hungry. Her foot was tapping. She wanted to find the highest building in town, cast Glide, and sail through the streets like a bird in flight.

"I'm going to the bathroom," Amy said.

"They don't have a bathroom," Elmore said.

Then I'm going outside.

As Amy squatted behind a dumpster in the alley, she pulled out a spell scroll and read over it carefully. It was newly purchased from a shop across the street. She couldn't help but buy a spell from every shop she found, as long as Elmore wasn't supervising her.

"Razor Nails…" Amy said.

While she was peeing, she cast the spell and two-inch steel blades stretched slowly out of her fingernails. The razor nails cut the scroll in half as they grew and the paper fell into the fluid pooling beneath her.

"God damn it," Amy said.

As she tried to pick up the paper with her long, dangerous fingernail, a figure stepped out of the pile of garbage behind her.

"What the fuck!" she cried, falling butt-first onto the pavement.

The man came at her, holding his arms up. He was naked and covered in garbage and human waste.

Amy jumped to her feet, pointing her razor claws at him with one hand while trying to pull her pants up with the other.

"Get back!" she cried.

But the filthy man was not aggressive. He just stared at her, drool leaking from his mouth.

"Mike?" Amy asked.

She didn't recognize him at first. The crazed homeless man was actually her stepfather.

"Is that you?" she asked.

But he didn't respond. He didn't have any memory of language.

"He's a Hollow," Hoggins told the two children.

Amy was back inside the restaurant with Elmore. They stared at their naked stepdad, staring at him through the window. He was like some kind of disgusting wild animal, walking through the alley, eating old food and smelling his armpits.

"It can't be him," Amy said, her eyes tearing up. "It can't be…"

The children both knew about the hollows. Ever since they arrived in Hell's Bottom, Elmore worried that something like this might have happened to Amy's stepdad. A lot of bad things happen to people in this city, especially newcomers.

"I'm real sorry, kid," Hoggins said, placing his pudgy hand on her shoulder. "It happened to a lot of people in this city. I feel so guilty about it. I'm almost responsible. If I'd only noticed sooner…"

"You know what caused this?" Elmore asked.

"How did this happen to him?" Amy asked.

Hoggins shook his head. He didn't really want to talk about it. He was still in shock from learning the truth himself. "One of my employees did this to all the hollows in town. She was addicted to a spell called Memory Theft, and drained the memories of many Hell's Bottom citizens."

"Where is she?" Elmore asked. "Is she still alive?"

"She's been locked up in the institution."

"What's her name?"

At first, Hoggins was worried the kid was going to take his revenge on Bee for what she did. "Look, kid. There's nothing that can be done to bring your stepfather's memories back. The woman who did this doesn't have the power to bring memories back to normal after she drains them, in the same way that you don't have the power to return a cheeseburger back to normal after eating it. His memories are gone. Permanently. He's become a newborn baby again."

Amy broke away from the window. She couldn't handle watching Mike dig through trash, shit smeared across his back, eating rotten meat from a garbage can and then puking it up.

Elmore went to Amy and said, "At least we found him. At least he's still alive."

Amy's face fumed red. "There's nothing left of him. He might as well be dead."

She ran out of the restaurant.

"Can you keep an eye on him until we come back in a couple days?" Elmore asked Hoggins.

The pig man nodded.

"Tell Mia we need her help, next time you talk to her," Elmore said. "It's really important that I return Amy to her mother as soon as possible."

Then Elmore rushed out the door and went after his daughter, before she did anything reckless.

"What's this?" Elmore asked Amy, lifting up her hand.

"Let go," Amy cried.

She pulled her hand away and walked faster up the street.

"Your hand," Elmore said. "Have you been using magic again?"

He grabbed her hand and showed it to her. The fingernails on her left hand had mutated. They were now made of stainless steel. When Amy touched them, she couldn't believe it. They looked like they were painted with silver nail polish but they were actually made of real metal.

"How did this happen?" she cried.

"I told you not to use magic. It transforms your body."

"But I only cast this spell once. It shouldn't have done anything yet."

"Sometimes once is all it takes," Elmore said. "That's why I said you should never use magic."

"Well, I don't care," Amy said. "They look cool anyway."

"You might not be able to go back home again. You must promise me never to cast a spell again. *Any* spell."

"*Fine*," Amy said.

"Say 'I promise.'"

"I *promise*."

Amy didn't need Elmore's bossy attitude anymore. She just lost her stepdad. She would rather be with Mike than Elmore any day. Mike was nowhere near as strict as the kid.

"So why are we going to the institution anyway?" Amy asked. "That pig guy already said she couldn't help Mike."

"This isn't about Mike. I need her magic. My mother told me that there are people out to get me. If I grow up, they'll be able to track me down. I need to know who they are and why they're after me."

"Are they dangerous?"

"I don't know. If I'm going to put you and your mother in

danger again, then I won't cast the spell on myself. I won't let myself grow up."

"But isn't that what you want more than anything?"

"No," Elmore said. "What I want more than anything is for you and your mother to be safe."

Amy laughed at him. She wasn't sure why she thought his words were funny. Perhaps it was because they came from the lips of an eight-year-old boy.

"Hungy, hungry…"

Bee was bound in a straightjacket, sitting in the lounge of Hell's Bottom mental care facility. Her short black hair was a frizzy mess. Her antennae hung down in her face. Her wings buzzed within the straight jacket.

"She's incredibly dangerous," said the nurse with one large eyeball for a head. "We usually keep her pretty sedated. It's the only way we can handle many of our patients."

"Are there a lot of powerful sorcerers here?" Elmore asked.

"They're all powerful sorcerers here," said the nurse. "But we know how to deal with them. Bee here is usually easy to deal with, when she's in the right state of mind."

"Hungry…"

The nurse went to Bee and snapped her fingers in her face. The woman blinked her eyes twice and returned to her old self. She sat up in her chair, tried to adjust her arms inside of the straight jacket. "You have visitors," the nurse told her.

Bee focused her vision on Amy and Elmore. "Children?"

"They said they need use of your magic," the nurse said. "The doctor agreed to let you do this, if you're willing to try. You'll be monitored. Do you think you can control it?"

"Control it? You want me to cast Memory Theft?"

"This boy has a lost memory that he needs you to find. If you remove it from his head then you can tell him what he needs to know."

A worried expression crossed the bee woman's face.

"I don't think I'm ready…" Bee said. "Besides, I can't take one spell at a time. I take whole years within minutes. I couldn't remove something so small."

"It's okay," Elmore said to Bee. "Just take any memories in my head that are older than eighty years. I'm supposed to have lived another life long before I can remember."

Bee shook her head. "I'm sorry. I can't do it."

"Well, doctor's orders," said the nurse. "You're going to do it and you're going to do it right, with no screw-ups."

The mental institution in Hell's Bottom was a private business. There was no government and no taxpayer money to keep the place running. The hospital was able to function because they sold the magical abilities of their patients. People came and paid quite a bit to have powers cast on them, such as healing spells or luck spells or body modification spells. The people here were more like slaves than patients, but it was a way to keep dangerous sorcerers off of the streets.

Elmore paid the hospital good money to have Bee cast her magic on him. They weren't going to let her get away with turning him down. She was now nothing but a spell-casting machine until she was fit to return to the streets and was no longer of any use to them.

"When do we begin?" Bee asked.

Elmore wished there was someone in the institution that knew age control magic. It would have been very convenient for them to return to normal if all they had to do was come here. But this institution was one of the first leads they followed; there were no patients that had a spell that could help them.

The nurse pulled up a chair for Elmore and he sat in front of Bee.

"This won't take long," Elmore told her.

Bee frowned at him. She never used her power on a child before, even if he was a ninety-year-old child. It didn't feel right.

"My mother told me there were people out to get me,"

Elmore said. "She said they would find me if I ever became an adult. I must know who they are and if they still pose a threat. I have no idea how long ago this was… at least eighty years ago. Probably more like a hundred."

"You're an old kid," Bee said.

"I've had a long childhood."

Bee leaned in close to Elmore. She paused for a moment. Then looked at the nurse. "Pull me off of him if my personality changes."

The nurse nodded.

Bee extended her long sticky tongue and attached it to Elmore's forehead. Then she began to drink.

As the bee woman sucked on the boy's head, Amy glared at her. She knew she was the one responsible for what happened to her stepdad. She wanted to rip her throat out. Her razor fingernails grew from her left hand, preparing to attack.

"Hungry…"

Bee's eyes rolled back. Even with the tongue sticking out of her mouth, she was still able to speak. It was as if the words came from deep within her throat, something else saying them.

"Hungry, hungry…"

Elmore could feel her drinking from his brain. It almost felt as if she were sucking fluids, but the fluids weren't wet. They were energy, as if she sucked electrical currents from his mind.

"Drinky, drinky…"

Elmore felt the bee woman lose control. He pulled back, but her tongue held him into place, slurping more of his memories. Amy lunged at Bee and wrapped her fingers around her neck.

"Let him go," Amy said, squeezing tighter.

Her razor fingernails cut into the patient's black and yellow skin.

"Hungry…" The voice faded from Bee's throat and her tongue retracted into her mouth.

Amy didn't let go. She squeezed tighter, her eyes turning red. Blood dripped down her chest from the thin cuts.

"Stop it, Amy," Elmore said.

The nurse removed Amy's hand from Bee's throat. The metal fingernails retracted into the girl's fingers. Bee seemed physically unharmed by the attack.

"Are you okay?" the nurse asked Bee.

Bee didn't even seem to notice the blood leaking down her neck. She stared at Elmore. Tears built up in her eyes.

"I saw her," Bee said to Elmore. "Your mother."

"What were in the memories? What was it like?"

"I'm so sorry…" Bee said, crying. It was as though she had experienced Elmore's childhood herself.

"Who are the people that are after me?"

Bee shook her head. "There are no people after you. There never have been." Bee looked away and tried to wipe her eyes against her straight jacket. "Your mother…"

"What do you mean?"

"Your mother convinced herself that you were some kind of powerful godlike being and there was an ancient society of evil sorcerers that were after you, who were planning to sacrifice you to their overlords. It was all in her head. She made it up."

"Why would she do something like that?"

"It was the only way she could justify what she was doing to her own son. Never letting you grow up, keeping you a child forever. It was selfish, but she couldn't help it. She was addicted to being a mother. She couldn't have any other children. She only had you. So she rebirthed you over and over again, so that she would never have to give up being a mom.

"She knew how cruel it was and couldn't even look at herself in the mirror, so that's why she invented the story. In her mind, she was saving you. If you grew up something horrible would happen. That way she was able to keep you a child forever without ever having to feel guilt ever again. By her death, she truly believed the story. She had created false memories of being on the run from these people. I'm sorry. It must have been so hard for you."

Elmore was not angry. He was actually relieved.

"So I'm safe? There's really nobody after me?"

"Nobody," Bee said. "You can finally grow up."

Two days later.

"Where'd you put my spells?" Amy said, just before they were getting ready to leave for Hoggin's restaurant.

"I threw them out," Elmore said.

Amy threw a fit. "Are you kidding me?"

"We're getting you home to your mother. I won't let you cast another spell."

"Those were my spells!" Amy cried, digging through the kitchen garbage. "I haven't even memorized all of them yet."

"You paid for those spells with my money. They were my spells. You don't need them. All they've done for you is turned you into a freak."

Amy kicked the garbage can over once she realized the spells weren't in there.

"I think my metal fingernails are cool," Amy said. "I don't care what you say. I want my spells back, even if I have to re-buy them all."

"Not with my money you're not."

"You're such a little asshole."

"Let's just go to the restaurant," Elmore said. "If we can get that shape changing magic you can go home to your mother tonight."

"I don't care about that. I just want my magic."

"Get ready. We're leaving."

Amy was still pissed off by the time they got to Le Petite Provence. She almost ran away from Elmore twice to go to a spell shop, but since he took all of her money away there wouldn't have been anything she could have bought.

"Are you Mia?" Elmore asked, as they entered the restaurant.

The girl smiled with deep dimples. "Uh-huh! Hoggins told me all about your problem. I can teach you my spell but only if you promise never to teach it to anybody else."

"Don't worry, we're go-betweens," Elmore said. "Once we return to our proper ages, we plan to leave Hell's Bottom and never come back."

"Okay," Mia said. "I normally wouldn't teach this to anyone. It's a very addicting spell. Being able to change shape into anybody else is really fun at first, but if you use it too much you lose touch with the real you. I recommend using this spell once and then forgetting all about it."

"That's what I plan to do," Elmore said, smiling. "I don't use magic."

Amy rolled her eyes at her eight-year-old father. He seemed like such a nerd, acting as if not using magic was something to be proud of.

"Let's go in the back so nobody else will hear," Mia said.

Once Amy and Elmore were taught the spell, they transformed into their former selves. Amy was in her old body again and Elmore had returned to his teenaged self, looking as he did when he was dating Amy's mother over a decade ago.

"You're both sixteen," Mia said, looking down at Elmore. "I thought you said you were really eighty years old?"

"I've been alive for eighty-nine years, but I've never been older than sixteen. My mother wouldn't let me grow up."

The teenaged Amy turned to teenaged Elmore.

"So this is what you looked like when you dated my mom?" she asked. "When you were David?"

"Yeah, exactly like this," Elmore said.

"I can see why she liked you," Amy said.

Being around Elmore never ceased to make Amy feel awkward. First he was her little brother, then a child-sized father, now a teenager her same age. He wished he would have turned into Mike instead. Then maybe her life would have gone back to normal, what it was like before Elmore came into her family.

They had to leave Mike in Hell's Bottom. Elmore thought of bringing him with them, but he wouldn't belong in the real world. He just would have been like a ghost in Rachel's house that only Amy could see.

"Now that it's all over, I think I'm going to miss it," teenaged Amy said, as they walked through the streets on their way home to Rachel's.

"Miss what?" teenaged Elmore asked.

"Hell's Bottom, casting spells, living in a world of magic, being a kid again."

"I thought you hated being a kid," Elmore said.

"It wasn't that bad, especially since it only lasted a month. Now that I don't have to grow up all over again, it was fun while it lasted. This whole experience will be a memory I won't soon forget."

"You should forget it, though. You need to think about the real world. Hell's Bottom is a place that traps people, like flies in a web. You never want to go back there. You're lucky to have gotten out when you did."

"I wonder what people are going to think of my nails," Amy said, holding out her hands.

"They'll probably love it," Elmore said.

When they got home, Rachel's eyes brightened. She saw Elmore as the teenager she knew in high school, the boy who knocked her up and changed her life forever. The boy she never stopped being in love with.

"David?" Rachel asked.

"Yes, I'm David again, finally," Elmore said. "Though you probably shouldn't call me David. It might be weird."

Rachel shook her head.

"I couldn't imagine calling you anything else," she said, smiling with glossy eyes.

Rachel stepped closer to him. She grabbed him by the hand and touched it against hers. It felt as if she'd gone back in time, to her high school days.

"It worked," Rachel said. "You finally found the magic to return you to your old self."

"Yes," Elmore said. "It wasn't the magic I was looking for, but it worked just as well."

"Why are you talking to yourself, Elmore?" Amy asked.

Rachel peeked over Elmore's shoulder, looking out the open door.

"So where's Amy?" Rachel asked.

"Right here." Elmore pointed at her. The smile fell from his face. "You don't see her?"

Rachel looked around, wondering what he was talking about. "No."

Elmore pointed at her. "She's standing right there."

Rachel looked where he was pointing, but she didn't see her daughter. Amy was invisible to her. She'd used too much magic. Like what happened to Mike before her, she no longer existed in the human world.

"Where?" Rachel said.

"What's going on?" Amy cried.

When she looked back at Elmore, he was shaking his head and backing away.

"I'm sorry…" Elmore said. "I failed you. I'm so sorry."

"Are you going to tell me where my daughter is?"

"She was eaten by the hungry bug," Elmore said.

"What does that mean?"

"She no longer exists."

POT LUCK

Big Strange wanted to make the absolute best dessert to bring to the Thanksgiving pot luck at Hoggin's restaurant, but every year everyone always thought the dish he brought was completely disgusting. It seemed unfair to him. Just because he had a gross-looking rhino beetle head instead of a human head, did not mean that his food was gross as well. Big Strange wasn't trained in cooking, he didn't have any magic food-conjuring spells like Angry Eddie, he didn't even have a human tongue to taste what he was doing, but he thought he still had what it took to create an excellent dessert because he put more love into his cooking than anyone he's ever met.

"Excuse me, fine sir," Big Strange said to the clerk at the spell shop. "I'm looking to acquire a spell that will return my tongue to its original human state."

"Huh?" said the clerk, rustling the pages on his book-shaped body.

"I wish to make the most splendid apricot dandies for this year's Thanksgiving pot luck, but cooking with my beetle tongue just won't do."

"What the fuck does *bloopa-bloo* mean?" asked the clerk.

"Please forgive my speech impediment," said Big Strange. "I would be most appreciative if you would sell me that bottle of tongue-shaping potion you have on the shelf there."

The massive wrestler-sized man with the beetle-shaped head pointed at a blue bottle behind the clerk.

"You want this?" the clerk asked, picking up the bottle.

"Indeed," said Big Strange.

"Does *bloo* mean yes or no?"

Big Strange nodded. "If you wouldn't mind, I am in quite a hurry."

The clerk wrapped up the potion and Big Strange paid the man.

"Good day to you, sir," Big Strange said as he left the store.

"Yeah, whatever…"

Nobody could tell with his beetle-shaped head, but Big Strange had the happiest smile on his face as he walked through the streets of Hell's Bottom. He was excited that he'd actually be able to taste as he was cooking this year. With a new tongue, he just knew he would prepare the most delicious plate of apricot dandies that anybody had ever tasted. This time, his dish would be a big hit with everyone at the party. Everyone would think he was super swell.

"It will be so divine to finally taste as a human again," Big Strange said, pulling the cap off of his potion. "This will surely be the greatest Thanksgiving ever."

But as Big Strange drank the potion, his tongue grew differently than he expected. It swelled out, wide as well as long. As it stretched out of his mouth, the growth seemed to be unending. His tongue kept getting fatter and bigger, until it was the size of his entire body, hanging in front of him like a warm wet blanket.

When Big Strange realized what had happened, he nearly fell over in shock. The spell transformed a beetle's tongue to that of a human; only human tongues are a hundred times larger than beetle tongues. Since he had a monster-sized beetle head, he was given a monster-sized human tongue.

Big Strange looked at the bottle and read how long the effects would last. He would have to put up with it for three days.

"Oh, dear…" he said with a muffled voice.

Big Strange wanted to cry. With his tongue so big, Thanksgiving would be ruined. Not only would he not be able to cook, but he wouldn't be able to attend. This was not fair. Thanksgiving was always Big Strange's favorite holiday, especially since he came to Hell's Bottom. He couldn't bear the thought of missing it.

He shook his beetle head and wobbling tongue.

"I will most definitely find a way," said Big Strange. "No setback will stop me from making the most delicious apricot dandies this world has ever seen!"

Wrapping his tongue into a ball and wearing it on top of his head like turban, Big Strange went forth and constructed his dish with utmost care, inserting as much love as he possibly could into every little action. His mother always told him that love was the most important ingredient to put into anything you cook, and Strange had a massive reserve of love built up over the years. He was sure they would be perfect.

Upon completion, Big Strange shoved one apricot dandy into his mouth and tasted it with his massive tongue. The flavor exploded in his mouth. He wasn't sure if it was his gigantic tongue or because he hadn't eaten with a human tongue for so long, but he'd never tasted anything so delicious. His dish would be perfect for the pot luck.

When he arrived at Hoggins' restaurant on Thanksgiving Day, Big Strange inhaled the rich scent of roasting turkey. Hoggins was a master of brining and rotisserie-roasting turkeys. The aroma saturated everything in the restaurant, creating a warm, comforting blanket of deliciousness that the large man could feel permeate his muscled skin. But it didn't just smell like turkey, flavors of two dozen homemade dishes brightened the room with such festive happiness that Big Strange couldn't help but giggle.

As Big Strange crossed the restaurant, carrying his basket of apricot dandies, he followed the spicy aroma of pumpkin pie until he found Angry Eddie.

"Happy Thanksgiving, Strange," Eddie asked, pulling pies out of the oven.

"Happy Thanksgiving, Edward," said Big Strange.

When Eddie saw the massive tongue on Strange's head, he did a double take. "What the heck happened to you?"

"A potion mishap," Strange said. "I thought a new tongue

would improve Thanksgiving for me this year, but my plan backfired in a most regrettable way."

Eddie cringed at the sight of the tongue hat. "Yeah, tough break, pal."

Big Strange held out his basket of treats to his best friend, "Would you care to try an apricot dandy?"

Eddie looked at the basket and then looked up at Strange's even-more-deformed-than-usual head, and said, "I'm kind of busy right now. Put them over with the other desserts."

Big Strange looked away with a frowning face as Eddie went back to work. "Very well…"

On his way to put his dandies with the other desserts, he passed Hoggins who was attending to the turkeys.

"Would you like to try one, Sir Hoggins?" Strange asked, holding out his basket.

Hoggins didn't even look at the food. "Damn it, Strange. You're getting drool all over the place with that thing. Get out of here."

He shoved Big Strange out of the kitchen so hard that he rammed right into the new waitress, Mia, and her boyfriend, Zach.

"A thousand apologies, madam," Big Strange said, nodding at the girl.

She just smiled and nodded at him as he squeezed past her.

When they thought he was out of ear-range, Zach asked her, "What did he say?"

"Boopa-poo or something like that," Mia said. "It's all he ever says."

Big Strange put his dish on the table where the desserts were supposed to go. He placed his directly in the center of the table, so that it wouldn't get pushed off to the side. Maybe people would try his food if they didn't know he was the one who made it.

As other guests showed up with their dishes, Big Strange's apricot dandies were immediately pushed to the side, far into the corner of the table.

"Fiddlesticks…" Big Strange said to himself.

At dinner, Big Strange had to sit at the table in the back of the dining room, away from most of the other guests. Even Eddie wasn't sitting with him, hanging out by Torko instead, his new best friend. Once Eddie had taken over Bee's job and Torko became his new partner, it made Big Strange feel like a third wheel. It wasn't fair. Eddie and Strange had been best friends for years, ever since they came to Hell's Bottom. He was paranoid they might've been drifting apart.

"Why aren't there more vegetarian options?" Janie whined, sitting in the seat next to Strange. "Tofurkey isn't hard to make or anything. Obviously. What is Thanksgiving without tofurkey?"

Brian sat down in the seat next to her, carrying a pile of meat on his plate.

"What is *that?*" Janie said when she saw all the meat. "Are you kidding me?"

"Bears are carnivores, babe," Brian said. "I gotta put on the pounds before hibernation season."

"If you weren't part bear I would be so pissed with you right now."

"It's good," Brian said, chewing with bits of turkey stuck to his cheeks.

Brian gobbled his meat so rapidly that it sprayed across the table. Then he laughed out loud and took a drink of mushroom whiskey.

"Do *not* kiss me after eating that," Janie said. "I swear I will freak out on you if you try it."

Brian made kissing expressions at her and she held out her hands, ready to fight him off.

Big Strange carefully ate his food, delicately using a fork and knife. He was very worried that he might gross out the people around him. But, luckily, nobody seemed to realize he was even there.

On the other side of Big Strange, the new go-between sat quietly with his family. They barely ate their food and barely spoke to one another.

"How's the support group been going?" Elmore asked Amy, breaking the silence between them.

Amy shrugged. "It's okay."

"Have you been casting at all?"

Amy wouldn't look him in the eyes. "No, it's fine. Everyone's real nice, especially Mia and Zach." There was no energy in her words. She was deeply depressed after learning she'd be stuck forever in Hell's Bottom.

"It'll take time, but you'll adjust," Elmore said.

Rachel took Elmore by the hand. "Leave her alone, David." Then she kissed his knuckles.

Amy was also depressed by the relationship that was forming between her mother and biological father. She thought it was sick and unnatural, since not too long ago she thought of Elmore as her eight-year-old little brother. But it just sort of happened. They couldn't control themselves. After all that time apart, they were still in love with each other.

"Please don't kiss in front of me," Amy said. "Don't even hold hands."

In order to see her daughter and be able to live in both worlds at the same time, Rachel had to use magic and become a go-between. So Elmore taught her Mimic and she transformed into her old teenage self.

Rachel swore that she did it by accident, but it was obvious she did it because of her deep desire to return to the days when she was with David, the love of her life. It was awkward for all of them at first. Rachel knew Elmore as a little boy, her foster son, and Elmore knew her as a grown woman, his foster mother. Not to mention that Elmore was actually twice Rachel's age based on the number of years he'd been alive. It was all confusing, disturbing, and perhaps morally wrong, but when they were with each other in their teenaged bodies, experiencing all that they missed out on for the past sixteen years, they just didn't care. They'd both gone back in time, reborn as their former selves. Outside of Amy, the two of them wished they could just forget the past sixteen years happened at all.

"It's ok," Rachel said. "You'll get used to it."

Amy shook her head. She couldn't believe her parents were the same age as her.

After dinner, Hoggins stood up and chimed his wine glass. Everyone quieted down. Everyone, that is, except for Janie who was drunk and giggling, playing footsie with Brian under the table.

"I'd like to thank you all for coming tonight," Hoggins said to his people. "It's always nice to have us come together during the holidays, as a family, to remember what having a family is all about."

"Getting drunk together!" Angry Eddie yelled out, and everybody laughed.

Hoggins raised his glass to Eddie for the comment, then continued. "After coming to Hell's Bottom, most of us lost our families. That's always the worst part about this place. It's not the magic, the poverty, the Arachne, the dolls, or the hard living. The worst part is knowing that we'll never see our loved ones ever again, unless they were misfortunate enough to share the same fate.

"We've left behind mothers and fathers, sons and daughters, lovers and spouses. That's why I like to bring us all together as a family at this time of year. A family isn't just the family you're born with. There's also the family you choose."

Hoggins stopped and choked on his words. At first, Big Strange thought the fat man was just coughing on his wine. But then he noticed that Hoggins was crying. Strange never saw the boss cry before.

"All of you are the family I choose," Hoggins said, covering his face so nobody could see the tears. "And I couldn't have asked for a better family to be thankful for."

Then he sat down. Nobody knew why he'd gotten so upset until they saw the empty seat next to Hoggins. It was where Bee always sat. Somebody mistakenly set her place and even set out a glass of her favorite honey wine.

"Now let's have some dessert!" Eddie yelled to brighten everyone's mood.

The crowd got up from their seats and headed toward the dessert table. Big Strange stayed back, peeking around the crowd to see which desserts they were choosing. He frowned when he noticed nobody was touching his apricot dandies. The basket was way off to the side, still covered in a flower-print cloth. Nobody even knew they were there. They all got their desserts and left. His apricot dandies completely untouched.

Big Strange lowered his head and turned away, his massive tongue drooping sadly, no longer hungry to eat any dessert of his own.

But then he heard someone say, "What are these?"

Big Strange turned and saw Mia opening his basket of apricot dandies. Excitement reappeared on his face as she took a bite.

"What…" Mia said, after tasting it.

Big Strange didn't like her response at first, but then Mia's eyes lit up.

"Mmmm…" Mia said, taking another bite. "This is really good."

"Bloo?" Big Strange said, as if surprised she actually said that.

She put the rest of the dandy to Zach's mouth and said, "Try this."

He took a bit and said, "Holy shit." Then he grabbed his own.

"These are amazing!" Mia announced to everyone.

People came back to the dessert table to see what she was talking about. Torko grabbed one, then Janie who brought two to give to Brian, even Hoggins grabbed one for himself.

"They're so good!" Amy said.

"This is the best dessert on the table," Rachel said.

Big Strange's face was exploding with smiles and happiness as he watched people eat his dish. His mouth was wide open. His eyes were glittering like crystal balls. It was a dream come true. People were actually eating a dish he prepared. It was all the love he put into it. Surely, it was all the love. They could taste how much he loved each and every one of them.

"I could eat a hundred of them," Mia said. "Who made these?"

"Eddie, probably," Hoggins said. "That man is one amazing pastry chef."

Eddie went to the dessert table, wondering which dessert he made that everyone was raving over. But he dropped his mouth in shock when they saw which one was the center of their affections. It wasn't his dessert.

"Oh…" Eddie said. "Big Strange made those."

When everyone heard the name Big Strange, they froze, looked at each other, and then spit their food all over the floor. They tossed their dandies into the trash, rubbing their mouths with napkins, and guzzled down whole glasses of wine. Then Big Strange let out the saddest bloopa-bloo that anyone had ever heard.

BONUS SECTION

This is the part of the book where we would have published an afterword by the author but he insisted on drawing a comic strip instead for reasons we don't quite understand.

I hope you liked my new book *Hungry Bug*. Wasn't it enchanting?

It's me CM3!

For some reason, this book was really hard for me to write. It took three times longer than any previous book I've worked on.

I think maybe it was because each chapter was structured like a stand-alone short story and I've always had a harder time with short stories than novels.

Or maybe it was because my computer kept coming to life and eating my hands.

I hate when my computer eats my hands. It's nearly impossible to get any writing done at all when that happens.

It's a good thing I have several clones in storage where I can get my hands replaced at any time.

Although having to deal with the clones is a pain in the butt. They always want me to bake them cookies and read them a bedtime story.

Then they want me to throw a disco taco party the next day.

And try to get me to invite Mr. T to dance at the disco as the guest of honor. But it's really hard to get Mr. T to come out, because he doesn't like disco music.

But every time I even suggest the idea, my computer gets really sad and I don't want to hurt its feelings...

THE END

ABOUT THE AUTHOR

Carlton Mellick III is one of the leading authors of the bizarro fiction subgenre. Since 2001, his books have drawn an international cult following, despite the fact that they have been shunned by most libraries and chain bookstores.

He won the Wonderland Book Award for his novel *Warrior Wolf Women of the Wasteland* in 2009. His short fiction has appeared in *Vice Magazine, The Year's Best Fantasy and Horror,* and *The Best Bizarro Fiction of the Decade*, among others. He is also a graduate of Clarion West, where he studied under the likes of Chuck Palahniuk, Connie Willis, and Cory Doctorow.

He lives in Portland, OR, the bizarro fiction mecca.

Visit him online at **www.carltonmellick.com**

Bizarro Books

CATALOG   SPRING 2013

ERASERHEAD PRESS

Swallowdown

Press

FunGasm

LAZY FASCIST

Your major resource for the bizarro fiction genre:

WWW.BIZARROCENTRAL.COM

Introduce yourselves to the bizarro fiction genre and all of its authors with the Bizarro Starter Kit series. Each volume features short novels and short stories by ten of the leading bizarro authors, designed to give you a perfect sampling of the genre for only $10.

BB-0X1
"The Bizarro Starter Kit"
(Orange)
Featuring D. Harlan Wilson, Carlton Mellick III, Jeremy Robert Johnson, Kevin L Donihe, Gina Ranalli, Andre Duza, Vincent W. Sakowski, Steve Beard, John Edward Lawson, and Bruce Taylor.
236 pages $10

BB-0X2
"The Bizarro Starter Kit"
(Blue)
Featuring Ray Fracalossy, Jeremy C. Shipp, Jordan Krall, Mykle Hansen, Andersen Prunty, Eckhard Gerdes, Bradley Sands, Steve Aylett, Christian TeBordo, and Tony Rauch. **244 pages $10**

BB-0X2
"The Bizarro Starter Kit"
(Purple)
Featuring Russell Edson, Athena Villaverde, David Agranoff, Matthew Revert, Andrew Goldfarb, Jeff Burk, Garrett Cook, Kris Saknussemm, Cody Goodfellow, and Cameron Pierce **264 pages $10**

BB-001"The Kafka Effekt" D. Harlan Wilson — A collection of forty-four irreal short stories loosely written in the vein of Franz Kafka, with more than a pinch of William S. Burroughs sprinkled on top. **211 pages $14**

BB-002 "Satan Burger" Carlton Mellick III — The cult novel that put Carlton Mellick III on the map ... Six punks get jobs at a fast food restaurant owned by the devil in a city violently overpopulated by surreal alien cultures. **236 pages $14**

BB-003 "Some Things Are Better Left Unplugged" Vincent Sakwoski — Join The Man and his Nemesis, the obese tabby, for a nightmare roller coaster ride into this postmodern fantasy. **152 pages $10**

BB-005 "Razor Wire Pubic Hair" Carlton Mellick III — A genderless humandildo is purchased by a razor dominatrix and brought into her nightmarish world of bizarre sex and mutilation. **176 pages $11**

BB-007 "The Baby Jesus Butt Plug" Carlton Mellick III — Using clones of the Baby Jesus for anal sex will be the hip sex fetish of the future. **92 pages $10**

BB-010 "The Menstruating Mall" Carlton Mellick III — "The Breakfast Club meets Chopping Mall as directed by David Lynch." - Brian Keene **212 pages $12**

BB-011 "Angel Dust Apocalypse" Jeremy Robert Johnson — Meth-heads, man-made monsters, and murderous Neo-Nazis. "Seriously amazing short stories..." - Chuck Palahniuk, author of Fight Club **184 pages $11**

BB-015 "Foop!" Chris Genoa — Strange happenings are going on at Dactyl, Inc, the world's first and only time travel tourism company.
"A surreal pie in the face!" - Christopher Moore **300 pages $14**

BB-032 **"Extinction Journals" Jeremy Robert Johnson** — An uncanny voyage across a newly nuclear America where one man must confront the problems associated with loneliness, insane dieties, radiation, love, and an ever-evolving cockroach suit with a mind of its own. **104 pages $10**

BB-037 **"The Haunted Vagina" Carlton Mellick III** — It's difficult to love a woman whose vagina is a gateway to the world of the dead. **132 pages $10**

BB-043 **"War Slut" Carlton Mellick III** — Part "1984," part "Waiting for Godot," and part action horror video game adaptation of John Carpenter's "The Thing." **116 pages $10**

BB-047 **"Sausagey Santa" Carlton Mellick III** — A bizarro Christmas tale featuring Santa as a piratey mutant with a body made of sausages. 124 pages $10

BB-048 **"Misadventures in a Thumbnail Universe" Vincent Sakowski** — Dive deep into the surreal and satirical realms of neo-classical Blender Fiction, filled with television shoes and flesh-filled skies. **120 pages $10**

BB-053 **"Ballad of a Slow Poisoner" Andrew Goldfarb** — Millford Mutterwurst sat down on a Tuesday to take his afternoon tea, and made the unpleasant discovery that his elbows were becoming flatter. **128 pages $10**

BB-055 **"Help! A Bear is Eating Me" Mykle Hansen** — The bizarro, heartwarming, magical tale of poor planning, hubris and severe blood loss... **150 pages $11**

BB-056 **"Piecemeal June" Jordan Krall** — A man falls in love with a living sex doll, but with love comes danger when her creator comes after her with crab-squid assassins. **90 pages $9**

BB-058 **"The Overwhelming Urge" Andersen Prunty** — A collection of
bizarro tales by Andersen Prunty. **150 pages $11**

BB-059 **"Adolf in Wonderland" Carlton Mellick III** — A dreamlike adventure that takes a young descendant of Adolf Hitler's design and sends him down the
rabbit hole into a world of imperfection and disorder. **180 pages $11**

BB-061 **"Ultra Fuckers" Carlton Mellick III** — Absurdist suburban horror
about a couple who enter an upper middle class gated community but can't find their way
out. **108 pages $9**

BB-062 **"House of Houses" Kevin L. Donihe** — An odd man wants to marry
his house. Unfortunately, all of the houses in the world collapse at the same time in the
Great House Holocaust. Now he must travel to House Heaven to find his departed fiancee.
172 pages $11

BB-064 **"Squid Pulp Blues" Jordan Krall** — In these three bizarro-noir no-
vellas, the reader is thrown into a world of murderers, drugs made from squid parts, deformed gun-toting veterans, and a mischievous apocalyptic donkey. **204 pages $12**

BB-065 **"Jack and Mr. Grin" Andersen Prunty** — "When Mr. Grin calls
you can hear a smile in his voice. Not a warm and friendly smile, but the kind that seizes
your spine in fear. You don't need to pay your phone bill to hear it. That smile is in every
line of Prunty's prose." - Tom Bradley. **208 pages $12**

BB-066 **"Cybernetrix" Carlton Mellick III** — What would you do if your
normal everyday world was slowly mutating into the video game world from Tron? **212
pages $12**

BB-072 **"Zerostrata" Andersen Prunty** — Hansel Nothing lives in a tree
house, suffers from memory loss, has a very eccentric family, and falls in love with a
woman who runs naked through the woods every night. **144 pages $11**

BB-073 **"The Egg Man" Carlton Mellick III** — It is a world where humans reproduce like insects. Children are the property of corporations, and having an enormous ten-foot brain implanted into your skull is a grotesque sexual fetish. Mellick's industrial urban dystopia is one of his darkest and grittiest to date. **184 pages $11**

BB-074 **"Shark Hunting in Paradise Garden" Cameron Pierce** — A group of strange humanoid religious fanatics travel back in time to the Garden of Eden to discover it is invested with hundreds of giant flying maneating sharks. **150 pages $10**

BB-075 **"Apeshit" Carlton Mellick III -** Friday the 13th meets Visitor Q. Six hipster teens go to a cabin in the woods inhabited by a deformed killer. An incredibly fucked-up parody of B-horror movies with a bizarro slant. **192 pages $12**

BB-076 **"Fuckers of Everything on the Crazy Shitting Planet of the Vomit At smosphere" Mykle Hansen -** Three bizarro satires. Monster Cocks, Journey to the Center of Agnes Cuddlebottom, and Crazy Shitting Planet. **228 pages $12**

BB-077 **"The Kissing Bug" Daniel Scott Buck** — In the tradition of Roald Dahl, Tim Burton, and Edward Gorey, comes this bizarro anti-war children's story about a bohemian conenose kissing bug who falls in love with a human woman. **116 pages $10**

BB-078 **"MachoPoni" Lotus Rose** — It's My Little Pony... *Bizarro* style! A long time ago Poniworld was split in two. On one side of the Jagged Line is the Pastel Kingdom, a magical land of music, parties, and positivity. On the other side of the Jagged Line is Dark Kingdom inhabited by an army of undead ponies. **148 pages $11**

BB-079 **"The Faggiest Vampire" Carlton Mellick III** — A Roald Dahl-esque children's story about two faggy vampires who partake in a mustache competition to find out which one is truly the faggiest. **104 pages $10**

BB-080 **"Sky Tongues" Gina Ranalli** — The autobiography of Sky Tongues, the biracial hermaphrodite actress with tongues for fingers. Follow her strange life story as she rises from freak to fame. **204 pages $12**

BB-081 **"Washer Mouth" Kevin L. Donihe** - A washing machine becomes human and pursues his dream of meeting his favorite soap opera star. **244 pages $11**

BB-082 **"Shatnerquake" Jeff Burk** - All of the characters ever played by William Shatner are suddenly sucked into our world. Their mission: hunt down and destroy the real William Shatner. **100 pages $10**

BB-083 **"The Cannibals of Candyland" Carlton Mellick III** - There exists a race of cannibals that are made of candy. They live in an underground world made out of candy. One man has dedicated his life to killing them all. **170 pages $11**

BB-084 **"Slub Glub in the Weird World of the Weeping Willows" Andrew Goldfarb** - The charming tale of a blue glob named Slub Glub who helps the weeping willows whose tears are flooding the earth. There are also hyenas, ghosts, and a voodoo priest **100 pages $10**

BB-085 **"Super Fetus" Adam Pepper** - Try to abort this fetus and he'll kick your ass! **104 pages $10**

BB-086 **"Fistful of Feet" Jordan Krall** - A bizarro tribute to spaghetti westerns, featuring Cthulhu-worshipping Indians, a woman with four feet, a crazed gunman who is obsessed with sucking on candy, Syphilis-ridden mutants, sexually transmitted tattoos, and a house devoted to the freakiest fetishes. **228 pages $12**

BB-087 **"Ass Goblins of Auschwitz" Cameron Pierce** - It's Monty Python meets Nazi exploitation in a surreal nightmare as can only be imagined by Bizarro author Cameron Pierce. **104 pages $10**

BB-088 **"Silent Weapons for Quiet Wars" Cody Goodfellow** - "This is high-end psychological surrealist horror meets bottom-feeding low-life crime in a techno-thrilling science fiction world full of Lovecraft and magic..." -John Skipp **212 pages $12**

BB-089 "Warrior Wolf Women of the Wasteland" Carlton Mellick III
— Road Warrior Werewolves versus McDonaldland Mutants...post-apocalyptic fiction has never been quite like this. **316 pages $13**

BB-091 "Super Giant Monster Time" Jeff Burk — A tribute to choose your own adventures and Godzilla movies. Will you escape the giant monsters that are rampaging the fuck out of your city and shit? Or will you join the mob of alien-controlled punk rockers causing chaos in the streets? What happens next depends on you. **188 pages $12**

BB-092 "Perfect Union" Cody Goodfellow — "Cronenberg's THE FLY on a grand scale: human/insect gene-spliced body horror, where the human hive politics are as shocking as the gore." -John Skipp. **272 pages $13**

BB-093 "Sunset with a Beard" Carlton Mellick III — 14 stories of surreal science fiction. **200 pages $12**

BB-094 "My Fake War" Andersen Prunty — The absurd tale of an unlikely soldier forced to fight a war that, quite possibly, does not exist. It's Rambo meets Waiting for Godot in this subversive satire of American values and the scope of the human imagination. **128 pages $11**

BB-095 "Lost in Cat Brain Land" Cameron Pierce — Sad stories from a surreal world. A fascist mustache, the ghost of Franz Kafka, a desert inside a dead cat. Primordial entities mourn the death of their child. The desperate serve tea to mysterious creatures. A hopeless romantic falls in love with a pterodactyl. And much more. **152 pages $11**

BB-096 "The Kobold Wizard's Dildo of Enlightenment +2" Carlton Mellick III — A Dungeons and Dragons parody about a group of people who learn they are only made up characters in an AD&D campaign and must find a way to resist their nerdy teenaged players and retarded dungeon master in order to survive. 232 **pages $12**

BB-098 "A Hundred Horrible Sorrows of Ogner Stump" Andrew Goldfarb — Goldfarb's acclaimed comic series. A magical and weird journey into the horrors of everyday life. **164 pages $11**

BB-099 **"Pickled Apocalypse of Pancake Island" Cameron Pierce**—A demented fairy tale about a pickle, a pancake, and the apocalypse. **102 pages $8**

BB-100 **"Slag Attack" Andersen Prunty**— Slag Attack features four visceral, noir stories about the living, crawling apocalypse.A slag is what survivors are calling the slug-like maggots raining from the sky, burrowing inside people, and hollowing out their flesh and their sanity. **148 pages $11**

BB-101 **"Slaughterhouse High" Robert Devereaux**—A place where schools are built with secret passageways, rebellious teens get zippers installed in their mouths and genitals, and once a year, on that special night, one couple is slaughtered and the bits of their bodies are kept as souvenirs. **304 pages $13**

BB-102 **"The Emerald Burrito of Oz" John Skipp & Marc Levinthal** —OZ IS REAL! Magic is real! The gate is really in Kansas! And America is finally allowing Earth tourists to visit this weird-ass, mysterious land. But when Gene of Los Angeles heads off for summer vacation in the Emerald City, little does he know that a war is brewing...a war that could destroy both worlds. **280 pages $13**

BB-103 **"The Vegan Revolution... with Zombies" David Agranoff** — When there's no more meat in hell, the vegans will walk the earth. **160 pages $11**

BB-104 **"The Flappy Parts" Kevin L Donihe**—Poems about bunnies, LSD, and police abuse. You know, things that matter. 132 **pages $11**

BB-105 **"Sorry I Ruined Your Orgy" Bradley Sands**—Bizarro humorist Bradley Sands returns with one of the strangest, most hilarious collections of the year. **130 pages $11**

BB-106 **"Mr. Magic Realism" Bruce Taylor**—Like Golden Age science fiction comics written by Freud, *Mr. Magic Realism* is a strange, insightful adventure that spans the furthest reaches of the galaxy, exploring the hidden caverns in the hearts and minds of men, women, aliens, and biomechanical cats. **152 pages $11**

BB-107 **"Zombies and Shit" Carlton Mellick III**—"Battle Royale" meets "Return of the Living Dead." Mellick's bizarro tribute to the zombie genre. **308 pages $13**

BB-108 **"The Cannibal's Guide to Ethical Living" Mykle Hansen**—Over a five star French meal of fine wine, organic vegetables and human flesh, a lunatic delivers a witty, chilling, disturbingly sane argument in favor of eating the rich.. **184 pages $11**

BB-109 **"Starfish Girl" Athena Villaverde**—In a post-apocalyptic underwater dome society, a girl with a starfish growing from her head and an assassin with sea anenome hair are on the run from a gang of mutant fish men. **160 pages $11**

BB-110 **"Lick Your Neighbor" Chris Genoa**—Mutant ninjas, a talking whale, kung fu masters, maniacal pilgrims, and an alcoholic clown populate Chris Genoa's surreal, darkly comical and unnerving reimagining of the first Thanksgiving. **303 pages $13**

BB-111 **"Night of the Assholes" Kevin L. Donihe**—A plague of assholes is infecting the countryside. Normal everyday people are transforming into jerks, snobs, dicks, and douchebags. And they all have only one purpose: to make your life a living hell.. **192 pages $11**

BB-112 **"Jimmy Plush, Teddy Bear Detective" Garrett Cook**—Hardboiled cases of a private detective trapped within a teddy bear body. **180 pages $11**

BB-113 **"The Deadheart Shelters" Forrest Armstrong**—The hip hop lovechild of William Burroughs and Dali... **144 pages $11**

BB-114 **"Eyeballs Growing All Over Me... Again" Tony Raugh**—Absurd, surreal, playful, dream-like, whimsical, and a lot of fun to read. **144 pages $11**

BB-115 **"Whargoul" Dave Brockie** — From the killing grounds of Stalingrad to the death camps of the holocaust. From torture chambers in Iraq to race riots in the United States, the Whargoul was there, killing and raping. **244 pages $12**

BB-116 **"By the Time We Leave Here, We'll Be Friends" J. David Osborne** — A David Lynchian nightmare set in a Russian gulag, where its prisoners, guards, traitors, soldiers, lovers, and demons fight for survival and their own rapidly deteriorating humanity. **168 pages $11**

BB-117 **"Christmas on Crack" edited by Carlton Mellick III** — Perverted Christmas Tales for the whole family! . . . as long as every member of your family is over the age of 18. **168 pages $11**

BB-118 **"Crab Town" Carlton Mellick III** — Radiation fetishists, balloon people, mutant crabs, sail-bike road warriors, and a love affair between a woman and an H-Bomb. This is one mean asshole of a city. Welcome to Crab Town. **100 pages $8**

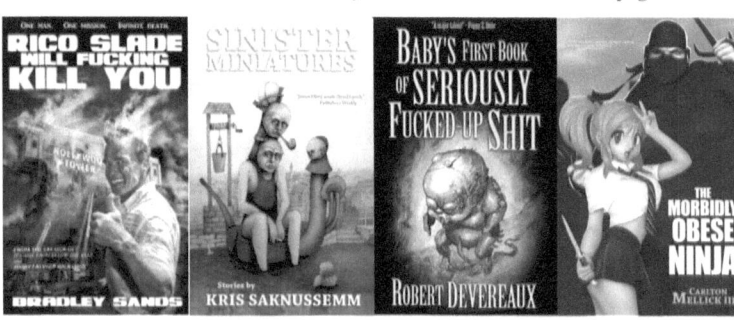

BB-119 **"Rico Slade Will Fucking Kill You" Bradley Sands** — Rico Slade is an action hero. Rico Slade can rip out a throat with his bare hands. Rico Slade's favorite food is the honey-roasted peanut. Rico Slade will fucking kill everyone. A novel. **122 pages $8**

BB-120 **"Sinister Miniatures" Kris Saknussemm** — The definitive collection of short fiction by Kris Saknussemm, confirming that he is one of the best, most daring writers of the weird to emerge in the twenty-first century. **180 pages $11**

BB-121 **"Baby's First Book of Seriously Fucked up Shit" Robert Devereaux** — Ten stories of the strange, the gross, and the just plain fucked up from one of the most original voices in horror. **176 pages $11**

BB-122 **"The Morbidly Obese Ninja" Carlton Mellick III** — These days, if you want to run a successful company . . . you're going to need a lot of ninjas. **92 pages $8**

BB-123 **"Abortion Arcade" Cameron Pierce** — An intoxicating blend of body horror and midnight movie madness, reminiscent of early David Lynch and the splatterpunks at their most sublime. **172 pages $11**

BB-124 **"Black Hole Blues" Patrick Wensink** — A hilarious double helix of country music and physics. **196 pages $11**

BB-125 **"Barbarian Beast Bitches of the Badlands" Carlton Mellick III** — Three prequels and sequels to *Warrior Wolf Women of the Wasteland*. **284 pages $13**

BB-126 **"The Traveling Dildo Salesman" Kevin L. Donihe** — A nightmare comedy about destiny, faith, and sex toys. Also featuring Donihe's most lurid and infamous short stories: *Milky Agitation, Two-Way Santa, The Helen Mower, Living Room Zombies,* and *Revenge of the Living Masturbation Rag.* **108 pages $8**

BB-127 **"Metamorphosis Blues" Bruce Taylor** — Enter a land of love beasts, intergalactic cowboys, and rock 'n roll. A land where Sears Catalogs are doorways to insanity and men keep mysterious black boxes. Welcome to the monstrous mind of Mr. Magic Realism. **136 pages $11**

BB-128 **"The Driver's Guide to Hitting Pedestrians" Andersen Prunty** — A pocket guide to the twenty-three most painful things in life, written by the most well-adjusted man in the universe. **108 pages $8**

BB-129 **"Island of the Super People" Kevin Shamel** — Four students and their anthropology professor journey to a remote island to study its indigenous population. But this is no ordinary native culture. They're super heroes and villains with flesh costumes and outlandish abilities like self-detonation, musical eyelashes, and microwave hands. **194 pages $11**

BB-130 **"Fantastic Orgy" Carlton Mellick III** — Shark Sex, mutant cats, and strange sexually transmitted diseases. Featuring the stories: *Candy-coated, Ear Cat, Fantastic Orgy, City Hobgoblins,* and *Porno in August.* **136 pages $9**

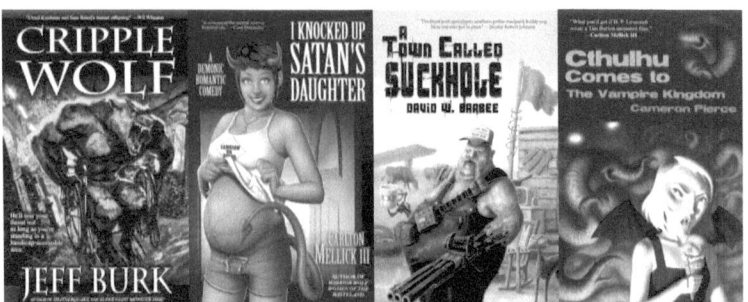

BB-131 **"Cripple Wolf" Jeff Burk** — Part man. Part wolf. 100% crippled. Also including *Punk Rock Nursing Home, Adrift with Space Badgers, Cook for Your Life, Just Another Day in the Park, Frosty and the Full Monty*, and *House of Cats*. **152 pages $10**

BB-132 **"I Knocked Up Satan's Daughter" Carlton Mellick III** — An adorable, violent, fantastical love story. A romantic comedy for the bizarro fiction reader. **152 pages $10**

BB-133 **"A Town Called Suckhole" David W. Barbee** — Far into the future, in the nuclear bowels of post-apocalyptic Dixie, there is a town. A town of derelict mobile homes, ancient junk, and mutant wildlife. A town of slack jawed rednecks who bask in the splendors of moonshine and mud boggin'. A town dedicated to the bloody and demented legacy of the Old South. A town called Suckhole. **144 pages $10**

BB-134 **"Cthulhu Comes to the Vampire Kingdom" Cameron Pierce** — What you'd get if H. P. Lovecraft wrote a Tim Burton animated film. **148 pages $11**

BB-135 **"I am Genghis Cum" Violet LeVoit** — From the savage Arctic tundra to post-partum mutations to your missing daughter's unmarked grave, join visionary madwoman Violet LeVoit in this non-stop eight-story onslaught of full-tilt Bizarro punk lit thrills. **124 pages $9**

BB-136 **"Haunt" Laura Lee Bahr** — A tripping-balls Los Angeles noir, where a mysterious dame drags you through a time-warping Bizarro hall of mirrors. **316 pages $13**

BB-137 **"Amazing Stories of the Flying Spaghetti Monster" edited by Cameron Pierce** — Like an all-spaghetti evening of Adult Swim, the Flying Spaghetti Monster will show you the many realms of His Noodly Appendage. Learn of those who worship him and the lives he touches in distant, mysterious ways. **228 pages $12**

BB-138 **"Wave of Mutilation" Douglas Lain** — A dream-pop exploration of modern architecture and the American identity, *Wave of Mutilation* is a Zen finger trap for the 21st century. **100 pages $8**

BB-139 **"Hooray for Death!" Mykle Hansen** — Famous Author Mykle Hansen draws unconventional humor from deaths tiny and large, and invites you to laugh while you can. **128 pages $10**

BB-140 **"Hypno-hog's Moonshine Monster Jamboree" Andrew Goldfarb** — Hicks, Hogs, Horror! Goldfarb is back with another strange illustrated tale of backwoods weirdness. **120 pages $9**

BB-141 **"Broken Piano For President" Patrick Wensink** — A comic masterpiece about the fast food industry, booze, and the necessity to choose happiness over work and security. **372 pages $15**

BB-142 **"Please Do Not Shoot Me in the Face" Bradley Sands** — A novel in three parts, *Please Do Not Shoot Me in the Face: A Novel*, is the story of one boy detective, the worst ninja in the world, and the great American fast food wars. It is a novel of loss, destruction, and--incredibly--genuine hope. **224 pages $12**

BB-143 **"Santa Steps Out" Robert Devereaux** — Sex, Death, and Santa Claus ... The ultimate erotic Christmas story is back. **294 pages $13**

BB-144 **"Santa Conquers the Homophobes" Robert Devereaux** — "I wish I could hope to ever attain one-thousandth the perversity of Robert Devereaux's toenail clippings." - Poppy Z. Brite **316 pages $13**

BB-145 **"We Live Inside You" Jeremy Robert Johnson** — "Jeremy Robert Johnson is dancing to a way different drummer. He loves language, he loves the edge, and he loves us people. These stories have range and style and wit. This is entertainment... and literature."- Jack Ketchum **188 pages $11**

BB-146 **"Clockwork Girl" Athena Villaverde** — Urban fairy tales for the weird girl in all of us. Like a combination of Francesca Lia Block, Charles de Lint, Kathe Koja, Tim Burton, and Hayao Miyazaki, her stories are cute, kinky, edgy, magical, provocative, and strange, full of poetic imagery and vicious sexuality. **160 pages $10**

BB-147 **"Armadillo Fists" Carlton Mellick III** — A weird-as-hell gangster story set in a world where people drive giant mechanical dinosaurs instead of cars. **168 pages $11**

BB-148 **"Gargoyle Girls of Spider Island" Cameron Pierce** — Four college seniors venture out into open waters for the tropical party weekend of a life-time. Instead of a teenage sex fantasy, they find themselves in a nightmare of pirates, sharks, and sex-crazed monsters. **100 pages $8**

BB-149 **"The Handsome Squirm" by Carlton Mellick III** — Like Franz Kafka's *The Trial* meets an erotic body horror version of *The Blob*. **158 pages $11**

BB-150 **"Tentacle Death Trip" Jordan Krall** — It's *Death Race 2000* meets H. P. Lovecraft in bizarro author Jordan Krall's best and most suspenseful work to date. **224 pages $12**

BB-151 **"The Obese" Nick Antosca** — Like Alfred Hitchcock's *The Birds*... but with obese people. **108 pages $10**

BB-152 **"All-Monster Action!" Cody Goodfellow** — The world gave him a blank check and a demand: Create giant monsters to fight our wars. But Dr. Otaku was not satisfied with mere chaos and mass destruction.... **216 pages $12**

BB-153 **"Ugly Heaven" Carlton Mellick III** — Heaven is no longer a para-dise. It was once a blissful utopia full of wonders far beyond human comprehension. But the afterlife is now in ruins. It has become an ugly, lonely wasteland populated by strange monstrous beasts, masturbating angels, and sad man-like beings wallowing in the remains of the once-great Kingdom of God. **106 pages $8**

BB-154 **"Space Walrus" Kevin L. Donihe** — Walter is supposed to go where no walrus has ever gone before, but all this astronaut walrus really wants is to take it easy on the intense training, escape the chimpanzee bullies, and win the love of his human trainer Dr. Stephanie. **160 pages $11**

BB-155 **"Unicorn Battle Squad" Kirsten Alene** — Mutant unicorns. A palace with a thousand human legs. The most powerful army on the planet. **192 pages $11**

BB-156 **"Kill Ball" Carlton Mellick III** — In a city where all humans live inside of plastic bubbles, exotic dancers are being murdered in the rubbery streets by a mysterious stalker known only as Kill Ball. **134 pages $10**

BB-157 **"Die You Doughnut Bastards" Cameron Pierce** — The bacon storm is rolling in. We hear the grease and sugar beat against the roof and windows. The doughnut people are attacking. We press close together, forgetting for a moment that we hate each other. **196 pages $11**

BB-158 **"Tumor Fruit" Carlton Mellick III** — Eight desperate castaways find themselves stranded on a mysterious deserted island. They are surrounded by poisonous blue plants and an ocean made of acid. Ravenous creatures lurk in the toxic jungle. The ghostly sound of crying babies can be heard on the wind. **310 pages $13**

BB-159 **"Thunderpussy" David W. Barbee** — When it comes to high-tech global espionage, only one man has the balls to save humanity from the world's most powerful bastards. He's Declan Magpie Bruce, Agent 00X. **136 pages $11**

BB-160 **"Papier Mâché Jesus" Kevin L. Donihe** — Donihe's surreal wit and beautiful mind-bending imagination is on full display with stories such as All Children Go to Hell, Happiness is a Warm Gun, and Swimming in Endless Night. **154 pages $11**

BB-161 **"Cuddly Holocaust" Carlton Mellick III** — The war between humans and toys has come to an end. The toys won. **172 pages $11**

BB-162 **"Hammer Wives" Carlton Mellick III** — Fish-eyed mutants, oceans of insects, and flesh-eating women with hammers for heads. Hammer Wives collects six of his most popular novelettes and short stories. **152 pages $10**

www.ingramcontent.com/pod-product-compliance
Lightning Source LLC
Chambersburg PA
CBHW021956010726
47494CB00003B/755